Kerrigan got a whiff of Rachel's perfume.

The scent rippled in a shock wave right down to his toes. It filled his senses with images of wild flowers and forest glades, of sweet, shared secrets and whispers in the night.

The memories grabbed him and wouldn't let go. He'd been her first lover. She'd been his. It had been like coming home, like finding heaven, pure heaven.

Now he felt as if he'd run to hell and back.

Damn her for doing this to him! If he had any sense, he'd get the hell out of there. But a burning shaft of desire speared through him, and there was a roaring in his ears.

And with a silent, savage curse, he brought his mouth to hers....

Dear Reader,

Welcome to Silhouette **Special Edition** . . . welcome to romance.

Last year, I requested your opinions on the books that we publish. Thank you for the many thoughtful comments. For the next couple of months, I'd like to share quotes with you from those letters. This seems very appropriate while we are in the midst of the THAT SPECIAL WOMAN! promotion. Each one of our readers is a *special* woman, as heroic as the heroines in our books.

Our THAT SPECIAL WOMAN! title for this month is *Kate's Vow,* by Sherryl Woods. You may remember Kate from Sherryl's VOWS trilogy. Kate has taken on a new client—and the verdict is love!

July is full of heat with *The Rogue* by Lindsay McKenna. This book continues her new series, MORGAN'S MERCENARIES. Also in store is Laurie Paige's *Home for a Wild Heart*—the first book of her WILD RIVER TRILOGY. And wrapping up this month of fireworks are books from other favorite authors: Christine Flynn, Celeste Hamilton and Bay Matthews!

I hope you enjoy this book, and all of the stories to come!

Sincerely,

Tara Gavin
Senior Editor

Quote of the Month: "I enjoy a well-thought-out romance. I enjoy complex issues—dealing with several perceptions of one situation. When I was young, romances taught me how to ask to be treated—what type of goals I could set my sights on. They really were my model for healthy relationships. The concept of not being able to judge 'Mr. Right' by first impressions helped me to find my husband, and the image of a strong woman helped me to stay strong."   —L. Montgomery, Connecticut

LAURIE
PAIGE

HOME FOR A WILD HEART

Silhouette®

SPECIAL EDITION®

Published by Silhouette Books New York

America's Publisher of Contemporary Romance

With thanks to
Okie, Bill and the gals
at the Prospect Inn in Oregon
for all the information

SILHOUETTE BOOKS
300 East 42nd St., New York, N.Y. 10017

HOME FOR A WILD HEART

Copyright © 1993 by Olivia M. Hall

ISBN: 0-373-09828-6

First Silhouette Books printing July 1993

All the characters in this book have no existence outside the
imagination of the author and have no relation whatsoever to
anyone bearing the same name or names. They are not even
distantly inspired by any individual known or unknown to the
author, and all incidents are pure invention.

®: Trademark used under license and registered in the United States
Patent and Trademark Office and in other countries.

Printed in the U.S.A.

LAURIE PAIGE

reports that life after a certain age (thirty-something and then some) keeps getting rosier. She was recently presented with the *Affaire de Coeur* Readers' Choice Silver Pen award for favorite contemporary author. Laurie gives the credit—and thanks!—to her romance readers, who are the most wonderful, loyal people in the world. She's also just had another super event—the birth of her first grandchild, a boy. "Definitely hero material!"

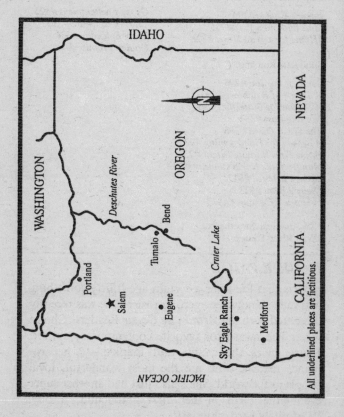

All underlined places are fictitious.

Chapter One

Kerrigan McPherson swore savagely. He'd have bet his last year's rodeo winnings that no animal could leap a rock face that high, but the cougar had cleared it with room to spare. Now she was in full stride, tearing off over the ridge as if she had turpentine on her tail.

Hell, at this rate he'd *chase* her off the ranch and into the rugged mountains of the Rogue River National Forest before he got a chance to hit her with a tranquilizer dart and transport her to a more remote region of the country.

He rested the rifle across his thighs and sat there on his pinto gelding for a few seconds, dragging air into his lungs and admiring the smooth perfection of the big cat in motion. A streak of sun pierced the clouds and hit the animal, turning her fur from soft tawny to bright gold.

God, she was beautiful. He'd once known a woman like that, with hair sun kissed into shades of light and dark— even at that sweet, secret woman's place, it had been deep tawny gold. She'd had the same fluid grace as the cat, her body lithe and streamlined. When they'd made love, she'd been like molten flesh under his hands.

She'd sometimes screamed with the force of the passion they'd shared. Then afterward, she'd purred. It had been the same for him—powerful, gripping, soul wrenching and then . . . contentment.

The vision congealed into a hard lump that moved from his chest to his throat. Pain mingled with memory, and for a moment he felt the old longing, the sharp ache of needing someone more than life itself. The sudden, restless movement of the gelding brought him back to the present.

Bloody hell, he was acting like some kind of moony-eyed fool, worse than ol' Hank back at the bunkhouse, picking out sad tunes on his guitar and mourning his lost love.

What he needed was some fun.

It had been months since he'd been to town with the men of the Sky Eagle ranch. Maybe when he got the cat moved and finished the repairs on the fence that ran the boundary, he'd go in and have a ripping good time.

Yeah, fun, he mocked. A brawl was the highlight of Saturday night. The town, a dot at the crossroads—population two hundred if the dogs were counted—was a mecca of highbrow entertainment. Not that he was personally into highbrow. . . .

The cougar left the ridge and started down, heading into a shallow ravine where the gully ran with spring melt. Her golden coat caught the sun again. She ran in splendor, a solitary queen at home in her vast domain.

She should have a mate.

The thought came to him suddenly, like the unexpected slip of a knife blade against the skin. He sucked in a harsh breath.

He'd wanted that woman so much that, for months after they'd parted, a weak feeling would come over him whenever he thought of her and he'd experience a sharp pain in his chest.

"Heartsick," his brother had diagnosed. "You'll live."

He had. She'd been a boy's dream, one that had been beaten out of him. Literally. The result had been a lesson in pain and humiliation he'd never forget ... nor would he forget the fact that any man who relied on a woman for his happiness was a fool.

But for that one month he'd believed in paradise. He'd held it in his arms. And then it was gone.

Story of his life. As a kid, he'd thought life was perfect, then his dad had died. At a time when his mother should have drawn closer to them, when her seven-year-old sons had needed her the most, she'd abandoned them to drown her grief in a bottle.

Years later, with that golden-haired woman, he'd grabbed at happiness with both hands, sure that this time it would last forever. What a sentimental dope. It had taken him a long time to catch on to life and love, but the final lesson had been pounded into him the night his beloved had failed to show up for their elopement. Instead, she'd sent three men to beat him up.

A cynical smile tugged at his mouth. She could have just *told* him she'd changed her mind.

Since then he'd learned to keep his sights trained on goals that were within his reach. Those didn't include beautiful, golden females from highfalutin families. . . .

The cougar disappeared behind some boulders, then reappeared on the other side of the ravine, leaping easily across the brook.

What the heck was he doing just sitting there? He had a mountain cat to catch. He watched her for a minute and calculated where she was heading.

For the past two weeks of this cold, miserable spring—the worst on record, with the most unpredictable weather he'd ever seen—he'd been trying to run her to ground, each time losing her over this ridge, but he'd seen her big paw prints in the mud near the boundary creek a week or so ago.

Making a quick decision, he decided to take a chance and head for the bluff about a half mile from there by way of the trail. That would be almost as fast as the cougar could make it going across country... if she was heading that way.

He shoved the rifle into the scabbard and wheeled the pinto to the west, urging him into a ground-eating lope when they reached a smooth patch.

Rachel Barrett checked the zipper of her green camouflage parka. It was closed to the top. She flipped up the collar with its imitation sheepskin lining to shield her neck from the breeze.

The wind was from the north. Must be blowing straight off Jackass Mountain, she decided, shivering. Nothing like southern Oregon in the spring. Crater Lake was to the northeast, about twenty-five miles...if one happened to be a bird.

She grinned. At the present moment she was sitting on a tree limb that seemed to be growing harder by the minute.

Lifting the binoculars, she perused the land from horizon to horizon. On the other side of the bluff was a narrow ravine where a sharply carved gully burbled with spring runoff. The temporary brook ran into Eagle Creek right below the rocky ledge. The creek joined the Rogue River a mile or so downstream.

It had been a wet spring. Cold, too. She shivered again.

The only sound was the high, keening cry of the wind through the gorges. A lonely sound. But she liked it.

She had a penchant for quiet, solitary pastimes. At twenty-eight, working as a naturalist sponsored by the Sloan Foundation and her own money, she'd found a life that satisfied her.

Like the eagle she was trying to observe, she preferred this high, rough country to the city. She scanned the skyline once more. Nothing. She put the binoculars in the case hanging from a tree branch. Another shiver rippled along her back.

Perhaps she should climb down and try another location. She hadn't seen hide nor hair...uh, feather...of the eagle for three days.

Besides, she was getting hungry. She'd eaten her trail mix hours ago. Keeping warm in this wind used up the calories. She'd hike back to her base camp and have lunch. Before she could act on this decision, she spied a cougar coming out of the ravine.

The big cat padded to the sandbar where the creek water ran clear and cold, her sides heaving as if she'd been running. She dropped into a crouch and drank rapidly.

Rachel watched, hardly daring to breathe, although she was well above the animal and partially hidden by the sparse branches of the ancient tree. The rush of water from the brook covered any noise she might make. One part of her, the scientist, automatically noted the cougar's physical condition.

The cat was a young female, sleek and well-groomed. Her stance was alert, her eyes bright with intelligence. She paused in her thirsty lapping and cleaned the fur between the toes of one large paw. That showed good sense and discipline.

Observing the creature in a natural setting like this caused a pang of remembered yearning to rise in Rachel's breast.

Oh, to be wild and free, to have no restraints but those of instinct and nature...

She'd tasted that exhilaration once, briefly.

Sudden tears misted her eyes, unexpected after so long a time. There was no need to become soggy. That had been years ago.

Since following her own instincts had led her astray, she'd given in to family urging and finished college. However, she'd made her own career choices, opting for wilderness and quiet.

Now she was happy... well, she was content. That was close.

The lioness finished grooming her paw and drank again. Rachel wondered if the lovely, tawny female had found a mate in this wild, lonely country.

A sound, muffled but distinct, caught her attention.

Rachel clutched a limb to keep her balance and peered over her left shoulder. A rider came into view, his big pinto picking out a path along the deer trail she'd followed to the bluff. She frowned as he came closer, intruding into her space.

The man's hat was pulled low over his forehead, hiding his face from her view. His body displayed the rawhide toughness and wiry strength she'd seen in the cowboys in town last Saturday.

She wondered if he'd been one of them—dressed in skin-tight jeans that hinted at maleness barely contained—their boisterous laughter indicating their carefree mood.

He rode easily, one hand on the reins, the other resting on his thigh, with the natural grace all cowboys seemed to have in the saddle. Through the tight denim of his worn jeans she could see the muscles contract like steel bands when the horse lunged over a boulder in the path.

Several emotions rushed through her, so fast and fleeting she couldn't identify them. She didn't want to. She stayed away from cowboys. They were deadly on untried, trusting hearts.

She remained still, undecided about whether she should call out to him or not. If she did, she'd frighten the cat away.

What was he doing here anyway? she wondered, growing more irritated by his presence. She realized she was possessive of the land. During the week she'd been there, she'd come to think of it as her private domain. It belonged to her, the cougar and the female eagle who soared above its narrow gorges. No males wanted or needed.

Actually, the land was part of the national forest. The cowboy was trespassing...maybe. Ranchers sometimes leased grazing rights from the federal government. She'd seen plenty of cow sign in the area. And hoofprints down at the creek where she'd set up camp. He was most likely checking on his cattle.

Maybe he wouldn't notice her.

She grinned at the thought of his surprise if he looked up and spotted her perched there like some strange bird.

He stopped his big pinto gelding beneath her tree and surveyed the area down in the gorge. She knew the moment he spotted the cat by the way his shoulders tensed. He went utterly still when the female glanced around before lapping the water again.

Rachel's eyes flew open when he drew a rifle from a leather scabbard attached to his saddle. Surely...surely he didn't mean to shoot the cougar. No one would hurt something so beautiful.

He hefted the weapon into place against his shoulder.

She glanced wildly around for a weapon of her own. The binoculars were all she had. She didn't think they were heavy enough to throw off his aim.

The man shoved his hat back and leaned his cheek close to the rifle stock. He lined up his sights on the cougar.

She had to do something . . . *now.*

Kerrigan squinted when the sun suddenly came out from behind a cloud. Lining the cougar's right hip in the cross hairs of the scope, he tightened his finger on the trigger.

An ear-piercing scream jarred every muscle in his body.

From the corner of his eye, he saw a flash of tawny gold coming at him from the tree, then something heavy and clinging and probably lethal landed on him.

Several sensations hit him at once. Foremost was the icy fingers of Death clutching at his neck. Another was the feel of the rifle being knocked from his grip. A third was the sense of falling. His last impression as he pitched out of the saddle was one of surprise. He'd never suspected the beautiful lioness had found a mate.

Rachel's jump was good. Triumph shot through her. She'd not only spoiled the cowboy's aim, she'd also kicked his rifle out of his hands. Then she saw the ground rushing up to meet her.

She held on to her opponent's neck with one hand, determined to take him down with her. With fatalistic humor, she realized she was on the bottom of the pile as they fell in a tangle of arms and legs. She hit and felt a burst of pain in her side, then, like an echo, in her head.

The man rolled out of her clutches and into a low crouch, a knife at the ready in his hands. She gaped up at him. For a split second, it was like looking into her past. Then the image divided into two, wavered and blinked out. . . .

Kerrigan thought he'd somehow gone to sleep and didn't know it. He stared at the woman. If he was in a dream or nightmare, it was hers, not his. She lay on the rocky ground in a relaxed pose, her eyes closed, her body limp.

After a stunned minute, thought returned to him. He swore and sheathed the knife. Glancing along her supine form, he saw no blood or obvious damage. Kneeling beside her, he said her name.

"Rachel."

His voice was a hoarse rasp. It had been seven, almost eight, years since he'd spoken to her. Even now, the memory of it burned like hot lead in his chest. He cleared his throat and tried again.

Her eyes fluttered open. He saw her pupils contract as the clouds parted and let in a dollop of sun, teasing them with the promise of warmth, only to disappear behind the clouds again.

Did she have a concussion? He tried to decide if her pupils were the same size. Yeah, they looked okay.

She blinked like an owl, slowly and deliberately, then stared at him some more. Her eyes were brown, striated with golden rays that ran from her pupils to the dark, velvety edge of her irises. Exactly as he remembered them.

It used to fascinate him when he looked into them, in the days when he'd been under her spell. He'd especially liked gazing into her eyes when she was tucked under him, his body warmly sheathed in hers, both of them moving slightly, holding on to that last burst of pleasure, not wanting it to end.

Way back then she'd been hot for him, eager and ready when they'd stolen away from civilization and found their own world.

Once upon a time, she'd told him a kiss was the meeting of the body and soul . . . and making love was the sweetest kiss of all.

Yeah, once upon a time, right out of a fairy tale. That fantasy had ended when she'd abandoned him, leaving him to the tender mercies of her three hired guns.

"Where do you hurt?" he asked, sounding angry rather than concerned. Hell, he was angry.

She opened her mouth, but no sound came out. "Can't breathe," she said, mouthing the words.

In that instant, he realized the breath had been knocked out of her. He hesitated, reluctant to touch her; then he moved behind her and propped her against his chest.

"Raise your arms," he ordered.

She lifted one, but winced at moving the other.

Damn.

He ran a hand over her left arm, but couldn't detect a broken bone. She unzipped her coat and clutched the turtleneck sweater at her throat, but no air rushed through her open mouth.

He grabbed both her wrists and raised her arms high over her head, then pumped them up and down. Her head rolled back and forth against his chest, telling him the maneuver wasn't working.

"All right," he said, "we'll have to use drastic measures."

Moving aside, he whipped off his jacket and put it under her head. He noticed a spot of blood on a small, sharp rock near her temple. Another rock, larger, its edges rounded by erosion, was in the right position to have done the damage to her midriff.

She was still trying to breathe without success. Her eyes had taken on a worried glaze. He clenched his fists, but there was nothing to strike at. Damn fate for doing this to him!

Bending over her, he pinched her nose closed with one hand, pulled her chin down with the other.

"Open your mouth," he ordered when she twisted her chin from his grasp.

He got a glimpse of the shock in her eyes when he covered her mouth with his. How the hell did she think he was going to help her? Dial 911 and wait for the paramedics to show up?

Her lips opened under his. They were soft, yet surprisingly cool. Memories rose out of his past. Touching her again was almost like being in a dream.

One he'd gotten over a long time ago, he reminded himself ruthlessly. He hadn't thought of her in years. Except at odd moments now and then, like with the cougar.

A premonition?

He didn't believe in them.

Against his forearm, he felt her chest lift as he carefully pushed air into her lungs. He automatically closed his eyes, as if they shared a real kiss. Sitting back on his heels, he watched her, hoping one breath would be enough to get her lungs working on their own again.

With one hand he felt for the pulse in her neck. It was steady and strong, no missed beats or erratic fluttering. Good. Then he ran both hands over her torso, searching her rib cage for obvious breaks. He could detect no sharp edges under the skin. He quickly checked the rest of her. Nothing out of place.

Thank heavens for small favors. It would be hell trying to get her out of here if she were seriously injured.

Realizing she'd exhaled the breath he'd given her, he leaned close and watched her try to draw breath.

"Breathe," he said, ordering her to do it as if she were a ranch hand under his command.

She couldn't.

He drew a deep breath and bent to her again. This time she opened her mouth and took his breath into her eagerly, greedily.

The way she used to take his kisses.

His temperature rose with the unbidden memory. He pushed it from his consciousness ruthlessly. He'd fallen under this woman's spell once. He wouldn't do it again.

When he levered himself up once more, he pulled the bandanna from his back pocket and wiped sweat from his forehead.

He dropped the bandanna beside his leg. The chill wind whipped it over the bluff and out of sight.

The cougar, too, was long gone. Nothing left but the deep gashes in the dirt where claws had dug in as the animal took off with a bound up the creek bank. After Rachel's screech, the cat was probably still running for her life.

Shaking his head in disgust for the wasted morning, he laid a hand on his assailant's abdomen, then blew air into her lungs. He sat back, his face grim. Her diaphragm was still stunned from her fall. If he could get it pumping, she'd be okay.

The sun disappeared behind the clouds. He scanned the sky. The weather might turn nasty at any moment. The approaching storm could dump inches of rain or snow on them. There was a line cabin about a quarter mile from there. He'd take her to it as soon as she was breathing well.

Resuming his task, he bent to her once more. This time he'd give her several deep breaths, hoping that would get her on her feet again.

He noticed she'd closed her eyes. Her lashes lay over her cheeks like tiny, exotic oriental fans. A blue tracery of veins ran through her eyelids. For some reason it made her look young and vulnerable.

A pang, strange and aching, attacked his chest.

Closing his eyes, he concentrated on breathing in and out, in and out, at a steady pace, lifting his mouth between each breath. He established a rhythm with her.

It came easily, as if they lived by the same internal clock, their time matching perfectly as it had in the past. . . .

He forced himself to think on the mechanics of breathing.

Breathing out, he gave his air to her. Then, while he drew his next breath, her body naturally exhaled. It was as intimate a sharing as making love.

Each time he took a breath, his nose no more than a few inches from her skin, he got a whiff of her perfume. The scent rippled in a shock wave right down to his toes. It filled his senses with images of wildflowers and forest glades, of sweet shared secrets and whispers in the night.

He'd been her first lover. She'd been his.

The memories grabbed him and wouldn't let go. Damn her for doing this to him. As soon as she was breathing on her own, he'd get the hell out of there, if he had any sense.

With a silent, savage curse, he touched her mouth and gave her the kiss of life. *Five,* he counted. *Six.*

The wind picked up. It blew her hair into his eyes. With fingers that trembled, he caught the strand and held it.

Seven. Eight. Nine.

There was a roaring in his ears. It was like drowning. The way she probably felt, he reflected. Looking into her eyes, he saw no signs of fear. He scored her a point for courage.

Her lips were warm now, moist with their mingled saliva. She gave him a slight, wry smile. A burning shaft of desire speared through him. Once she'd begged for his kisses.

Again. Kiss me again, Kerrigan!

And he'd quit his teasing and kissed her until neither of them could breathe. It hadn't mattered. The universe had narrowed to that moment and the joining of their yearning flesh. He'd slid into her, and it was like coming home at the end of a grueling day and finding heaven, pure heaven.

He jerked his mouth from hers and sat up, drawing in a deep, shaky breath, feeling as if he'd run to hell and back. When he licked his lips, he tasted her. Vanilla. It was the flavor of the lip gloss she'd always used.

Double damn!

"Can you breathe yet?" he asked almost in a snarl.

She blinked at him in that wide-eyed, deliberate way she had. Her eyes were one of the first things he'd noticed about her....

She'd been sitting on a stool at the local diner, over in the bar area, her chin propped on her hand when he'd walked in, dressed in his best jeans and ready for some Saturday-night fun. He'd known a couple of the girls in the group she was with. He'd gone to school with them.

After ordering up a beer, he'd moseyed on over, nonchalant outside, while inside his heart was going like a trip-hammer. He'd been hotly aware that her gaze hadn't left him for an instant.

She was new in the area. The rumor was that she and her brother had inherited their uncle's spread south of town. She apparently knew nothing about the fighting McPherson twins—rough kids that other parents wouldn't let their daughters date.

From that first instant, he'd noticed her long, dark lashes and the heavy-lidded look she'd given him. She'd blinked once, owllike, then stared at him while a soft, lazy smile formed on her lips. It was like she'd known the minute their eyes had met that they'd be lovers. By dawn, they were. It had happened that fast....

He almost groaned as hunger licked hotly along his veins. "Can't you breathe yet?" he snapped.

She tried and shook her head.

Muttering a succinct expletive, he pinched her nostrils closed and pressed his lips over hers once more, giving her a deeper breath this time. His hand shook when he pushed his hat back off his sweating forehead. He swiped at his face with his sleeve.

Studying the sky, he saw the clouds had closed off the sun completely. They were building rapidly. A storm was just what he needed to complete his day.

She licked her lips and tried to breathe. A faint gasp came from her.

At last she was beginning to get some air on her own, he noted with savage satisfaction. He was damned tired of playing doctor and patient.

What would you like to play? The question echoed in his skull. *Lovers,* the answer immediately followed.

No way.

"Again," she gasped.

For a heart-stopping second, he thought she was asking him to love her the way she'd once done, her hands running down his back, her body writhing under his, demanding satisfaction.

Longing poured through him like a spring flood. Then he realized she still needed him to breathe for her.

He laughed at his wild leap of imagination. *Get real,* he advised. She didn't give a damn about him except as a pair of lungs to get hers to work again.

Putting his lips over hers, he gave her a quick breath and another, then withdrew.

She smiled at him. He recognized the gesture for what it was—a smile of thanks. But knowing that didn't stop him from thinking of other smiles she'd given him. She'd drawn him into her web of deceit so deftly he hadn't given it a second thought.

Woman-magic.

He wouldn't fall into that spell again.

He shifted restlessly, a sense of self-preservation urging him to get on his horse and ride out of there.

Her gaze flickered over him, paused and glanced away. She had probably noticed the desire he couldn't completely control. He resented her for being the cause of it.

"I don't usually touch a woman like this and not go all the way," he told her, deliberately crude.

Her eyes, when she looked back at his face, weren't shocked. Instead she nodded solemnly. If she could speak, would she tell him she regretted the loss of that mad passion they'd shared for a wild, insane month one brief summer?

Struggling, she tried to force a breath, then gave him an expectant glance.

Calling himself all kinds of a fool, he held her nose and breathed into her mouth again. He laid his left hand on her abdomen, over her diaphragm.

Her body heat warmed his palm. He wanted to slip his hand under her turtleneck sweater and caress her skin. He knew how she would feel. Smooth as new saddle leather. Soft as cottonwood fluff. Without conscious volition, he stroked down her, noting the way her body sloped in a gentle curve down from her rib cage. Her abdominal muscles clenched, then relaxed, then clenched again under his hand.

He paused, remembering the pleasure of pressing his face into the soft tangle of tawny curls and hearing her gasps of rapture.

Sudden rage joined the passion that trumpeted through him. He had a mad urge to take her, right there on that stony bluff and show her she was still his, that he could still make her helpless in his arms, a captive to their hungry need.

Yeah, he could do that. Then he'd have to live with himself.

He forced himself to breathe...in...out...in...out....

When he felt a slight heaving movement in her diaphragm, he gave a sigh of relief. His insides were in more tangles than a kitten in a knitting basket.

He'd vowed not to let a woman do that to him ever again. He wasn't a green kid, twenty-three years old, fresh off his first big winning season on the rodeo circuit and thinking himself in love, thinking he had to have this one woman or die.

He heard her catch her breath, then felt the full expansion of her chest against his arm as her breathing resumed. Lifting his head, he watched as she inhaled and exhaled in a deep, oxygen-absorbing sigh. He hadn't realized how pale she'd been until the color returned to her face.

"Thanks," she said and took another deep breath.

Reaching up, she laid the tips of her fingers against his lips, then rubbed back and forth, her touch so gentle it almost unmanned him.

Hell, he hadn't cried since he was ten years old when his mom had died and he and Keegan had gone to live with their harsh, unforgiving grandfather.

There had been no regrets from the old man or the twins when they'd driven off in their used pickup truck to make their fortunes rodeoing immediately after graduation from high school. There would be no regrets over this incident, either. He wouldn't be trapped in the magic spell she wove this time. Catching her wrist, he pushed her hand away from his mouth.

Rachel had thought she was hallucinating when she'd first opened her eyes and seen the cowboy kneeling beside her. When his mouth had touched hers, she'd been sure of it. But this was no dream. He was here. He was real.

"Kerrigan McPherson," she murmured.

"In person," he mocked.

She could only gaze at him as if spellbound. Kerrigan, her first love...Kerrigan, the man she'd promised to elope with, the man who hadn't come for her, or so she'd thought.

Her brother had made her late for the elopement, arguing that Kerrigan wanted her money to save his ranch. When she'd arrived, there'd been no sign of her lover.

A week later, she'd discovered that her brother had sent three of his security men to intercept Kerrigan. Kerrigan and the three men had fought. That was why he hadn't been at their meeting place.

By the time she'd found out the truth, it had been too late. He'd refused her call and hadn't answered the two letters she'd sent.

If Kerrigan had truly loved her, wouldn't he have responded to her attempts to contact him?

Chapter Two

"Yeah, I don't believe it, either," Kerrigan continued when she was silent. "The gods must be laughing." He laughed, too, a brief, mocking sound of irony, not humor.

Rachel found herself staring at his lips, drawn now into a tight slash across his face. The lower lip was slightly fuller than the upper, both cleanly delineated. When he kissed, they were mobile, tender, fierce . . . a sorcerer's magic.

She pushed herself upright, unable to suppress a groan as her side protested the effort. Her head throbbed with an insistent ache that scattered all thoughts, past and present.

"Can you move everything?" he asked, standing and backing up a step.

She gingerly rotated her shoulders, then flexed her elbows and wrists. "Yes. Thanks for your help." She smiled at him.

He didn't return it. Instead he turned and walked away from her. She knew he'd felt emotion while breathing for her. She also knew he was angry about it.

When he turned back, she hauled herself into a standing position, as near as she could get, anyway. She leaned in a slight stoop to her left, a hand pressed to her side.

"I may have a cracked rib," she said. "And a cracked skull." She raised her free hand to her head.

"Let me see." He stepped close and lifted the tangled strands of hair. "You have a goose egg. The skin's broken, but it doesn't look serious."

"I have a headache."

"Probably a mild concussion." He looked her over with his wintry blue eyes, his gaze assessing, his expression grim. "I've had one or two of those after being tossed from a horse." He glanced around, his expression irritated. "Speaking of which, where's your mount?"

"I don't have one."

"How did you get up here?"

"I hiked."

"Hiked?" he snorted. "It's five miles from the dude ranch."

"I'm not staying at any dude ranch." She forced herself to her full five feet six inches. Kerrigan, at six feet, seemed to loom over her. "I've got a camp down where Sky Creek runs into the Rogue River."

"Well, your camping buddies shouldn't have let you go off on your own. It's too dangerous." He gave her a sarcastic grin. "Especially since you've taken to jumping on people from trees."

"I don't have any camping buddies. I'm alone," she informed him. "I had to jump on you. You were going to shoot the cougar. I couldn't let you."

He swore, as one might say, a blue streak. She listened, impressed with his command of the language. He spoke of the chase after the cougar, of days spent tracking the animal, of the wasted time and energy he'd expended on the task.

"I was going to *tranquilize* the cat and move her to higher country so the rancher down from us wouldn't have her killed. He thinks she's been after his calves and has given orders to his men to shoot her on sight."

"She has every right to be here," Rachel said, starting out indignant, then quietening as the pain in her head increased. "This is national forest land—"

"This is McPherson land," he corrected.

"It isn't."

"You left the national forest when you crossed to the south side of Sky Creek and west of the Rogue. Didn't you know that?"

She shook her head, then pressed a hand to her temple.

"Now you do." He assessed the black clouds directly overhead. "There's a storm brewing. Let's go."

"Where?"

"We have a line shack not too far from here. I'd planned to sleep there tonight. I suppose you'll have to stay with me."

"I'll go to my camp—"

"The hell you will. You'll come with me. I'm going to get you to a doctor and have you X-rayed from head to foot. That way, you won't be able to sue for damages that mysteriously show up later as soon as your lawyer checks our assets."

She couldn't believe how hard and cynical he'd become in seven short years. "I wouldn't do that."

His expression was skeptical. "Stranger things have been tried," he remarked.

Rachel took a few experimental steps. A thousand questions buzzed in her head, but the dull throb of pain stopped her from asking. Later, she thought. When she could think straight. When her control was better.

It wasn't until she acknowledged the shaky state of her emotions that she realized just how stunned she felt at seeing Kerrigan. All the time he'd breathed for her, she hadn't let herself think of anything but getting air into her lungs.

Now there was the storm to think about. They had to get to shelter. Later, they would talk.

It came to her that if she'd fallen out of the tree, instead of flinging herself out like a heroine in some old Western movie, she could have died out here alone. It might have been months before she was found.

Well, probably not months—other people did know where she was camped and how long she planned to stay there—but certainly it could have been days.

"You saved my life," she said.

He turned his winter blue gaze on her. Once, she remembered, he'd looked at her with warmth in his eyes, while the fire of their joined passion blazed between them.

What, she wondered, was he thinking as he watched her, his manner so impersonal she might have been a stranger? Surely his memories were the same as hers.

"Come on," he said. "I'll help you up."

"Up?" She looked at the tree. "Oh, yes. My binoculars."

His gaze followed hers. He muttered something. The next thing she knew he was in the tree. After hanging the binocular case around his neck, he climbed down, lightly landing on the ground with the grace of a cat.

"You're still lean and wiry the way you used to be," she said without thinking. She bit her lip as he gave her another icy glance. Then she shrugged. It was true.

She'd loved to run her hands over his body, marveling at the hardness of his muscles. A tiny chasm of pain opened within her. She decided she'd better not think of the past. There were too many hurtful things between them.

He recovered his rifle, looked it over, then shoved it into the scabbard. After storing her binoculars in his saddlebag, he picked up the reins of his horse, which was cropping the grass in a rock crevice, and turned to Rachel. "Get on," he ordered.

"On your horse?"

"Of course on my horse," he snapped. "Step on it. I'd like to get to the cabin before that cloud dumps on us."

Lifting her face toward the wind, she sniffed. The air was heavy with the ozone odor that heralded rain. Lots of rain by the looks of that cloud.

She put her left foot into the stirrup and reached for the saddle horn, clamping her teeth against the pain that racked both head and side. Before she could give the agonizing leap that would propel her onto the back of the tall horse, a large, warm hand settled familiarly on her bottom and lifted her into the saddle.

For a second, she slumped over the pommel and gasped for breath again. Definitely a cracked rib, she decided.

"You'd better take it easy," he advised, but not very sympathetically, she thought. Still, he had spoken.

He pulled on his jacket and swung up behind her. His thighs encased hers. She felt the incredible hardness of his muscles as he tightened his knees on the horse.

Her hips fitted snugly into the V formed by his legs, making her aware of his body heat. Then his arms came around either side of her, and he set the horse in motion with a click of his tongue.

The gelding bounded into a trot, eager to head for home. Rachel cried out and held herself stiffly, fighting the movement. Kerrigan reined the big horse in.

"We're going to have to hurry to beat the storm," he said, his cheek touching her hair as he spoke close to her ear. "Lean into me. Let your body ride with mine."

"I...I can't."

He laid his hand flat on her waist, his long, slender fingers spread over her, and pulled her against him. She tensed.

"Relax," he ordered. "I'm hardly going to ravish you on a horse with a helluva storm ready to break over us."

She twisted her head around to look at him. Their faces were two inches apart. She faced the front again. Slowly, with an effort of will, she forced her body to conform to his.

"Good," he said.

He slid his arm around her and held her firmly against him, then she felt his thighs tighten once more. The gelding swung into a ground-eating lope until they hit rougher terrain in the stand of trees. Then they slowed to a walk.

With the relaxing of his hold on her, Rachel was able to rest more easily in his embrace. The first pellets of hail struck them, causing the gelding to shake the reins and snort.

"He wants to get to his hay," Kerrigan said near her ear.

She nodded and shivered. The air was much colder.

"I have a poncho," he added and pulled the horse to a stop under cover of some thick fir branches.

He untied the poncho from the back of the saddle and pulled it over her, tucking the edges between her shoulders and his chest to hold it in place.

The tears burned behind her eyes at this act of kindness. "Thank you," she murmured, becoming entangled in a welter of emotions, not the least of which was an overwhelming desire to let herself sink into the safety of his arms and never leave.

"I don't want you catching pneumonia and adding that to your lawsuit," he stated, his voice rough, as cold as the storm.

"A williwaw," she said.

"What?"

"That's what the mountain men used to call a fiercely cold north wind," she explained. She referred to him rather than the storm, but she didn't say that.

He gave a grunt and was silent.

For the next few minutes the only sound was the chatter of the ice particles hitting the ground. The hail resembled tiny snowballs, a quarter inch across. They hit and bounced, some of them skipping two or three times before coming to rest among the pine and fir needles.

The sense of isolation was complete.

She became aware of his hand at her waist, his fingers splayed across her abdomen. He was lightly stroking.

Turning her head and glancing up at him, she saw he was staring out at the hail-whitened landscape, apparently not conscious of the tantalizing caress. Instead, he seemed lost in his own deep thoughts.

She studied the hard, clean lines of his face with its square chin, thin, hawkish nose and high cheekbones. He had a scar, an inch long, on the underside of his chin. Probably due to a fall from a bucking bronco.

She'd followed his career on TV and in magazines. He and his brother had been in the top-ten contenders for the title for several years. Keegan had dropped out after a serious injury three or four years ago. Kerrigan had been grand champion last year with winnings just over a million dollars.

In all the articles about him, he'd never mentioned a woman in his life—the reporters had asked every time—but his name had been linked to some movie star briefly. He was a handsome man.

His hair was dark, almost black, with a stubborn cowlick over his forehead. His eyes were blue, changing to silver near the pupils, which gave them their wintry hue. He could make a person shiver with just a glance from those frosty eyes.

However, she was far from cold now. Warmth began to percolate through her, aided by his body behind her and his poncho in front. She drew a shaky breath and was rewarded with the masculine scent of him surrounding her. He wore no cologne that she could detect.

He had on their dates, though. A heady after-shave lotion that had reminded her of the crisp smell of the outdoors. It had suited him. He belonged to the rugged land around them.

His glance suddenly shifted from the distant ridges to her. He caught her studying him. She couldn't look away.

A hum invaded her ears, like the sound of a high-tension power line. She could almost feel the electricity arc between them. In his eyes she saw the same questions she would ask when the time was appropriate.

"Ready to go on?" he asked.

She realized he'd been letting her rest. Tears clogged her throat, so she nodded.

He clicked, and the gelding obediently went forward into the pelting hail. The sound changed. It beat against the gray felt of his Stetson. He held his head forward slightly in order for the wide brim to shield her from the frozen droplets.

Some things hadn't changed, she mused, holding on to the saddle horn while the gelding picked a path along the rocky trail. Kerrigan might be harder, tougher, but there was still that core of old Western courtesy toward women she'd trusted from the very first moment they'd met.

Then she remembered that later he'd left town without a word and that her letters had gone unanswered. She admitted there had been mitigating circumstances, but why hadn't he answered her letters? Maybe she'd ask him. When she was feeling strong enough to accept his answer.

"Is it much farther?" she asked.

"No. Are you hurting?"

"Yes."

Five minutes later they turned onto an equally faint trail and came out of the trees next to a house, a one-room, split-log cabin used by cowboys who rode the fence line making repairs.

"Sit still. I'll help you down."

So saying, he swung down, then reached up for her. When she slid her right leg over the saddle, he tightened his hold on her waist and lifted her down.

She nearly cried out from pain. "Ribs," she gasped and swayed against him.

"Sorry," he said in a husky voice just above her head. "I didn't realize you hurt that much."

Pulling herself upright and out of his arms, she started for the cabin.

"There's some snow pack under the trees back there. That might help stop the bruising. Let's go inside, then I'll get it."

He held her arm as if she were some feeble grandma he was helping across the street. They went into the cabin, where she sank carefully into a straight chair pulled up to the fireplace.

"There's dry wood. I'll get a fire started." He was busy for a few minutes with wood and pine needles and matches.

When the flames were curling around the logs, he stood and went outside.

Rachel closed her eyes and wished she hadn't jumped out of the tree. Stupid. Really stupid. He was only going to tranquilize the cat and move the animal to safety.

Yes, but she hadn't known that. Under the circumstances, she had hardly had time to inquire what his intentions were. If she'd known it was him, would she have trusted his judgment?

Before she could answer this, he returned. He carried another bandanna, blue rather than red this time. It was full of snow, the ends tied so none would fall out.

"Lift your top and we'll put this on your side," he said.

She pulled her cotton turtleneck out of her jeans and lifted it to the curve of her breasts. He placed the snow pack against her, causing her to gasp at the cold.

"I'll hold it," she said, slipping her hands under his.

He backed off. "I have to see to the horse." He went outside again. Through a window grimy with age, she saw him lead the gelding to a shed next to a corral. He went inside with the animal. In a few minutes he came out carrying the saddle and rifle. He brought them into the cabin.

She noticed some hay and oat seeds on his jeans. The horse was probably happy to be out of the weather and munching on his dinner. She remembered the lunch she hadn't gotten around to eating. Glancing at her watch, she saw it was almost four.

"I can't believe it's this late."

He made a sound deep in his throat that could have meant anything or nothing, dropped the saddle near the hearth, propped the gun in the corner and headed back outside. He returned with an armload of straw and the saddle blanket.

While she watched, he spread the straw in front of the saddle, then laid the saddle blanket over it. Two more blankets were tied behind the saddle in a waterproof wrap. Those he dropped at the foot of the straw bed.

"You can lie down whenever you want."

She swallowed hard. It had finally dawned on her they'd both have to sleep on the pallet. There was nothing else but a makeshift table and two chairs in the tiny room.

"I have a sleeping bag at my camp—"

"That's three miles round-trip in a hail storm. If you think I'll take an animal, who's already put in a full day's work, out in that, think again."

She gave him a resentful glance. He made her sound like a heartless wretch. "I wouldn't think of it," she said succinctly.

"Temper?" he inquired with savage gentleness. "Save your energy. We have a long night before us and a rough ride out tomorrow." He studied her for a minute, then shook his head as if wondering what ill fate had brought him to this.

His gaze took on a brooding, angry quality—not directed at her perhaps, but at life and its quirks—and it came to her that he hated having to deal with the situation, with her and her injuries, that he wished he'd never seen her again.

Sadness echoed through her like the lonely cry of the wind through the river gorge. So much between them . . . gone . . . gone forever. . . .

"Kerrigan—" she began, the questions refusing to stay inside a minute longer.

Again he cut her off. "We'll eat, then talk."

"I don't remember you being so bossy," she grumbled. It was clear he intended to call the shots between them.

"The circumstances are different," he said, acknowledging the changes in him and in his life. "This is my cabin and my land. You're the one who's trespassing this time."

As he'd been trespassing on Barrett land the day of their elopement? She wanted to ask, to bring the past into the open between them. She wanted to tell him she'd been heartbroken when he hadn't shown up. She'd thought he'd changed his mind about the marriage. Until a ranch hand had told her the truth.

After hanging the poncho and her jacket on a nail she found sticking out of a log, she sat on the pallet and leaned on the saddle. The snow pack had numbed her aching ribs. Her head still hurt, though, as if she were feeling the steady *thwack* of an ax against a tree.

She was silent while he knelt by the saddlebags and removed his camping gear. Laying a macaroni dinner on the hearth, he took a bucket from a peg by the door and went out. A minute later, he returned with it full of water.

It was evident he knew what he was doing. In no time, it seemed, he was serving her a portion of macaroni and cheese on an aluminum plate along with a sourdough roll he'd retrieved from his saddlebags. He placed a cup of coffee on the floor beside her.

"I only have one cup," he said, "so you can have coffee first. I'll have some after you."

She started to protest, but closed her mouth when he gave her a hard look. He hooked his toe around the chair rung and pulled it closer to the fire. He ate from the cooking pan, using the stirring spoon. She used his fork, an act that seemed terribly intimate.

They ate quickly, hungrily. Although her head still pounded, she thought she could go to sleep. With the crackle of the fire and the chatter of hail and sleet on the tin roof, she felt snug and as comfortable as she was liable to get that night.

"Do you think I could take some aspirin?" she asked.

"Not with a chance of a concussion. The doctor'll give you something tomorrow." He finished his meal.

He took her plate and the fork, efficiently washed them in a thimbleful of water and placed them on the table. He cleaned the pan, spoon and his knife. The pan and spoon joined the items on the table. The knife went into the sheath attached to his boot.

"The meal was excellent," she said. She lay down against the saddle and pulled a blanket over her. "Sometime I'll cook dinner for you at my camp." She closed her eyes.

"Don't go to sleep," he ordered. "There's a few details I want to find out first."

"My head hurts, Kerrigan."

He ignored her complaint. "What are you doing on our land?"

She opened her eyes. Her lashes felt weighted. She let them drift closed. "Observing an eagle."

"You're up here bird watching?" He gave a snort of disbelief.

"Sort of." She smiled and forced herself to look at him. He was studying her through narrowed eyes, his glance suspicious. "I have a grant to study the migration and—" she was surprised to find the word hard to say "—mating of a female eagle I'd tracked to this part of the country last year. She winters over in central California and heads back here usually in March."

"A grant?" he questioned.

"Yes. After you...we..." She cleared her throat. "I returned to school, changed my major from literature to biology and got a degree. I'm a naturalist."

"The eagle is the subject of your study? That's why you came back here?"

"The eagle nests here," she explained with simple logic.

"I heard you'd sold the ranch you inherited."

"Yes. I didn't want to, but my brother was in charge. The ranch was losing money."

Kerrigan nodded. "I can identify with that."

Pain beat against her eyes. "I'd really like to go to sleep now," she requested.

"No," he said sharply. He picked up the coffee, which she'd only sipped once, and took a drink. "You'll stay awake until I'm sure you're okay."

"Then talk to me. Tell me about your ranch."

"What do you want to know?"

"Everything. Start at the beginning."

"The beginning," Kerrigan repeated. He poured hot coffee into the cup and took a drink, staring into the fire.

The beginning was too dismal. He could just remember the early years with his father—the happy years. After his dad died in an oil well blowout, their lives had gone downhill. When his mother had died of an overdose of sleeping pills and alcohol, he and Keegan had been dumped on their grandfather.

Rachel was interested in his ranch. He'd start with the summer they met. "When the old man died—"

"Your grandfather," she interjected as if he were telling a story and had left out an important part.

"When my grandfather died," he began the tale anew, "I came home to take care of the legalities."

"Your brother was in the hospital in Denver. His leg had been gored by a bull."

"Who's telling this story?" he demanded.

She smiled sleepily and settled more comfortably against the curve of the saddle. The snow had melted in the bandanna, soaking her cotton top. She laid the bandanna on the hearth.

He wrung it out over the bucket and hung it up to dry, some part of him acutely aware that the cloth was warm from her skin.

"My grandfather's place had been mortgaged to the hilt," he said. "We were going to let it go back to the bank. Then we realized it would be cheaper to save it and add land, if we could. The ranch next to it was for sale. Keegan and I had a small nest egg, not much, because we'd just started winning the bigger purses. We paid off the mortgage, but we were broke."

"You won five rodeos later that year. Keegan won three. You both moved up in the standings."

"Yeah, well, we had a hard time convincing the bank to back us in buying more land. We had to show them our winnings could be relied upon."

"You did. You were number one and two for two years in a row. Later, after your brother was hurt again, he retired and you've been in the top five since, winning around a million dollars a year for the past five. Is it true that you've retired?"

"Yes."

"Why?"

"It's a young man's game."

She laughed. The sound reminded him of a waterfall, a rushing, rippling murmur of delight. "You're so old?"

"Thirty-one soon."

"In three days," she said. "April sixth. I remember."

She turned her head from the fire and gazed at him with eyes like dark honey. A stricture formed in his chest. She'd always made him think he could perform impossible deeds of courage.

"I'm twenty-eight," she said.

He remembered. The reason she'd been in the bar was to celebrate her twenty-first birthday. They watched the blaze in silence. The sleet had stopped and the wind had died.

After a while, she asked, "Is there a Mrs. McPherson?"

"Neither Keegan nor I have married, if that's what you're asking."

"Why not?"

He tightened his hold on the tin cup. "I learned my lesson about women a long time ago."

"You mean because of the beating?"

The hot coffee splashed on his hand, and he cursed under his breath. He wiped his hand with the bandanna. "I'd wondered if you knew about that." Every muscle in his body ached with the need to hit something.

"Not until later. One of our ranch hands didn't think it had been exactly a fair fight—three against one."

His brother had agreed. "When we're both prime, we'll go back and clean out that bunch of polecats," he had said, just out of the hospital and still limping.

"She's not worth it," Kerrigan had replied.

He looked at her, the curves of her body drawing his gaze against his will. She was fuller in the breasts, he thought. Her hips were rounder. An ache started low in his gut.

He forced himself to remember that this was the woman who had vowed her love, then had failed to appear at the crucial moment.

So what else was new? he questioned with bitter amusement. His mother had abandoned her sons in favor of the bottle. That had been due to grief, and he had forgiven her.

Rachel had abandoned him on the way to the altar. He'd never understood her motives. He still didn't.

"I wrote you," she said softly, an accusation in her tone.

Strange to be having this conversation after seven years. He shrugged as if none of it had mattered to him.

"You never answered my letters."

"I was moving around a lot in those days."

"I see." She sounded sad.

Words rushed to his throat and choked him with the need to explain, to apologize for failing her . . .

Hell, he'd shown up, hadn't he? The welcoming committee had been a little rough. It had been all he could do to drag himself to his truck and drive the fifty miles to his grandfather's old homestead. Yeah, he'd learned his lesson.

A person was a fool to think love was more than an itch below the belt, not all that important in the scheme of things. He stood, gulped the coffee and flung the cup on the table.

"Damn you," he said. "Of all the eagles that must live in all the national parks in the United States, why the hell did you have to choose *that* one to follow?"

He jerked his jacket off the hook and headed out the door.

Chapter Three

Rachel rose to her knees and watched Kerrigan through the window. She could barely see him in the dim twilight. He went into the shed, presumably to check on the horse. A few languid snowflakes drifted to the ground.

She saw him come out after a minute, scan the sky with weather-wise eyes, then go off into the woods. Hmm, that was something she was going to have to do before she settled down for the night. She'd wait for him to come back, then she'd go.

After adding another log to the fire, she sat down to wait.

Glancing at the makeshift bed, she admitted she was going to have to face what lay ahead. She and Kerrigan were going to have to sleep together. There was no help for it.

They would just have to be adult about the situation. *He* seemed to be handling it with no problem. She was the one who hadn't dared think on it.

What was there to think about? Even if Kerrigan did have ideas—which he didn't . . . well, maybe he did, but he certainly wouldn't act on them—anyway, *she* had a pounding headache.

A bubble of laughter, rather sad, more than a little desperate, rose to her lips. A headache. That was an old, shopworn excuse . . . and very true.

She yawned and snuggled down against the saddle. It was like him, she thought, closing her eyes. Hard, toughened by life and strictly functional. Like its owner. No silver or flashy touches, just sturdy, hardworking leather.

She woke with a start and glanced wildly around. It took her a few seconds to get her bearings. Oh, yes, the cabin on McPherson land. Kerrigan!

He wasn't inside.

The fire had burned low. She added two pieces of wood to it, then pulled up her top to check her ribs. A bruise, roughly the size and shape of a large grapefruit, discolored her skin. Drawing a deep breath, she felt the spot but couldn't detect a jagged edge of bone. Nothing broken.

Frowning, she picked her jacket off its nail and pulled it on, careful of her injured left side. The side nearest her heart, she thought, then grimaced at the inane reflection. After zipping her coat, she pulled open the door and stepped outside.

"Oh," she said, startled.

Kerrigan leaned against a post that supported the roof overhang. "What is it?" he asked.

"I . . . I need . . ." A flush rose to her face. Considering what they'd once been to each other, it was ridiculous to be embarrassed about needing to answer nature's call. She lifted her chin and spoke with dignity. "I'm going to the woods."

He pushed away from the post. "I'll go with you."

"Uh, no, you can't. I need . . . privacy."

"I'm only going to walk you to those trees over there to make sure you don't trip in the dark. Then I'll come back. You can call me when you're ready to return."

He took her arm. She went quietly, as they used to say in the old Westerns. No use trying to argue with a Mc-Pherson. The people in town said the boys had been prone to fight at the drop of a hat when they were young. Kerrigan had been only gentle with her, especially when he found out she was a virgin.

True to his word, he dropped his hold on her at the edge of the woods and returned to his post. She walked a bit farther.

Although the wind was still, the air was cold. She quickly finished and returned, not bothering to call for her escort. When she stepped into the clearing, he left the little porch and came to her. They crossed the open space in silence.

"It's lighter now than at twilight." She stopped at the roof overhang and leaned against the post to gaze at the sky.

The clouds had cleared. The moon was visible, full and huge and very bright, so beautiful it made her want to weep.

"It looks like a big snowball, doesn't it?" she remarked. Her voice sounded husky. She cleared it self-consciously.

He gave a sort of grunt or snort, she couldn't tell which. "You'd better go in," he said. The remark wasn't in the nature of a polite suggestion, but an order.

"What about you?"

"I'll be in soon."

"You've been out here for more than an hour. I went to sleep," she added. She realized she sounded as if she were accusing him of being derelict in his duty toward her.

"You seem all right to me," he said coolly. "Are you dizzy?"

"No." She went inside and banged the door shut. "Oh," she groaned, pressing her fingertips to her aching temples.

She folded her coat to use as a pillow in place of the saddle, which was too high and too hard for her comfort, and spread both blankets over their bed. After removing her shoes, she lay down, leaving him as much room on the crackly straw pallet as she could.

The fatigue seemed to radiate from her body. She hadn't realized how tired she was. She yawned once and closed her eyes.

Kerrigan stayed outside until he was so cold he couldn't feel his toes in his boots. He wasn't numb all over, which was what he'd hoped, but it was a start. Heaving a sigh that indicated his feelings about life's dirty tricks, he went inside and slid the bolt closed, locking them in for the night.

He stopped dead still when he looked at Rachel.

That she expected him to sleep with her was obvious. Both blankets were spread out over the pallet, and she'd left enough room behind her for him to lie there, too.

His mouth went as dry as thistledown. He rubbed his suddenly moist palms up and down his thighs. Slowly, he hung up his hat. After a short, furious argument with himself, which he lost, he took off his boots. With a cynical grimace, he lifted the blankets and crawled under the covers with her.

Well, there he was—in bed with the woman who'd robbed him of several years of peaceful dreams. There was an old saying for a situation like this. *Out of the frying pan and into the fire?* Yeah, that was it.

He'd no sooner lain down than Rachel, who was lying on her side with her back to him, scooted her feet over against his leg. Even through her socks and his pants, he could feel how cold they were.

Next thing he knew, she'd moved her tush over, too. Now it was nestled against his hip. She sighed and mumbled something.

"What?" he asked.

Her reply was indistinct.

"What did you say?" Was she dreaming? he wondered.

She rolled half over so that she rested against him and opened her eyes, startling him. "Nothing. I must have been dreaming."

"Yeah, you must have been." When she moved away, he said, "You can keep your feet against me. I don't mind."

For a long ten seconds, she didn't say anything. "Thank you," she said, very softly. She put her feet against him again and sighed wearily.

"Head still hurt?"

"Yes," she said.

He was hurting, too. Only it wasn't his head. Maybe he'd better go back to Plan A, which was for him to wrap one of the blankets around him and sit on the other side of the fireplace, his back to the wall, for the night.

Rachel stirred and moved her curvy little tush against him again. They'd spent lots of nights together, he suddenly recalled, talking and making love. They'd slept very little that month.

He almost groaned as his body roused to full, painful life. He would probably break through the zipper before morning. If he lived through the night, there was still the ride to the ranch . . . another four or five hours of temptation. And he'd never had any notions of sainthood.

Rachel woke with the dawn. She was instantly aware of the solid warmth behind her. Kerrigan's lean, hard body was cupped around hers. One arm was thrown carelessly over her waist. His hand rested on the pallet but was tucked under her breast, holding its weight in his palm.

Her heart set up a raucous beating in her chest. For a moment longer, she lay there, enjoying the tactile sensation of his touch, her skin tingling through her clothing. If they'd been married, she would have turned to him and wakened him with a kiss.

They would make love....

His hand moved and his thumb glided over the tip of her breast. Her nipple sprang instantly to life. Her breath caught in her throat. Without conscious thought, she pushed against his hold, enraptured by desire.

Suddenly he cursed under his breath and withdrew his hand. He lifted the blankets and rose, letting in a draft of cold air.

She turned her head and met his furious gaze.

"So you're awake." He almost growled the words. The tone of his voice accused her of trying to seduce him.

"Yes," she said coolly. He had been just as guilty—if guilt was the proper term—of adding fuel to the situation between them as she was.

He stomped into his boots and zipped his jacket. After adding wood and building up the fire, he headed for the door, taking the bucket with him when he left.

Rachel grimaced and sat up. Pushing her fingers through the heavy tangles of her hair, she smoothed it as best she could, then put on her shoes and jacket and headed outside to the woods.

He was returning just as she was leaving. They passed each other under the narrow overhang without a word. When she came back inside after washing her face in a rocky basin hollowed out of a boulder in the rushing little creek, he had oatmeal ready.

"Head still hurt?" he asked, handing her his bowl.

"Like the devil was inside and trying to get out," she replied. She ate without much interest.

Kerrigan took the bowl when she finished, added more instant oatmeal and poured water over it from the bucket. He wolfed the meal down. "Let's be off," he said with a grim frown.

They left as soon as he got the fire drowned and the horse fed and saddled. She thought each movement was more painful today than it had been yesterday.

"Do we have to go so fast?" she demanded after what seemed like hours of pounding along the rocky trail.

"We aren't," he snarled next to her ear. "Lean into me like I showed you yesterday."

"My ribs ache," she complained. She realized she sounded sulky, but it was the truth. She hurt all over. And he, the brute, was apparently indifferent to her pain.

"We'll see Dr. Dennison this afternoon. If we ever get to the ranch so we can switch to the truck."

A tremor ran through her at the thought of the doctor. She pushed the memory aside. "Good," she said, matching Kerrigan's sarcastic tone perfectly. "I was afraid we'd have to ride the horse all the way to town."

His chest heaved in a put-upon sigh against her back, but he didn't say anything. Tired of holding herself erect and trying to counter every jounce of the gelding, she relaxed against him, letting her body curve into his completely.

She felt his chest rise in a sharply drawn breath. Then she became hotly aware that he wasn't as indifferent to her as he was pretending. He was blatantly aroused.

Blood rushed through her and gathered deep inside. Her body prepared to welcome him into her.

No. Her instincts had been wrong before. She wouldn't trust them again.

"Don't worry," he drawled in her ear. "I don't act on my impulses anymore. I've learned there's more to a relationship than sex . . . hot and sweet as that might be."

She twisted her head to look at him. He gave her a one-sided smile, hard and cynical.

As they rode down the trail, she thought of that young man she'd met and made love with within hours of their first meeting. There'd been warmth in him, then, and caring and gentleness. She'd missed that man when he'd left. She still did, she realized.

The pain in her left side seemed to increase. Kerrigan was right. Of all the eagles she could have observed, why had she come here to find one to study?

"Good for you," she said defensively, angry with her body's response to his. "It seems we've both learned a lot."

"Right."

He was so cold, a chip off the old glacier, one might say. She didn't find the thought humorous at all.

"Are we getting close to your place?" she asked.

"Halfway. We'll rest up the trail a ways. I know a meadow with a couple of fallen trees."

He didn't explain that statement, and she didn't ask. When they got there, she saw the trees had formed a natural bench and backrest. After getting off the gelding, she sank wearily onto the seat and laid her head back on the huge trunk of the upper tree.

"You'll get resin in your hair," he advised.

She kept her eyes closed. "What does a little fir sap matter in the grand scheme of things?" she questioned philosophically, not expecting an answer.

"The hell if I know," he muttered, opening one of his saddlebags. He tossed a granola bar into her lap and took one for himself. After running his hand over the horse's hocks, he sat down a couple of feet from her and ate.

Not hungry, she stuck the granola bar in her pocket and rested, afraid to let herself think, because her thoughts suddenly seemed too sad to contemplate at this moment.

She would remember the past, she mused, and remembering, she would relive the days and nights she'd known him and the ones after he'd left. But not now. When she was stronger, maybe. If she thought about it now—she bit into her bottom lip to stop the tremble that threatened her composure—if she thought about it now, she might cry, and she'd vowed never to cry over a man again.

They arrived at the ranch in time for the noonday meal. Rachel gazed at the activity below, when they paused on the crest of a hill. The hill overlooked a long, narrow valley. A creek, lined by cottonwoods, meandered through the meadows. Several buildings dotted the area. One of them was a large house of natural stone with a wide bank of windows on the south side.

Horses and men seemed to be everywhere.

"The remuda," Kerrigan said. His chest moved against her back as if he drew a deep breath of pleasure.

She knew what a remuda was. It referred to the herd of working horses on a ranch. There must have been over a hundred cow ponies in the pasture. Several cowhands divided and moved them by groups into corrals.

Suddenly one man on a magnificent roan stallion peeled off from the group and headed in their direction, riding hell for leather and whooping at the top of his lungs. She tensed, not sure what was about to happen.

Kerrigan chuckled and pulled the reins tight on the gelding who seemed to want to join the wild race.

The other rider charged up to them and came to an impressive stop, with the stallion rearing and pawing the air before settling lightly to the ground.

"Keegan," she said. "The other McPherson twin."

The cowboy doffed his hat. "At your service, ma'am." He had the same mocking quality in his voice as Kerrigan.

The men were within a half inch of height and five pounds of weight to each other, she guessed. Both had hair that was almost black. Their facial features were very similar. Keegan's eyes were gray, though, shading to blue at the outer edges.

"You're not identical twins," she murmured.

"Brilliant observation," Kerrigan remarked. "Looks like you've got everything under control," he said to his brother.

"Yeah, the vet just left." His gaze took in every detail of Rachel's appearance. His smile was lazy, assured, curious. "Who's this, and where did you find her? Is there another one out there like her?"

"Rachel Barrett. Keegan McPherson," Kerrigan introduced them. He reined the gelding into step with the stallion, and they started down the hill.

Rachel said hello. The brother's smile disappeared. The sardonic humor left his expression, to be replaced by a cold, hard perusal. Well, no need to ask. He knew who she was.

"What the hell is going on?" Keegan asked.

"She fell out of a tree," Kerrigan replied. "I'm taking her in so the doc can have a look at her."

"What was she doing in a tree?"

"Eagle watching."

"Care to explain that?"

Rachel didn't appreciate being discussed over her head. "I have a grant to study an eagle in the national forest—"

"She was on our land, out near the number four line shack," Kerrigan interrupted. "That's why I'm taking her in."

"Good thinking. Is she hurt?"

Rachel felt Kerrigan shrug. They rode to a gigantic stable and stopped at the open doors. Keegan shouted, and a young cowboy came out. He stopped in surprise when he saw her.

"Don't stand there catching flies in your mouth," Keegan advised. "Take care of the horses, will you?"

The two brothers swung down. Kerrigan reached up for Rachel. He set her gently on the ground. She held on to him for a second while strength returned to her legs. When she looked up, Keegan was watching. His eyes, she noted, were as cold as a winter storm.

"Dinner ready?" Kerrigan asked.

"In the cook house," his brother replied.

"I'll bring two plates over to the house. We'll eat, then I'll take her into town."

"I'll get the plates." Keegan walked toward a building that formed the third side of an open quadrangle, with the stables and main house filling in the other two sides. Trees, edging the road to town, irregularly completed the fourth side.

"Come on." Kerrigan led the way into the house.

They went in a side door into a huge room that was evidently the family room and office. Hardwood floors gleamed. A Persian rug of deep blue and burgundy was flanked by two sofas of blue velvet. A stone fireplace took up one wall.

A glass-walled room divider held what looked like hundreds of rodeo trophies plus a large television. On the other side of the divider was a desk, file cabinets and several chairs.

"Functional, tasteful and comfortable," she remarked.

His gaze swept the room and landed on her. "I'll call the doctor," he told her. "Make yourself at home."

Home. His home, not hers.

She took a seat in one of the leather easy chairs in front of the desk. A wave of longing swept over her. If things had worked out differently, she and Kerrigan would be sharing a home. They'd have had children.

Nausea rose in her throat. She pressed a hand to her mouth until the feeling passed. When she glanced up, Kerrigan was watching her from behind his desk. He had the phone in his hand and was dialing a number.

While he spoke with someone at the doctor's office, she gazed out the broad bank of windows at the activity in the stable yard. The horses had been put into corrals. The men unsaddled their mounts and stored their gear. They went to the cook house.

From the back of the main house, she heard Keegan yell, then the sound of a door slamming. All was silent.

Kerrigan finished the call and gestured for her to precede him down a short hall. They went into the kitchen. Two plates were on a round oak table.

"Milk or tea?" he asked.

"Milk," she requested.

He poured a large glass for her and chose a beer for himself from a paneled refrigerator that blended with the oak cabinets that surrounded it.

"Who did your house?" she asked. "It's marvelous."

"Keegan and I picked it out of a magazine of architects' designs. Keegan supervised the construction, even did a lot of it himself." Kerrigan smiled cynically. "It was good therapy for him. Riding bulls did the same for me."

There was more to his statements than she understood, but it seemed too much effort to pursue the matter. Not that he'd explain anything to her. He and his brother struck her as self-contained men who shared little of themselves with others.

Had knowing her done that to him? She sighed, filled with the sadness of it all.

"Sit." He put the milk down by a plate.

She took her place. They ate without speaking. When they were through, he put the dishes in a dishwasher.

"I'll get the truck. There's a bathroom through there. Come outside when you're ready." He walked out.

Rachel went into the bathroom. It was tiled in white with blue flocked wallpaper on the upper third and blue towels on the racks. She noticed there was a shower. A blue terry bathrobe hung behind the door. She wondered whose it was.

When she went back into the kitchen, she saw Kerrigan in a four-wheel-drive utility vehicle, waiting for her. She stepped out on a wooden deck and quickly climbed into the truck.

The road was a two-lane blacktop, narrow and curving in places, roaming over hills and through thickly wooded areas. Forty minutes later they reached the first houses of the town. He drove along Main Street, which was also the highway, and parked at the doctor's office.

After turning off the engine, he rested his hand over the steering wheel and studied her. "Relax," he said. "It's just a checkup. I didn't know you were scared of doctors."

He climbed down and came around the truck. She unclenched her hands, realizing how cowardly she must appear. She got out when he opened the door, but before he could touch her.

They went inside. No one was in the waiting room.

"This is his afternoon off," Kerrigan explained. "Doc's getting old. He works short hours now and sends the serious stuff down to Medford."

She nodded.

Kerrigan left her and went through a door and down the hall. She heard him calling the doctor. An answer came from the nether region of the building.

"You can come on back," Kerrigan said, sticking his head around the hall door.

Heart pounding, she went with him to a room at the back. The doctor was there, a gray-haired, kindly man nearing seventy. He looked up and smiled at her. She held her breath, afraid of what he might say.

"Rachel," he said gently, "it's good to see you again."

"You, too, Doc." Her voice was husky. She cleared it and glanced around. The room held an X-ray apparatus.

"There's a gown in that first cubicle. You can change there." He looked at Kerrigan. "You can go to the waiting room."

A flush rose to Kerrigan's neck. He nodded and headed out.

"Kerrigan tells me you had a fall out of a tree," the doctor said when she returned. "From the sounds of it, you're a real heroine, trying to save the cat from getting shot."

"Except he wasn't going to shoot it, not to hurt it, anyway. He was going to move her to the back country. I ruined his chance, I'm afraid. He'll have to track her all over again."

"Well, no great tragedy, I should think."

He had her lie on the table while he examined her head and side. After checking her reflexes, he positioned her for the X rays and took three pictures.

"You can dress and wait in my office, third door to the right," he said. "I'll run these through the developer."

Kerrigan was in the office when she entered. She paused on the threshold, then went in. She noticed her file was on the desk, amid a litter of other folders and reports.

She'd been there twice in the past. The first time, she'd thought she was pregnant. Doc had said she wasn't, she was just suffering from emotional stress. He'd held her while she cried out her grief. She had wanted the child, she'd realized.

There had been anger in her as well as grief—Kerrigan had left without a word to her—and guilt over the beating.

Back at the ranch, she'd gone for a ride on a half-wild stallion. Racing across the rough country, the horse had stumbled. They'd gone down in a heap. Her brother had rushed her to the doctor's office, not knowing of her earlier visit that same day....

"Her injuries don't look too serious," Doc said when Kerrigan came in. "Mostly painful. Lots of contusion, probably a concussion, but a mild one. Now I have a few questions." He took his chair, picked up a pen and frowned at Kerrigan. "We'll call you when we're through."

Kerrigan ignored the dismissal.

"I don't mind if he stays," she said after a tense silence.

Doc flicked her a keen glance, then nodded. "Let's see, you must be twenty-seven or -eight?"

"Twenty-eight."

"Married?"

"No."

"Any major illnesses or surgery since the last time you were here?"

"None," she replied.

"No aftereffects from your previous fall?"

"No."

"What previous fall?" Kerrigan broke in.

She and Doc exchanged glances. "I fell from a horse once, when I was here before," she answered.

Kerrigan frowned. "When?"

"After . . . after you left town for the rodeo circuit. The ranch was sold and we were preparing to leave. I went for a ride one day on a stallion that was still half wild."

"That was a stupid thing to do," Kerrigan snapped at her.

"I know," she said quietly, not looking at him.

The doctor resumed his questions. No, she had no allergies to drugs. She'd always brimmed with health, rarely even having a cold or the flu.

"I'll check on those X rays," Doc said and left the room.

Kerrigan moved restlessly behind her. She fought a need to turn to him, to ask him to hold her and share the pain of their mutual past. She locked her hands together. If he had cared, if he had truly cared, wouldn't he have called or written later, after she'd tried to contact him?

"What is it?" Kerrigan asked, dropping to his haunches beside her chair. "Is your head still hurting?"

She nodded, unable to speak. They heard footsteps in the hall. She was relieved.

"You have two hairline cracks in your lower ribs," Doc said, returning to the office. "Nothing to worry about. Just take it easy for the next month. I want you to rest. Do you need something for that headache so you can sleep?"

"No."

"Yes."

She glared at Kerrigan. "I can speak for myself."

"It's a long drive to town. I don't want to dash back in at midnight to get something in case you can't sleep. If you don't need it, fine. If you do, we'll have it."

Doc agreed with that logic, so she acquiesced.

"She's staying by herself out in the woods," Kerrigan told the doctor. "Is that safe?"

"I'll be perfectly fine," she quickly said.

"Well, maybe you shouldn't be alone for a few days. If you fell again or lifted anything heavy..." He frowned at her from under his white eyebrows.

"I'll see that she stays at the ranch where we can keep an eye on her," Kerrigan decided, giving her a narrow glance when she opened her mouth to argue.

"Good idea," Doc approved. He patted her shoulder. "Let the boys take care of you for a few days. Do them good to have female company on that ranch." He chortled as if he thought that a brilliant idea.

Kerrigan tucked the packet of pills in his shirt pocket. He thanked the doctor for taking care of her, then they left.

"Don't you have any women on the ranch?" she asked on the way to the truck.

"Does the thought of being the only woman on the place bother you?"

"Yes," she said truthfully.

His face set in hard lines. "You don't have to worry. No man on the Sky Eagle ranch would dare touch you."

She didn't explain that it wasn't the cowhands she worried about. Or even him. It was her own reactions that upset her.

"I have a few things I need to pick up at the feed store," Kerrigan said when she didn't reply. "You can wait in the diner."

"I'd rather stay in the truck."

"We'll be loading sacks of feed. You'll probably get bounced around. It'd be better if you waited inside."

"All right."

He walked her across the street. In the restaurant, she sat at a rickety table. Kerrigan ordered her a cup of cocoa when she indicated that was what she wanted. He tossed a bill to the waitress and left.

Rachel sipped the soothing drink when it arrived. She finally looked through the archway at the stools that lined the counter of the bar. There, the third one—that's where she'd been sitting when he'd walked in.

She remembered the scene in detail. Kerrigan had worn tight jeans and a white shirt. While several men had sported string ties, he'd had his shirt open at the collar with a blue bandanna tied around his neck.

He'd been different from the others—contained, self-possessed, his gaze cool as he swept the room...and lighted on her.

He'd come over and introduced himself. Ignoring her friends, they'd talked for hours and had left together when the bar closed at two in the morning. They'd talked some more, sitting in his pickup truck and dunking doughnuts in coffee. While the sun rose over the mountains, they'd become lovers.

It was as if she'd been set free, as if she'd found the missing part of herself she hadn't known was lost, as if time had begun at that moment. It had been wild...incredibly sweet...and foolish. For a month they'd seen each other every night.

She sighed, fighting the ridiculous tears that kept coming to the surface. It was over long ago. A summer fling.

And yet...she couldn't help wondering how it might have been for them. They'd have been married seven, almost eight years by now.

"Ready?" Kerrigan stood beside her. She'd been so lost in contemplation, she hadn't heard his approach. She looked into his eyes. If there'd been a child, would it have had blue eyes or brown? Dark hair or light? So many possibilities...

Chapter Four

Rachel could barely slide out of the utility truck when they arrived at the ranch. Her body ached from top to bottom. If she could have breathed without moving her chest, she would have.

Kerrigan took one look at her and muttered a succinct curse. "Let's get you to bed before you pass out," he said.

"I don't think there's any danger of that. I'm far from being unconscious. But I wish I were," she added, following him inside.

The house was built on two levels, with the kitchen and living quarters on the lower one. Six steps led up to the bedroom level. Five doors opened off the hall. Bedrooms, she assumed.

Between the two doors to her left was a reading alcove with built-in bookcases wrapped around the three walls. It was both cozy and functional. The soft slate blue shades of the family room were echoed here in striped wallpaper and the brocade upholstery of the easy chairs.

He opened a door to the right. "You can use this room. It has a private bathroom."

"Are there bedrooms behind all those doors?" she asked, going in behind him.

"Yes." He crossed the blue Berber carpet and closed the blinds against the late-afternoon glare of the sun. "Three guest rooms on this side. The other two guest rooms share a connecting bath. Keegan's room is the second left. Mine is the first."

She glanced out the door. "Across from here?"

"Yes." He yanked the bedspread back and folded it at the foot of the queen-size bed. A tall chest of drawers, a full-length mirror, two armchairs and a piecrust table with a Tiffany lamp completed the furniture.

Peeking into the bathroom, she saw it had a white tub surrounded by blue tiles. "Could I take a shower?"

He glanced at her, then away. The frown etched deeper into his brow while he thought her request over. "I suppose it would be all right. Do you feel dizzy?"

"No, only achy." Her smile was rueful.

After nodding, he left the bedroom and closed the door behind him. She shed her jacket, shoes and clothing. In the tall mirror, she surveyed the damage.

The bruise on her side was interesting shades of purple, sort of green around the edges. There was another one on her hip, a third on her thigh. They weren't as colorful, nor as large as the one that had cracked her ribs.

She went into the bathroom and started the shower. Fifteen minutes later, feeling more human, she headed for the bed. There, on the blue velour blanket, was a man's shirt, a soft blue-plaid flannel. She stared at it for a long second before putting it on.

The flannel covered her tired body like a comforting caress. She grimaced at herself in the mirror. The tails of the shirt reached almost to her knees. After rolling the sleeves back, she pulled the sheet and blanket down and sank onto the firm mattress.

For all that he was—a hard-driving, ex-rodeo jock—Kerrigan McPherson was a considerate man, she mused, closing her eyes.

Ten minutes passed. She opened her eyes and glanced at the clock on the mantel. Mid-afternoon. Perhaps she shouldn't try to sleep now. She could go to bed early.

A soft knock thudded on the door.

She had to clear her throat before she could invite in whoever it was. Kerrigan entered. He carried a glass of water.

"I brought you a pill. In case you can't sleep."

Well, he seemed to know her physical condition better than she did herself. "Thanks." She took the pill and drank the water.

He stood there a minute after she handed the glass back. "That should give you about four hours rest. I'll get you up for supper after that. I've arranged for someone to stay with you during the day. One of the cowhands said his sister has agreed to drive over after her kids leave for school."

"I don't need a baby-sitter," Rachel protested.

"You're going to have one. I don't want to take a chance on your passing out and falling down the steps."

He was so dictatorial she wanted to leave just to defy him. But it was too much effort. The pain receded until it was only the distant sound of surf pounding in her skull. The last thing she saw before she went to sleep was Kerrigan sitting in one of the chairs, watching her with his icy gaze.

The ice enclosed her completely, and she knew nothing else.

* * *

"Rachel."

The soft sound of her name spoken in a rough, masculine purr fitted in with her dream. She snuggled deeper into her lover's embrace as the fire of passion burst through her....

She woke with a start. Kerrigan was bending over her. Gazing into his eyes, she felt the remembered warmth of her dream spread softly over her. She smiled to welcome her lover. Something wild and fierce flickered in his eyes, then was gone.

"Wake up," Kerrigan snapped, jarring her out of her trance.

She groaned and held her head. "Must you yell?"

"I wasn't yelling. I have some supper for you. Can you sit up?" He was the soul of cool, impersonal patience.

She pushed herself to an upright position. A callused hand tossed the pillows against the headboard. She leaned into them and let him place a bed tray across her lap.

The side panels that supported the tray were intricately carved. So was the surface of the tray that she could see around the edges of the bowl of soup and plate of crackers. The carvings were rodeo scenes, as detailed as a Remington sketch.

"This is beautiful," she remarked, tracing the graceful line of a cowboy and horse caught in midjump.

"Thanks."

Something in the way he said the word triggered a question in her. "Did you do it?"

He hesitated, then nodded.

"You're very talented."

"It was something to while away the time between rides."

"When you were rodeoing?"

"Yes." His expression was closed and remote. "Is your head still hurting?" he asked, stepping back from the bed and jamming his hands into his hip pockets.

"Yes, a constant, dull ache."

"The doc said it'd hurt for maybe three or four days."

She stared at the soup. There seemed nothing left to say. He pulled one of the chairs closer to the bed and sat in it, waiting for her to finish the meal. She wasn't hungry, but she ate, anyway, forcing the hot tomato soup past the tightness in her throat. More than words had been lost between them, she couldn't help thinking.

When she laid the spoon in the empty bowl, Kerrigan stood at once. He got a glass of water from the bathroom and gave her a pill, then watched to see that she swallowed it. "Do you need anything else?"

"No, thank you," she replied. She watched him take the tray and leave, his stride long and easy, his shoulders outlined by the blue chambray shirt, every flex of his lean, narrow hips visible under his jeans.

Glancing across the room, she looked directly into a mirror. She saw hunger in her eyes—a stark, lonely need.

Don't be foolish, she cautioned. His concern wasn't really for her. He just wanted to get her well and off his hands.

Tears rushed into her eyes. Once he'd been so gentle with her. She longed for that gentleness again. If only they could go back. But of course they couldn't.

She woke with the playful beams of the sun in her face. Her head still hurt, but the throb was less this morning, only a dull beat of pain across her temples. She rose, showered and dressed in her clothes, which had been washed, dried and folded while she slept. Kerrigan, the thoughtful host.

Leaving the bedroom, she noted the door across the hall was open. Curious, she paused and looked in. The bed was king-size, of a dark wood. A wall unit housed drawers, a bookcase and a small television. A sofa faced the unit. A cushioned parson's bench was placed at the foot of the bed. An open door to the left gave a glimpse of his bathroom.

A creak of timber made her jump guiltily. Hearing voices and laughter, she headed toward the sound. When she entered the kitchen, Kerrigan and a young woman stopped speaking and looked around. The silence swept over her. *Intruder,* it whispered.

Kerrigan rose. "Welcome to the land of the living," he said with a sardonic smile. "I was wondering if I should have Sita check on you." He smiled at his companion.

Rachel tore her gaze from his face and perused the other occupant of the room. Sita was in her twenties. Her hair was thick, black and wavy, her eyes large, brown and merry.

"Hi," she said.

"Hello."

"Sita is the one I told you about last night," Kerrigan continued. "Do you remember?"

Rachel managed a smile. "The sister to one of your cowboys. She has children to get off to school."

"Right. A boy and a girl," he confirmed, looking relieved that her brain seemed to be functioning okay.

"Does your husband work on the ranch?" Rachel asked.

"We're divorced," Sita said.

"Oh. I'm sorry."

She shrugged. "It was a long time ago."

"Sita manages the diner," Kerrigan said. "She also gives us a hand when we need it."

"We're planning the twins' birthday celebration," Sita told her. "Would you like breakfast? I can fix eggs or pancakes."

"Just juice and cereal, if you have it," Rachel broke in. She glanced at the clock. Almost ten. "I haven't slept this late in years."

"How's your headache?" Kerrigan got out a bowl, spoon and a box of cereal while Sita poured orange juice.

Rachel noticed they worked together without need for words. The painful throb in her head briefly included her entire body.

"Still there," she answered, smiling to show it wasn't anything she couldn't handle.

She took a seat at a round oak table when he placed the bowl on the shining surface. He got out the milk and brought it and the juice to the table. She glanced at the gleaming vinyl floor and neat room. "Who takes care of your house?"

"One of the men."

"There really are no women on the ranch?"

Sita laughed. "That's right. You've fallen into an all-male bastion. The women in the county make bets on who will be the first female brave enough to take on the fightin' McPhersons."

Rachel frowned at Kerrigan. What was he thinking, to agree to keep her here until her headache cleared? He gave a nonchalant shrug, obviously not caring what she thought. He offered her a cup of coffee and refilled his own cup.

He and Sita went back to their list.

After she ate and placed her dishes in the sink, Rachel took her coffee outside and stood on the broad wooden porch that ran along the entire south side of the house. Two men—one of them Kerrigan's brother—were in a corral, working with a colt who was only a few weeks old. She realized they were training it.

After crossing the yard, she leaned her arms on the fence rail and watched. While the cowboy held the halter, Keegan threw his leg over the colt. He was tall enough to straddle the animal without putting any weight on the young gelding's back.

The colt tossed his head, rolled his eyes at the man, then took a playful nip at his leg. Keegan laughed and slapped the youngster on the neck. The cowboy stepped aside, and Keegan moved the reins and clicked his tongue. He and the colt walked around the corral several times until the colt got the idea of responding to the bridle and ignoring the closeness of the man's body.

A truck cranked up behind her. She turned around. Kerrigan slammed the truck door, spoke to Sita, then stepped back while she drove off on the road to town. He came over to the fence.

"Spring training." His smile softened as he gestured toward the corral.

"Do you train all your horses this way?"

"Yes. We believe in starting them off young and developing a partnership between the horse and rider. It builds trust." The smile disappeared. "That way the horse isn't likely to run off and leave the cowboy in the lurch."

Was that an accusation in his tone?

They watched the proceedings in silence. While Keegan led the colt through the gate and into the pasture, another man brought the next horse into the corral, a big stallion with white markings on its auburn coat, and tied it to a post with no slack in the rope.

Several men joined Rachel at the rail. A stir of excitement went through the group when the cowboy brought out the saddle. She saw the big stallion tense. He moved away from the saddle and tried to throw his head up. The lead rope held him still.

In a minute the saddle was on. The stallion whickered and shook his head. She could see the animal becoming more and more riled up. Keegan returned to the corral. She knew that his thigh had been permanently injured during his rodeoing days. Surely he wasn't foolish enough to tackle the big stallion.

When the other cowboy climbed the fence, then dropped lightly into the saddle, taking the stallion by surprise, she let out a breath of relief. Keegan released the lead rope, freeing the animal, then leapt over the fence.

The horse stood there a second, not sure what was happening. Then the cowboy nudged the stallion with his knees.

All hell broke loose.

The stallion threw up his head and let out a scream of rage. Next, it dropped its head between its front legs and kicked out with the back two.

"Ride 'em, Hank," one man yelled.

"Tighten up," a wizened old-timer beside Rachel advised.

The stallion worked himself into a spinning, bucking fury. She clutched the rail and wondered how Hank could stay on. Of course, getting off might be worse. The stallion would probably kick him to death before anyone could help him.

"Why is the stallion being broken like this?" she yelled at the old man.

"He's a wild 'un," he yelled back.

More cowboys gathered. The place sounded like a real rodeo. The infuriated stallion lurched toward her, close enough that she felt his hot breath against her face when he reared, then threw himself into another spin near the fence. Adrenaline shot through her, and she clenched the rail harder.

Kerrigan tapped the back of her hand. "Watch that the horse doesn't catch your fingers against the fence with a flying hoof. More than one cowhand has had a couple of fingers broken that way."

She moved her hands back. "Thanks."

As they watched the wild ride, she was entirely aware of him at her side. He rested one arm on the top rail and turned his body toward hers, almost as if prepared to shield her in case of danger. She felt . . . safe . . . cherished.

Glancing up, she found his eyes on her, dark and intent, fathoms deep with some emotion she couldn't define. A tremor ran over her. She couldn't look away.

"Pull up," the old man screamed in a high pitch, bringing her attention back to the ruckus at hand.

Too late. Hank went flying over the head of the maddened horse. He landed in a roll and didn't stop until he reached the fence. Still on his back, he scrambled under it just as an ironclad hoof clanged against the bottom rail. The horse kicked a few more times, then trotted around the corral, his head high while he trumpeted his victory.

The men all looked at Hank.

The cowboy stood and brushed the dust off. He took a couple of steps. It was obvious he wouldn't be going back in the corral. He had a definite limp. Scowling in disgust, he shook his head.

"Well, big fella," Keegan commented, "looks like you're a candidate for the rodeo circuit."

She felt Kerrigan shift beside her. "Not yet he isn't," he contradicted his twin.

All eyes went to him.

"Grab him," he said when the horse came close to the fence.

Keegan snagged the reins, snapped on the lead rope and wrapped it around a post. The stallion whickered in warning, letting them know his temper wasn't spent.

Rachel wanted to protest when Kerrigan slid along the fence into position. She bit her lip and kept silent. He secured the reins around one hand. When he dropped onto the horse's back and jammed his feet into the stirrups, she stepped onto the bottom rail so she would have a clear view.

"Okay," Kerrigan called.

As soon as he was free, the stallion twisted sideways, lowered his head and kicked his hind feet straight at the sky. She didn't understand what kept Kerrigan on, but he stayed in the saddle.

"He's superglued," the cowboy on her left shouted and laughed like a maniac.

While she worried, ten grown men screamed and cheered at the top of their lungs. They went silent all at once when the horse suddenly dropped to the ground as if its legs had given out; then it went into a roll.

Kerrigan was ready, though. He kicked one foot out of the stirrup and stood when the horse went down. He gave a hard yank on the reins, and the stallion lunged to its feet, sides heaving. Kerrigan dropped back into the saddle. The battle was on again.

"He's tiring," the old man yelled. "Hold on, he's giving up."

Rachel could see no signs of it. The stallion was turning in a circle, his hooves kicking just as high. The fight raged from one side of the corral to the other.

All at once it was over.

The men quietened. They all watched intently to see what would happen next. The horse stood, his head down, his sides heaving. Kerrigan stayed in the saddle, alert for whatever trick the horse would pull next. It didn't move.

She saw him nudge the stallion. It brought its head up, then walked around the corral. When Kerrigan pulled back on the reins, the horse stopped. He started and stopped the spirited stallion several times; then he swung to the ground.

The men let out a chorus of congratulations.

"All right, fun's over," Keegan called out, a smile on his face. "You bums get back to work."

The men drifted off, still talking about the ride. Rachel didn't take her eyes off Kerrigan. He stood quietly talking to the horse and rubbing the animal's neck.

"You want me to cool him out?" the old man beside her asked.

Kerrigan looked up. He shook his head. The old-timer strode off and disappeared inside the long stable. Kerrigan's gaze came to rest on her. She realized she was leaning over the top rail, her fingers still clutched around it in a death grip.

"You're still the champ," Keegan said with mocking humor in his tone. "In case that was what you were wanting to prove."

Rachel watched the two brothers exchange glances. A wordless communication passed between them. She discovered she was envious of that closeness of spirit.

Her parents were close, both involved in her father's career as a diplomat. Due to the demands of that career, Rachel and her brother had been sent to boarding schools. Her closest companions had been the two guards who had accompanied her everywhere until she'd refused to have them anymore when she turned twenty-one.

Turning from the brothers, she realized her head was pounding, probably from the excitement. She skirted the corral and walked toward the creek that ran down the middle of the property.

The sky was a flawless blue, the air calm so that the sun warmed her enough without her jacket. The beauty of the ranch hit her anew as if she'd just recognized it. Painfully awake, she thought of dreams that would never come true.

She would have been happy on this land, she mused. She and Kerrigan could have made a home together, raised their

children here. Instead, she'd had seven years of solitude...contentment, she corrected. Most of the time, she
liked being alone.

It was only recently that she'd become restless and
haunted by a loneliness she didn't understand. Since she'd
returned here where she and Kerrigan had met and loved,
she admitted.

The attraction that had captured them from the first moment was still strong between them. She'd thought it was
love all those years ago. She knew better now.

Kerrigan had wanted her—maybe he'd even wanted her
money like her brother had said, although she'd never truly
believed that, not after the passion they'd shared—but he'd
never loved her.

Reaching the creek, she realized it was much colder in the
shade on the rocky bank than in the sun.

"Here," a masculine voice said behind her.

She spun and found Kerrigan standing behind her. He
held out his coat to her, then draped it around her shoulders when she didn't move. A whiff of cologne and sweat,
of horses and leather came to her. She drew a deep breath
and let it out slowly. Desire flooded her, gathering in a tight,
hot bud inside her.

"Does the smell offend you?" he asked. "Sorry."

"Not at all. It's...a working man's scent, clean and...and
somehow honest." She smiled, embarrassed at the erotic
pleasure that coursed through her. She realized she wanted
to make love right there. She looked away.

He laughed briefly. "What would a woman like you know
about a working man's sweat?"

The question puzzled her as much as his bitter tone.
"What do you mean, a woman like me? I've been around
men who worked."

"When?" The challenge was immediate, direct and doubtful.

"On my uncle's ranch that summer."

The cynical smile disappeared. "Yeah, that must have been a new experience—watching men earn their living by the sweat of their brow. Some women find it fascinating, hanging out with the redneck bunch."

Rachel reached up and twiddled a strand of hair between her fingers. He was attacking her for some reason. She detected more than a trace of hostility in his manner.

"I had several new experiences that summer," she said softly, deliberately reminding him of what they had shared. She watched closely for his reaction.

His lips compressed angrily; then he relaxed and gave her a slow once-over. "Too bad you had to give up your virginity for a few cheap thrills."

A pain sliced right into her heart. That answered any lingering questions she'd had about them. "They weren't cheap," she corrected softly. She managed a smile.

He would never know just how much their month-long affair had cost her. Remembering the pain of that summer, she swallowed hard and walked blindly away. His hand on her arm stopped her as she headed back toward the house.

"Don't get any ideas about us," he warned. "I don't have time to continue your education in how the working class makes out. Not that you probably need educating. By now, you must have tried several different types."

She stared at his tanned hand against her fairer skin. "What are you talking about?"

"Slumming." He released her and started walking.

"What?" She had to hurry to catch up with him. Her head pounded as if the wild stallion were inside her skull.

"That's what your bodyguard said you were doing that summer. I'm too busy to fool with you this year. You'll have to go elsewhere for your lessons."

She stopped and stared at his back as he stalked off toward the stable. Did he truly think she'd only been amusing herself with him that summer? A tiny light flicked on inside her.

Perhaps she could explain . . . no, it didn't matter now. If he thought that of her, it was as well it had ended when it did.

The ranch bustled with increasing activity the rest of that day and the next. Rachel watched it all from an emotionally safe distance, like a tourist observing the rituals of some strange tribe she'd come across.

Sita and Kerrigan seemed to be in charge of the festivities for the birthday party. They consulted constantly, laughing and joking in easy familiarity with one another. Three other women appeared Saturday right after lunch and started preparing dishes in the kitchen at the house. Sita told her the fun began with a big cookout that evening at seven.

Rachel stayed out of the way. After a long afternoon nap, she rose and went into the shower. Returning to the bedroom, she noticed her clothing—jeans, turtleneck, socks and underwear—were on the bed, fresh and clean, just as they had been yesterday and the day before. She didn't know who washed and returned them to her. It was almost like having elves in the house.

When she went down the steps into the lower hall, she heard the women chattering in the kitchen. She saw her jacket on a coatrack and pulled it on, then slipped quietly out the family room door to stroll around the ranch.

The wooden floor of the hay barn was being swept clean, she noted. An old-fashioned barn dance? It sounded like fun. She wondered if Kerrigan danced. He never had with her.

At that moment, he came out of the barn, saw her, hesitated, then came over. "How are you feeling?"

His standard question whenever he saw her.

"Fine. My headache is actually gone."

"Good."

They stood there in the April sun, looking past each other. She couldn't think of a thing to say. Apparently neither could he. Why, she wondered, had they spilled their hearts to each other when they'd first met and now they couldn't find anything to say? Perhaps the oddity was the past, not the present.

"Are you expecting a lot of people for your party?"

He shrugged. "A few cowboys—friends, mostly."

"I see." She looked at the sky. Clear. "It looks like a good night for it."

"Yeah." He followed her gaze.

She stared at a dot high over them. "Strange," she murmured, "that we can't talk anymore."

"Our lives are different."

"They were different then, too," she reminded him. "What *did* we talk about? I seem to recall there weren't hours enough to discuss all we wanted to say."

A cynical grin etched attractive lines in his lean face. "We didn't talk *all* the time," he said very softly.

A tremor went down her spine. She twiddled a strand of hair.

"Sorry," he said. "That probably wasn't the gentlemanly thing to say."

"It doesn't matter. If nothing else, we can at least be honest with each other." She glanced from the dark shape in the sky to him. "Can't we?"

"If you prefer."

She sighed at his stiff reply and returned to her study of the sky. "Where are my binoculars? Do you still have them?"

"Yes. In my saddlebag," he said. "I'll get them."

He strode off and returned in a few minutes. She took the binoculars out of the case and put them to her eyes. After adjusting the focus, she studied the speck she'd been watching.

"An eagle," she said. "Young, I think. Maybe a male, judging from his size." She handed the binoculars to Kerrigan.

He watched the bird for a couple of minutes. "You're right. He still has some of the markings of an adolescent." He handed the binoculars back to her.

A stirring of excitement beat through her. "I've got to get back to my camp. The female's mate was killed last year." She frowned. "He was shot."

"None of our men did it," Kerrigan informed her. "Keegan and I've given strict orders to leave the wildlife alone."

Rachel turned the lenses back toward the sky. "Maybe she'll take this one, assuming he's a male and ready."

"Why shouldn't she take him?" Kerrigan demanded, sounding defensive on behalf of the young bird.

Rachel lowered the binoculars. "Eagles mate for life," she said quietly. "Sometimes, when one dies, the survivor won't accept another in its place, especially if the one left is a mature female. I don't know why..."

Her voice trembled, and she had to stop as emotion filled her. She'd never been able to accept another, either. Foolish, really, to be so selective. There must be hundreds of acceptable males in the world.

She looked at Kerrigan, then away. He looked so hard and self-contained, as if nothing could touch him. Perhaps nothing ever had. Perhaps the feelings she'd thought they'd shared had been in her imagination.

He'd wanted her with a burning hunger, a passionate intensity that had seared right down into the soul of her, but passion was no substitute for love. She knew that. In the future, she'd look for other qualities in a mate.

Lifting the binoculars, she watched the eagle until it disappeared from sight.

Chapter Five

"Rachel?" Sita came into the family room where Rachel sat looking through a ranching magazine.

Rachel smiled at the woman. "Yes?"

"I've brought something for you to wear to the party tonight." She held out a full skirt in bright woven cloth and a white peasant blouse. "There's shoes, too."

"Oh, I don't think—" Rachel stopped, unsure how to tell Sita that she didn't think the clothes would fit.

Sita giggled. "These belong to my little sister. She's not so full in the bust and hips as I am. The shoes are made like ballerina slippers, but of some stretchy cloth." She dropped the items in Rachel's lap.

Rachel stood. "Thank you. That was thoughtful of you, especially with all the work you've done the last two days."

Sita headed back for the kitchen where she was directing the women in last-minute preparations. "It was Kerrigan's idea. He thought my sister's things would fit you. He said you were as skinny as a half-grown filly.''

Rachel headed for her room to change, her lips compressed with anger. Skinny! Half-grown! She examined herself in the mirror after she'd taken off her jeans and top. True, she wasn't as voluptuous as Sita, but she wouldn't be taken for a half-grown adolescent, either.

Her breasts were high, firm and womanly...a handful, she thought defiantly, and remembered Kerrigan's hand cupped gently around her. He had liked her hips and the length of her legs. He'd told her how beautiful she was—

She broke off the evaluation as heat shattered her anger and left her aching with needs long unmet. Absolutely no good came of remembering the past.

Quickly she slipped on the blouse and skirt. The skirt was lined with a ruffled petticoat that caused it to flounce out around her knees in a flirtatious manner. The shoes fit fine.

After brushing her hair smooth, she put on the pink lip gloss she carried with her. That was all the makeup she had. It was all she needed, she realized. Her cheeks were already flushed with nervous excitement.

Heading for the kitchen, she decided she would only stay long enough to eat and say hello. Would any of the people she'd met seven years ago be present? She hoped so.

Kerrigan was in the kitchen with Sita and the women. He picked up two huge bowls of food and started for the door. He paused when she entered.

"Can I help carry anything out?" she asked.

"No," he said.

"Yes." Sita spoke at the same time. She smiled as he scowled. "Could you take the chips and salsa? Kerrigan will show you were to put it."

Rachel picked up the indicated items and looked expectantly toward Kerrigan. Sita held the door open for them. Rachel followed her host. They crossed the yard silently.

The stars were out in profusion. The moon wasn't as full as three nights ago, but it was still big and beautiful. The wind was fresh off the snow-dappled mountains.

Her heart stirred uneasily. She'd loved this country from the moment she saw it. There was something here that called to something inside her. A wildness. A yearning of the soul for some elusive something just beyond her grasp....

They reached the open door of the barn. Kerrigan glanced over his shoulder, his expression bland, his eyes angry. She realized he didn't want her here, involved with his life and his friends. She was a complication he hadn't counted on.

And he resented the desire that stirred between them.

When he turned around, she grimaced at his back. Then she saw the other brother looking at her. He was as unreadable as his twin. And just as hard.

Two untamed rogues, she thought. They certainly fit right in with the territory. Had the Rogue River been named for such as these? Probably.

"Here, you can set those down on this end of the table."

She followed Kerrigan's directions. The table was laden with his favorite foods—burritos, tacos, fajitas, plus platters of fresh vegetables and all kinds of chips and dips.

Couples were already eating, seated on bales of straw artfully placed around the perimeter of the dance floor. The men were mostly cowboys she recognized, some from the ranch, others she thought she'd seen in town on her two visits there. The party looked like any Saturday-night get-together at the bar in the diner—the locals called the bar a saloon, she remembered—except this get-together was in a barn.

While she watched, Hank turned on a stereo system that had been hooked up at one end of the building. In a minute, a rap song blared over the speakers.

"You look surprised," Kerrigan observed, offering her a plate.

"I...everyone is younger than I expected. I thought there would be families and some older people...ranchers and maybe some of the townspeople." She took the plate.

He raised one eyebrow. "Why would you think that?"

"Well, you and your brother are ranchers now, not drifters like many of the cowboys seem to be."

His expression hardened. "You think we should hobnob only with the bankers and other ranchers now that we own the place?"

"I'm not being snobbish," she said, realizing that was exactly how she sounded. "It's just that I thought there would be more variety. Why didn't you invite any of your neighbors?"

"When we were growing up here," Kerrigan told her, "Keegan and I weren't good enough to be invited to their parties. Why should I invite them to mine?"

He laid a tortilla on his plate, covered it with the makings of a fajita and ladled a generous serving of sour cream and salsa over it, his anger visible in his actions.

"The Fightin' McPhersons," she said softly.

He froze for a second, then turned his wintry gaze on her. "So you know about that. I suppose everyone in town advised you that you were making a terrible mistake, dating one of the wild McPherson twins. Is that why you sent your security chief and his friends to meet me instead of showing up yourself?"

She shook her head. "I knew about you from the first. I'd made friends with a local girl that summer. Suzannah

White. She went to school with you. She told me about you and your brother."

He laughed without humor. "Yeah, the banker's daughter. A perfect smile. A perfect figure. Sexy as hell. I wanted to take her to the homecoming game."

"Did you ask her?"

"No. Who would let their daughters go out with guys known to fight at the drop of a hat?" He shrugged as if it hadn't mattered.

Rachel knew that it had. She wanted to comfort him, that young boy whose dreams had been destroyed before they'd ever begun.

She also knew why the twins had fought. Suzannah had told her a local bully had made remarks about their deceased mother and the twins' legitimacy.

"I think it was rather noble to defend your mother's honor," Rachel said, unable to keep the admiration from her voice.

A flush crept up his face. "My mother was a pushover for anyone with the price of a drink that last year," he said in a voice so devoid of emotion, it hurt Rachel's heart. "I guess it's a McPherson trait. I was pretty easy pickings for you. I was so far gone, I even thought we were in love." He gave a harsh laugh.

He selected a beer from a cooler and chose a bale of straw to sit on. Several people glanced at him curiously, but no one came over. No wonder. Kerrigan looked like a thunderstorm ready to crackle with thunder and lightning.

Rachel stood frozen to the spot for a second. Kerrigan had thought they were in love, too, that summer long ago. It hadn't been a fantasy on her part. That he'd felt the same somehow made her feel better about it.

She joined him, determined not to drop the subject. "We *were* in love." The memory of it haunted her—the freedom she'd felt, the pure exhilaration of loving and being loved...

"I got over that fantasy pretty fast," he informed her, "and I learned not to barge in where I wasn't wanted. I found out life is a whole lot safer that way."

"I know." She smiled and wondered if he could see the sadness in it. "We both lost something that summer. Our virginity. Our innocence, perhaps. Certainly some of our belief in love." She looked him in the eye. "Do you really think I could have sent someone to hurt you after all we'd shared?"

"It sure seemed that way to me," he drawled. "Look, that's ancient history. I've forgotten what all the fuss was about. This is my birthday party. I'm ready for some fun."

He walked off. Rachel saw him toss his half-eaten food away, then grab Sita when she came through the door. He danced with her and several other women and never once looked at Rachel, sitting alone on the straw bale, watching him.

His brother came over to her after a while. "Is your head better?" he asked politely.

"Yes, much better, thanks."

"Feel like dancing?"

She looked at him in surprise. "I think I'd rather not."

He sat beside her, plucked a straw from the bale and stuck it in his mouth. "Are you leaving soon?"

Kerrigan was dancing body to body with some young woman. The music was slow and dreamy. Rachel looked down at her hands.

"Yes," she said. "Tomorrow, if possible."

The twin nodded. "I can take you across country by horse. That's faster than going by truck around the road and hiking in."

It was obvious his brother wanted her gone. Was he afraid she'd get Kerrigan in her clutches and make off with his money or something? "Fine." She stood. "I think I'll say good-night."

The party was beginning to get rowdy she noticed while she walked across the barn toward the door. There were perhaps fifty people there, a young, high-spirited group. She felt old compared to them. She'd always preferred solitude, anyway.

Outside, the moon turned the night into mysterious patterns of silvery silhouettes against velvet shadows. A horse whickered from the corral. On an impulse, she got a handful of oats from a bin in the stable and went to it.

The stallion sniffed at her cautiously before taking a dainty bite from her hand. For two days, she'd watched Kerrigan work with the animal, training it to the bridle and saddle, currying and feeding it, talking quietly to it all the while. The stallion had come to trust him. It no longer fought the bit.

"Another one falling under his spell," she murmured, reaching up to scratch the animal's ears, pleased when he let her.

Light spilled across the yard when the barn door opened. Someone came outside. The door swung closed. She recognized Hank when he ambled over. He peered at her, seemingly drunk.

"Kerrigan's girl," he said, swaying slightly. He held on to the fence as if to steady the world.

"No."

"He found you in the woods. That makes you his."

Rachel realized Hank had his own brand of logic. There was no use in arguing with him in his present condition. She smiled and remained silent.

"If you were my girl, I wouldn't leave you alone out here in the moonlight," he announced solemnly.

"She isn't your girl," a voice said from the shadows. "Rachel belongs to me." Kerrigan came around the corner of the barn and leaned carelessly against the fence next to her.

Hank nodded and ambled off toward the barn. He disappeared inside.

Kerrigan faced her. "You're asking for trouble standing around out here alone. The men think that's an open invitation to join you."

"Is that why you came out?"

"Maybe. Are you issuing an invitation?"

The air grew tense between them. She shivered and rubbed her arms against the cold. "I don't know."

Longing flared in her, flinging outward from her heart to run along hidden pathways of yearning and need. She stared at the hills, outlined in stark splendor against the star-bright sky, then gazed upward. The heavens seemed to move, to spin slowly, then faster. She turned from Kerrigan and grasped the fence.

She wanted him to kiss her madly, passionately. She wanted to feel all the joy of falling in love again, the sheer wonder of simply being when she was in his arms.

"If you're heading for bed, you'd better go now," he advised harshly. "Else you might not make it."

She realized he considered her his responsibility. He'd brought her in. He'd have to look after her.

The melody of a love song drifted from the barn, haunting her with its poignant loveliness. "I want to dance," she said. She faced him, a slow pirouette that sent the stars into new, fascinating patterns.

She saw his chest lift in a deep breath, then drop as he let it out. He was going to refuse. She sensed it.

Before the disappointment hit her, he held out his arms. "Never let it be said I refused a guest any reasonable request."

She measured the distance between them—one step and yet, an abyss of distrust as wide as the sea. She took the step.

He held her at a polite distance, almost formally, one hand warm on hers, the other at her waist. Staring up at him, she could see the stars behind his head and over his shoulders, seeming to move with them...dancing...around and around.

It was almost like a dream.

"We never danced," she whispered. "Why didn't we dance?"

"We ran out of time."

It seemed unbearably sad. All their passion, all their sweet promises...wasted. All the things they'd never done together. And never would, because tomorrow she'd be gone.

The pasture came into view as they moved to the music.

They'd never race like the wind across green meadows, she realized. They'd never roam the hills, laughing and carefree, creatures of the earth and the sky, driven only by nature's wild impulse.

She saw the house.

They would never share a home. They'd never have children. There would be no holding hands and strolling quietly into the twilight of age, still in love....

A tremor went through her. He drew her closer. They almost touched, not quite. If she tried, she could imagine them back in the past, back at the time their passion had flared like gently exploding rays from a benevolent sun.

Heat radiated over them, shutting out the night's chill. She could feel the tension in him, in her. There was still passion between them. A spark could ignite it.

They danced around the dusty stable yard while the stallion watched from the corral, his ears pricked to catch any remark they might make. But there were no words to hear. Only the music and the mad pounding of her heart as she waited...

The barn door opened. "Kerrigan, it's time," Sita called.

The spell was broken.

Rachel pulled out of his arms and put a hand over her eyes as tears rushed to the surface. She needed to be alone.

But Kerrigan kept a grip on her arm and guided her inside the building with him. His possessive manner was startling. She stared at him, but could read nothing in his gaze.

In the brightly lit barn, a monstrous birthday cake held the place of honor at the long table, she noted. It was aflame with candles, thirty on each side and one fat one in the middle.

"Make a wish and blow them out," Sita ordered, laughing when the twins complained about the impossible task.

The brothers paused, looked at each other, then took a deep breath, bent over the cake... and blew out every single candle in one breath. Their friends applauded and cheered.

Kerrigan cut two pieces of cake and brought one of them to her. Rachel felt the heat sweep up her neck and into her face as she sat beside him on a bale of straw. Several of the women gave her a disappointed glance. Some of them looked angry. Sita grimaced, then shrugged and smiled.

The other brother cut two pieces of cake and chose to share his treat with Sita. After that, the party got into full swing. As the music and noise rose in decibels, Rachel's headache returned with a vengeance.

"Tired?" Kerrigan surprised her by asking.

"Yes."

"I'll walk you to the house."

They stood and headed for the door. Kerrigan caught the frosty gray eyes of his brother and called out, "I'll be back."

His twin nodded, his gaze flickering to her.

In silence, she and Kerrigan walked across the quadrangle to the house. The stars stayed in their places.

She sighed as fatigue drifted over her. Yet she wasn't ready to go to bed. She wanted more....

Kerrigan gave her a sardonic smile. "Sorry to bore you with the locals."

"Don't," she said, pressing her fingertips to her temples.

His smile disappeared. "I'll get you a pill."

She went to her room. Going into the bathroom, she changed to the flannel shirt, brushed her teeth with the toothbrush her host had thoughtfully provided and returned to her room, expecting to find the pill on the table by the bed. Instead she found Kerrigan.

His eyes roamed down her and paused on her bare legs and feet. When he looked back at her face, his expression had changed. He blinked, looked away, then back.

"You look like a girl," he said in a tight, deepened tone, "young and innocent, still expecting the good things from life."

"No." She crossed the room and stood next to him by the bed, aware of the emptiness of the house, the proximity of his strong male presence. "I don't expect anything, not anymore."

"Why? Because of me?"

"Because you never came back."

He touched a strand of her hair, smoothing it back from her temple. He looked younger all at once. Vulnerable. The way she felt. She stared at him helplessly.

"We never really had a chance, you and I," he murmured. "We were worlds apart."

"We weren't," she whispered in a ragged voice.

"Worlds," he repeated. "But it was a lovely fantasy."

He stroked down her cheek and settled the tips of his fingers on her mouth, like a blind man discovering the feel of her again. Slowly he caressed her lips until they trembled and parted.

Words rushed to her throat. *Stay with me. Love me.* But she didn't say those words. She chose others.

"You wouldn't talk to me. The man at your grandfather's ranch said you didn't want to talk to me."

The longing cleared, and his eyes narrowed. "I couldn't talk. I thought my jaw was broken." He moved back from her with a harsh laugh. "Doc said it wasn't, just bruised and swollen to the point I had to stay on a liquid diet for a couple of days."

"I'm sorry for that. My brother was, too."

"Yeah? You couldn't prove it by me."

"It was later, when he realized how serious things were between us. When I wrote that second letter, he knew about it. If you'd have come back, he wouldn't have stopped you from seeing me."

Kerrigan handed her the pill and a glass of water. "I wasn't feeling up to taking any chances right then. A man needs to be in one piece if he's planning on winning a rodeo."

"He said if you'd loved me, you would have come back." She put the pill in her mouth and took a drink of water to wash it down. It was terribly hard to swallow, as if she had a sore throat. She set the glass on the table.

Their conversation was ironic, almost as if they spoke of other people rather than themselves. It had been too long. What did explanations matter now?

Kerrigan walked toward the door. He paused before going out. "I learned a valuable lesson that night. Don't fight over a woman, any woman. They aren't worth the pain."

She took a step toward him. "Did you fight for me?"

He gave her a self-mocking smile. "Why do you think they beat me up?" He left and closed the door.

Feeling that her legs might give out at any moment, Rachel sank onto the bed. She lay down, turned out the light and pulled the covers up to her neck. Shivers continued to run over her for several minutes before she felt warm.

He'd tried to come to her. Didn't that prove he had really cared? Something that had been hard and angry and hurting in her began to dissolve.

The sound of singing echoed off the walls in the wee hours of the morning. "Shh. Dammit, be quiet," Kerrigan said.

"Chill out," his brother advised. "It's our birthday. Oh, I have a present for you."

"You've already given me the big stallion."

"This is more personal." Keegan chuckled slyly. "It's in my room. And, we have one other item to discuss. Come on."

The light was on in the family room. The two brothers went in. Kerrigan was in a bad mood. His twin was baiting him.

"Forget the bet," he snapped.

"We agreed. Five years ago, remember?"

"Get on up to bed," Kerrigan ordered, "before you fall on your face. How much beer did you drink tonight?"

"Not so much that I can't remember our agreement," Keegan asserted. He grinned. "Afraid? That city gal got you tied into knots again?"

Kerrigan tensed. "No female's got a rope around me."

"Too bad. She looks healthy enough."

"Damn you, Keegan—" He stopped abruptly, knowing it was useless to argue with his twin in his present state.

Five years ago, at a boozy birthday party in some rodeo town neither of them could remember, some bronc rider had teased them about what they were going to do with their winnings, which were rather substantial by then.

The discussion had ended in an argument on who was going to produce their heir. Each twin had declared his intention never to marry. That impasse had led to the agreement Keegan referred to.

On their thirty-first birthday, if neither of them had wed by then, they'd agreed to flip a coin to see who had to find a woman and marry her—the idea being that an heir would soon follow.

If the loser hadn't found a wife in a year's time, he had perforce to leave the ranch and not return until he had one.

"We must have an heir for all our riches." Keegan swept his arms out to encompass the ranch.

"How about if I just concede the honor to you?"

"No. We got to be fair." Keegan grinned at his twin. He reached into his pocket and brought out a new, shiny penny. "Call it," he said, balancing the coin on his thumb.

The two men squared off and proceeded to stare each other down. Kerrigan had assumed his brother was spouting off in an alcoholic haze. Now he wasn't so sure. Keegan's gaze was serious, in spite of the half grin that curled his lips.

"That was a stupid agreement," Kerrigan muttered.

"Maybe, but we shook on it, so it stands. Call it," Keegan challenged, refusing to back down.

"Heads," Kerrigan gritted.

His brother flipped the coin without bothering to catch it. Both men watched as the penny hit the carpet, rolled, then fell to one side.

"Tails," Keegan said in satisfaction. "You lose."

Kerrigan's face darkened. He muttered several curses. None of them relieved his temper.

"One year, brother," Keegan reminded him unnecessarily. He chuckled and bounded up the steps to his room.

Rachel woke to the sounds of footsteps in the hall and a door closing. The birthday party was over, she assumed.

The house settled into silence. She listened to the small creakings and groanings of the wood. The wind carried the whisper of loneliness to her. She thought of snuggling up to a warm body, an arm reaching out to gather her close and comfort her.

Kerrigan was asleep right across the hall, but she couldn't go to him. Tears pressed close. She pushed them back. He'd been right. The time for them was past.

Settling herself, she waited for sleep to come.

After a while, realizing she was hungry, she climbed out of bed, pulled on her thick socks and crept down the dim hallway. In the lower bathroom, she found the blue terry robe and pulled it on over the flannel shirt. She headed for the kitchen.

The light was on in the family room. She glanced in as she passed. Her heart nearly stopped when she spotted Kerrigan.

He stood rigidly in the center of the room, lost in thought, then with an oath, he scooped up an object from the carpet and slammed it on the desk. He saw her. "What are you doing up?"

He was so obviously furious, she found herself hurriedly stuttering an explanation. "I...I woke up and was hungry."

Folding his arms across his chest, he put his anger under tight control and resumed the role of host. "There's soup in the refrigerator. I'll fix a bowl and bring it to you in your room."

"That's all right. I can manage. You don't have to wait on me." It occurred to her that the hour was late and they were alone. She felt very vulnerable all at once, the way she had when they'd danced. A premonition of danger flicked through her.

A mocking gleam came into his eyes. His gaze roamed over her, stopped at her feet and returned to her face. The heat in that intense perusal seared her. "I said I'd do it."

His voice was quieter, deeper. The earlier longing became a rush of need cascading over her, shattering her defenses.

"No, really, I'd rather," she insisted.

He pivoted suddenly and hit the desk top. "Stop looking at me as if I'm Attila the Hun. I'm not going to attack you."

"I didn't think you were. I'm not afraid of you," she said, more to reassure herself than him. "Only myself."

The words slipped out, a confession she didn't want him to hear. His eyes arrowed in on hers. She whirled to leave.

A hand caught her before she could retreat up the steps. "Don't make remarks like that, then scuttle off to hide. This is beginning to get interesting. Why are you afraid of yourself?"

She raised her chin defiantly. She'd hadn't asked for the situation between them any more than he had. "Because being around you makes me want you all over again. Like we were before."

He cupped her chin and leaned close, so close she could feel his breath on her forehead. She stared into the drowning depths of his stormy gaze.

"It'll never be like that again." He was cruel, cold.

Tears sprang into her eyes. A muscle in his jaw clenched. Time spun out of control between them, somehow becoming the past, the present, the lonely future.

"You could drive a man over the brink," he muttered. "Right over the brink." He let out a string of curses.

"Let me go," she pleaded, wanting him with a need so great she was afraid she'd faint with longing. "Or hold me."

The tears spilled over and ran slowly down her face.

"Heaven help me," he said and pulled her into his arms. "I want you. I want it the way it was before, too," he whispered. "So hot and sweet, it drove me crazy to be away from you."

"Yes," she admitted on a sigh.

They held each other. A tremor ran through her. She felt an answering one in him.

He drew a quick, hard breath. "Do you remember that first time?" he asked in a hoarse, low voice.

She wrapped her arms tightly around his waist and laid her head against his chest. She could hear his heart beating. "We were both trembling...with need, not fright."

"The dawn came, and it was like the day had just been created. The world was new...and all for us."

"You were so gentle, concerned about me..."

"I'd never been with a virgin...I'd never been with any woman."

"I know. I was glad when you told me. It seemed right, that we should be the first for each other."

She leaned her head back and felt his arms tighten across her back. He felt strong and solid, a man to depend on. His eyes blazed over her, touching her mouth, her throat, the low V of the robe and shirt. He smoothed his hands along her hips and pulled her closer.

Desire spiraled into her. She was as ready for him as he was for her. She moved against his hard body, knowing she was inviting his passion, unable to stop.

"Ah, Rachel," he breathed in defeat against her lips just before his mouth settled on hers.

This time the kiss was one of passion—pure and deep and burning hot, melting barriers, destroying common sense. Oh, the wonder of his lips! It was like the first time all over again, the same hot, probing magic that careened right down to the depths of her, making her weak.

She wrapped her arms tightly around his neck and let her body form to his, each curve and plane fitted and molded to each other.

A tremor went through her when he bent slightly and pulled her upward so that she was on tiptoe, her weight resting on his strength. The hard shaft of his desire nestled against her. When his hands slipped down along her hips and gathered her even closer, she couldn't keep from crying out in ecstasy and entreaty.

He lifted his head and stared down into her passion-drugged eyes. His gaze wasn't icy now.

"You used to cry out for me, wanting me so much you were wild in my arms," he said hoarsely.

"Yes," she moaned helplessly, feeling the wildness, wanting the exhilaration she'd once found with him.

"You said I could make you fly into the sun." He moved against her intimately. "Do you feel the heat?"

"Yes."

"You send me up, too. I feel like a puff of smoke, as if everything has been burned off and there's only this left."

He bent to her mouth again. The kiss went white hot. His tongue stroked hers, each thrust possessive and hungry. She clung to him, moved against him until he groaned with rampant hunger.

Suddenly he lifted and pivoted with her. She found herself sitting on the edge of the desk. He pushed impatiently between her knees, claiming his place in the heated jointure of her thighs.

The robe and flannel shirt slid upward. When he touched her bare skin, she gasped against his lips. He rested his hands on her thighs, then began to caress her slowly... so slowly.

He broke the kiss and stared into her dazed eyes while he moved closer and closer. "Come to my room," he said, his voice thickened and low with need.

She wanted to. Oh, how she wanted to!

"A-hem."

She pulled her gaze from the mesmerizing intensity of his and looked toward the stairs. Keegan stood there, watching them with a cynical smile on his face. His eyes were shadowed and not at all smiling, though.

She could have wept at the loss when Kerrigan jerked from her arms. He kept his body between her and his brother while he lifted her to her feet and saw that the robe fell into place over her thighs, properly concealing her from sight. The passion drained from him, and she realized he looked unbearably weary.

Instinctively she reached out to caress his brow, but he drew back and turned toward his twin. "What's the problem now?"

"I forgot one little thing," Keegan announced with a mocking smile. He tossed a small gift-wrapped box of condoms to his brother. "Here. Don't leave home without them."

Kerrigan caught the box and placed it on the desk. "A strange gift, considering the outcome of the...agreement."

"Just a reminder to be careful. Make sure you pick the right person for the job." On this cryptic note, the brother retreated up the steps and went to his room, closing the door with a firm bang behind him.

Rachel felt blood rush to her face.

Kerrigan pivoted to her. "If you can find your way around the kitchen, I'll go on to bed."

He'd become cold again. She drew a shaky breath, sorry for the loss of his passion and, at the same time, relieved that they'd been brought to a screeching halt in time. She couldn't let herself give in to impulse like that. "Yes, I'll be fine."

He studied her for several long seconds, looking as if he would disagree; then he leapt up the steps in two bounds and disappeared into his bedroom.

Rachel went into the kitchen, but her appetite had fled. She settled for a glass of milk and sat at the table with the light out and looked at the moonlight flooding the quadrangle.

All quiet on the western front, she thought. No battles won or lost, just interrupted. But would there have been a battle? Neither she nor Kerrigan had been fighting their hunger at that point.

How could she have succumbed like that? Hadn't she learned anything from that long-ago summer?

She'd be more careful around him in the future, knowing how volatile they were together. Tears pressed against her eyes.

No use crying over spilled milk…or past love affairs, she thought, trying to be as hard and cynical as Kerrigan obviously had become. She realized she hated old sayings. They were so often right.

Chapter Six

Rachel found pancakes and sausage waiting in the oven for her the next morning. A note on the table said Kerrigan would be back soon to check on her. She looked at his strong pen strokes. His hand was legible but spoke of impatience as he wrote. Not a man who liked to get hung up on details.

She ate and put the dishes in the dishwasher, then took her cup to the family room and looked out the windows at the activity. Two men were leaning on a rail, watching the horses. One of them was Hank. The other man was the wizened old man who'd shouted advice on riding the wild stallion on Friday.

Glancing at the calendar, she idly noted it was Sunday. She wondered what she should do with herself. She felt useless.

The back door opened and closed. She heard footsteps in the kitchen. She quickly went down the hall. Keegan was there.

He finished pouring a cup of coffee, then glanced over his shoulder at her. "You look rested," he commented.

"Yes." She swallowed, then asked, "Are we leaving today? You said you'd take me back to my camp."

"Are you sure you want to go?" He leaned against the counter and watched her over the edge of his cup as he took a drink.

The question caught her by surprise. "I think it would be for the best . . . for everybody."

"Didn't look that way to me last night," he said.

She tried to read his reaction to the passionate interlude he'd interrupted, but couldn't. Whatever he felt he was keeping it to himself, but she had no doubt he wanted her gone. Resentment welled in her. She hadn't asked to come here.

"I'm ready whenever you are," she informed him coolly.

He nodded. "Little brother may get angry if we leave without saying goodbye."

She studied his impassive expression. "Why do you call him little brother?"

"I was born first, about fifteen minutes before him. That makes me the big brother and him the little brother," Keegan explained in simplistic terms.

"I didn't know that. Kerrigan and I didn't discuss birth order." Realizing where that subject could lead, she changed topics. "Your house is very nice. Was this the original site of the one owned by your grandfather?"

"Good heavens, no. This is the ranch we bought with our rodeo winnings. The old homestead is farther back, its acreage smaller, too small really, to be a successful operation."

"Kerrigan said it was mortgaged when you inherited it."

Keegan looked grim for a minute. "It was. The old man was probably laughing in his grave at the legacy we got from him."

"Why didn't he like you?" she probed, wanting to understand this man and his twin.

"We were too much like our mother. Granddad liked to keep everyone under his thumb. She got out as soon as she could. Kerrigan and I did, too. He hated us for it."

"That's sad." She rinsed her coffee cup and put it in the dishwasher. "Families should be close."

Keegan shrugged, a movement so like Kerrigan's that it brought the sting of tears to her eyes. "I'll get the horses ready."

He left. She saw him go to the stables. She got her coat and binoculars. In less than thirty minutes, he returned to the house.

"Ready?"

The sound of a galloping horse directed their attention to the quadrangle. Her heart sped up when she recognized who it was. Longing ate at her while she watched Kerrigan tie the big gelding to the corral fence.

"He grieved for you," Keegan said, pausing by the back door before opening it.

She stirred from her preoccupation with the man outside and concentrated on the one inside. "I doubt it."

He shrugged. The back door burst open, letting in a blast of cool air. She glimpsed three horses tied to the porch railing. Kerrigan strode into the kitchen.

He gestured to the horses before slamming the door. "What's going on?" There was a curious note of suppressed anger in his voice. His gaze was cold as he faced his brother.

Keegan answered. "I promised Rachel I'd take her back to her camp today if the weather was clear." He glanced outside. "Looks about perfect to me—fifty degrees, sunny, light wind."

Kerrigan swung his hard gaze from his brother to her. "You're supposed to stay until you've recovered from the fall."

"My headache is gone. I need to get back," she explained, dry mouthed. "I want to see how the eagles interact."

"If you wanted to leave, why didn't you ask me to take you?" He leveled an icy glare at her. She felt as if she'd committed a crime.

"The way you've been acting," Keegan interceded on her behalf, "she probably thought she was under house arrest. She's old enough to decide for herself what she wants to do."

The brothers glared at each other with jaws set and eyes narrowed. It was a good thing, she thought, that they weren't wearing six-shooters like the cowboys in Western movies.

Kerrigan jerked his head toward her. "If she wants to go back, I'll take her."

Blue eyes and gray eyes clashed. "All right," his twin finally acquiesced. "I put on a load of supplies. I thought she might as well use the line shack since she's up that way."

Kerrigan nodded. "That's what I was thinking."

"Figured it was." A pause, then, "Watch yourself." The warning was delivered deadpan. Keegan was warning his brother to be careful of her, she realized. Kerrigan nodded, his face so hard, it was like a carving.

"I have my own things," she said, needing to break the tense silence that ensued.

The brothers turned to her simultaneously. A shiver went down her spine. They'd make formidable enemies. Individually, each man looked strong and tough. As a fighting unit, they could probably take on a platoon of marines.

"You have if the animals haven't ransacked your supplies," Kerrigan informed her. "Chipmunks have been known to chew through backpacks to get at the stuff inside."

Keegan stretched and yawned. "Everything's packed and loaded. Will you be back today?"

Kerrigan shook his head. "I may as well track the cougar if I'm going up that way again."

"Good idea." With a curt nod and, to her surprise, a smile that wasn't totally without sympathy, Keegan strode out.

Kerrigan frowned, then glanced at Rachel. "I'll check the horses. When will you be ready?"

"Now," she said stiffly, not meeting his eyes.

If Kerrigan had grieved, it hadn't softened him enough to forget his pride and come to her.

The horse she rode was a docile, older one, a gelding like Kerrigan's big pinto, but without his energy. It plodded along at the pinto's flank, happy to follow.

Rachel found that easier, too. She didn't have to worry about Kerrigan catching her looking at him. She felt vulnerable around him. Last night had proven beyond any doubt that she couldn't resist his arms. Sighing dispiritedly, she scanned the sky.

No sign of either of the eagles.

The morning waned. He pulled to a halt at the fallen trees where they'd rested on their previous journey. Her horse stopped behind his and patiently waited.

Kerrigan twisted around in the saddle and studied her face. She looked at him without speaking.

"We'll rest here," he decided.

She nodded and climbed off the horse.

"Just drop the reins," he advised. "He's ground hitched."

She followed orders, then went off into the woods by herself. When she returned, he was gone, but there was a packet of trail mix on the trunk of the fallen tree. She sat down, pulled it open and began to eat.

When Kerrigan returned, he did the same.

The air around them seemed to hum with tension. She noted he looked tired, as if he hadn't slept. He turned his head and caught her gazing at him. His expression hardened before he turned away.

"Last night was a mistake," he informed her.

"I know."

"It won't happen again."

She was silent.

He swung around, his glance darting over her. She gave him a weary smile, wondering if he believed his own words, then finished her snack, stood and stretched.

"It won't," he repeated.

"Okay." It wasn't a topic she wanted to argue about.

He stood and gave her a speculative perusal. "If I tried to take you away again, your family would probably send out a hit man after me."

"Nah." She lifted the hair off the back of her neck and let the mountain breeze blow across her heated skin. She managed an impudent grin. "My father would just ask one of his CIA buddies to take care of it. As a personal favor."

A moment passed, then he grinned—reluctantly but with wry humor. "Then I'll watch my step."

"Ready to go?" she asked. "I'm anxious about my gear."

He folded and put away their empty trail mix bags, earning her approval. They mounted up and resumed their journey. It took longer this time, since they were going up into the mountains, rather than down into the valley. The trail grew rougher.

They arrived at the line shack at midafternoon.

"We'll unload the supplies first," he decided.

"I'd like to go check on my things."

He frowned, then said, "You can stay here. I'll go over and pack up."

She shook her head. "I'm going, too."

"It's three miles round-trip."

"We'd better get started then."

He was clearly irritated by her stubborn refusal to stay behind, but he let her go with him. After unloading the pack horse and putting him in the makeshift corral next to the shed, they watered the two geldings and started off once more.

Rachel's rear protested when she swung into the saddle, but she ignored the soreness. They rode the mile and a half in silence.

Kerrigan was surprised by Rachel's campsite. She'd dug a small hole and rimmed it with one layer of rock for a fire pit. Her tent was on a bed of pine needles with a rain trench dug around it. Her backpack was a good twenty-five feet in the air, safe from all predators but the human kind.

He scanned the ground. "Bear sign," he said.

"Deer tracks," she added, also surveying the area.

"Cat paws, not big enough to be the cougar, probably a bobcat," he continued.

"Chipmunks," she said with a laugh. "Get out of there."

She backed out of her tent, leaving the flap open. Going to the back side, she unzipped that end and clapped her hands. Two tiny chipmunks ran out the front entrance, paused when they spied Kerrigan, then headed for their home.

"Any damage?" he called.

"No. I apparently didn't have the zipper pulled tight. The little devils wiggled through. They were building a nest in my sleeping bag, judging by the leaves." She laughed. "They must have thought they were in seventh heaven to find a snug home like this, just waiting for them to move in."

He ducked his head and torso into the tent and examined her sleeping bag. He couldn't find any rips. After tossing out the dried grass and leaves the animals had brought in, he couldn't stop himself from noticing the inside of the shelter.

First of all, it was a two-person tent. Had anyone shared it with her? A surge of pure jealousy heated his blood to red hot. He tamped it down. He wouldn't expect a woman of her passionate nature to be celibate for seven years.

He swallowed against a sudden constriction in his throat. Well, hell, he'd been to town a few times himself. A ranch with only men on it could get to be a lonely place.

Taking the sleeping bag outside, he shook it well to make sure no other varmints lurked inside its folds. Rachel had lowered her backpack and was checking the contents. He knelt with his knees inside the tent and rolled up the bag.

After stuffing it inside its nylon cover, he picked up a pair of long johns. They were white and smooth as silk. With a ripple of shock, he realized they really *were* silk. He pulled them across his palm. Their texture was like a cool whisper over his skin.

The way she would feel.

Until he warmed her up, he thought, then her flesh would become warm and melting against his, giving him heaven.

His body went into immediate reaction. He gave an involuntary jerk and cursed his lack of control. He tossed the sleeping bag outside, crammed the long johns into a small duffel and threw it over to join the pile.

By the time he had the tent in its cover, she'd tied the other stuff onto her backpack, put the plug of earth back over the fire pit and scattered the rocks. There was no sign that anyone had been there. He grunted, surprised at her ability.

When she looked at him, he brought the tent over and observed as she efficiently tied it into place. "Ready," she announced, glancing around one last time.

He lifted the pack and swung into the saddle. She climbed on her mount. He didn't miss the grimace on her face when she settled onto the hard leather of the saddle. He could take her to the warm springs.... Forget that.

But once the thought entered his mind, his imagination took over and supplied picture after picture of her, of them, relaxing in nature's steaming bathtub.

If he'd answered her letters, if he'd tried once more, would they be married now? Would they have the heir that Keegan was so set on? Maybe he should have talked to her....

The vision of being beaten, and helpless to do anything about it, returned to haunt him. No woman was worth making a man crawl. He'd trusted her, had gone to her with his heart in his hands. For that one month, she'd made him forget all he'd learned about love and life. It was a lesson he wouldn't have to repeat.

Rachel was aware of Kerrigan behind her on the ride back. She tried to concentrate on the scenery around them. Yarrow and other wild flowers pushed up fresh green heads along the trail. Wild dogwood and willows were plump with flower buds.

Coming out into the open on a rocky ledge, she halted the horse and squinted at the sky. "Where are my binoculars?"

"In your saddlebag, the one to your left."

She twisted around and fumbled it open. Putting the glasses to her eyes, she focused on a speck in the sky. "The young eagle."

The bird flew closer, gliding on the thermals with his wings barely moving. He dipped and turned, then rose again. She rested the binoculars on her thigh and watched the eagle, close enough now that they could watch him unaided.

"Oh-oh," she said, catching sight of another dot in the sky. Raising the binoculars, she watched the female zooming in on the unsuspecting male, who was peering at the ground.

"Is that the female?" Kerrigan asked.

"Yes."

"She's coming in from an attack position."

"Yes. I don't think she'll hurt the other one."

"But you don't know."

Rachel lowered the binoculars at the embittered tone. "If the young one is a female, the older one will drive her away. If it's a male, she might accept him."

A lump came to her throat as the female dived on the other eagle. The younger one, intent on dinner, didn't even realize the danger until the last minute. Unsheathed talons swept perilously close, but the female veered off, rose and circled.

Rachel breathed easier.

The other eagle, after a panicky bank and turn, flapped its wings until it caught the thermal updraft again. It rose to the same height and circled in a wider arc. The female maintained her advantage by going higher.

The young eagle took off in a swooping dive all of a sudden, threw its wings back into a stall, then soared upward like a feather caught in the wind. He pulled out before going higher than his companion. The other eagle watched.

Rachel held her breath. "Join him," she heard herself say. "Go to him."

"Is the young one a male?" Kerrigan asked.

"Yes, else she would drive him out. This is her territory. She won't share it with another female."

A minute passed while the two birds circled warily over the winding gorge, their wings moving only slightly while they looked each other over.

The female banked and went into a dive. She pulled out at the last possible minute and wafted upward. The male followed suit at once, diving, then pulling upward to join her in a lazy circle. The aerial show went on for several minutes.

The male dived and rose once more. He acted as if he wanted to land on her back, but the female quickly disabused him of that notion. She gave him a flogging that had him backing off in midflight. He dropped down a few feet and lowered his head, obviously having a sulk.

Rachel laughed in delight.

"I take it the courtship is going well?" a dry baritone voice inquired.

Rachel put the glasses away. "Well, it wasn't love at first sight—" She stopped abruptly, glanced at Kerrigan, then away. "But she didn't run him off, either."

She saw the sardonic smile disappear, replaced by a frown, and wondered what he was thinking. Of their first meeting when she'd taken one look into his eyes and had known he was the one?

She turned her face up to the sky. The female eagle was wiser than she had been. The eagle would think twice before taking this cocky young male to be her partner. The tears rose into Rachel's eyes as she watched them continue to circle each other.

The female flew to a dead tree clinging to the steep side of the gorge. She settled on the topmost limb. The male descended more slowly. He seemed to be thinking about joining the female, but at last decided to play it safe. He chose a nearby tree.

"Good," Rachel said. "Ready?" She wiped the moisture from her eyes and smiled at her companion. Her lips trembled slightly.

Kerrigan gave her a harsh, penetrating look she couldn't decipher. Let him think what he wanted about her tears over the eagles. She didn't care if he thought she was a sentimental sop.

She wanted the eagles to succeed. She wanted the young male to do the right thing. It seemed so important. She lifted her chin into the air, daring Kerrigan to ridicule her.

They rode on to the cabin, which was only a short distance.

"Why do women always get emotional over acts of nature?" he asked sardonically when they dismounted. He set her backpack by the cabin. "That display was nothing but hormones and instinct."

"Mating is basic to life," she argued, her voice quiet in the deepening twilight. "Maybe it is instinct, but it also signifies the future. For the eagles, it will be a lifelong commitment to meet here each spring and raise the next generation."

"Poor fool, a lifetime of work for one moment of enjoyment."

She raised her eyebrows at the disgruntled tone. "Oh, it probably isn't so bad as all that. They'll mate more than once before she lays her eggs. Then he gets the pleasure of seeing his offspring grow and fly off on their own."

Kerrigan snorted and took the reins to the horses. He led them off toward the tiny creek near the cabin.

Rachel lugged her backpack inside and propped it against the wall in the corner where he'd put the other supplies. She looked at the area in front of the hearth. Her heart skipped several beats before she busied herself with supper.

Taking the bucket from the wall, she went to get water. The horses were still drinking. Kerrigan stood braced against a tree, his arms crossed, his foot drawn up and resting on the bark. He was lost in thoughts that obviously pained him.

When she approached, he stirred and changed position. His face became closed. She got the water and headed back to the cabin. "Supper in twenty minutes," she called over her shoulder.

He appeared at the door right on time.

She noted his hair was damp when he hung his hat on a nail. He must have washed in the creek. She'd wiped her own face with a wet bandanna. She surveyed her preparations.

The table was set with their camping plates and utensils. The pan of noodles and chicken, spiced with pepper and garlic, was on the table along with another of mixed vegetables. She'd found a salad of spring cress and tossed it with powdered dressing mixed with water. She'd made hoecakes in a skillet.

He waited until she'd poured their coffee and taken a seat in one of the rough chairs before sitting down.

"Your manners were the first thing I noticed about you," she remarked, giving him a smile. "You held the door for a woman who was going out when you entered the saloon."

"A cowboy of the old school," he drawled with a mocking bow in her direction.

His cynicism bothered her. He'd been wary when she'd first met him, but there had been an inner warmth. Had he grown cold because of her? She picked up her fork and began eating.

When they finished, she washed her plate and fork. To her surprise and quiet amusement, he did his own. He went outside and returned with more wood.

"I'll chop you some fresh firewood before I leave in the morning."

Her heart nearly stopped. She hadn't allowed herself to think about the night. "Thanks, but you don't have to bother. I have a hatchet with me."

He gave her an annoyed glare, and she subsided. He checked the cabin. "Well, I'll be off."

"Off?" She stared at him blankly.

"I'll sleep under the stars tonight. You can have the cabin."

"It's too cold to sleep outside."

He shrugged. "I've slept through worse weather."

"But . . . you can sleep in here."

He paused before reaching for his hat. "Can I? After what happened between us last night? I don't think so."

A flush ran under her skin. She busied herself doing chores that were unnecessary—arranging the plates on the table, putting away the cornmeal. "We made it the other time."

"You were hurt." He cocked his head slightly to one side. "Of course, if you're all that eager for me to stay, I will. A gentleman doesn't disappoint a lady."

His emphasis on the word *gentleman* didn't escape her. Neither did his wolfish grin. Nor the quick flare of heat in his eyes.

"You can use my tent," she said at last.

"I already have a tarp thrown over a line strung between two trees. I'll be fine," he ended on a softer note.

"Good."

They stood there awkwardly; then he nodded his head, grabbed his hat and went out into the dark.

Rachel spread her ground pad and put her sleeping bag over it. She heated the rest of the water in the bucket and washed before putting on the silk long johns that she used as pajamas. She brushed her teeth in a cup of water, tossed the used water out the door and went to bed.

A nerve-lashing scream woke her at dawn. Without stopping to think, she grabbed the hatchet from her pack and headed outside. Kerrigan met her halfway across the yard. She flew into his arms.

He held her for a few seconds; then he set her away from him.

"Are you all right?" she asked. "I heard the cougar."

"Yeah, she's close. I'm going to track her. Maybe I'll get lucky and get her moved up country today."

"How will you carry her? Will your horse take her without getting spooked?"

"Yes. He's dependable." Kerrigan let his gaze run down her. "Those silk things don't leave much to the imagination."

She glanced down. While the knitted material wasn't thin enough to see through, the cold had caused her nipples to contract into tight buttons which stood out in bas-relief against the cloth.

Quickly she crossed her arms over her chest.

"Watch it," he yelped, jumping out of range of the hatchet. "You're going to unman me yet," he stated, but a smile curled up the corners of his mouth.

"Sorry. You shouldn't make suggestive statements when I'm armed and dangerous."

"I'll remember that."

She headed back inside. "Are you ready for breakfast?"

"I'll be moving out as soon as I get packed."

That, she assumed, was supposed to be a no, but she went inside, slipped on fresh jeans and a shirt, then put on coffee, made biscuits, cooked some bacon she found in his pack and stirred oats into boiling water. When he came inside, the meal was ready.

He looked hesitant, as if he were a wary animal who suspected a trap. At last he sat and ate. In five minutes he rose, cleaned and packed his dishes, went through the saddlebags and left her most of the supplies.

"I have enough food for another week," she told him when he placed a sack of beans and meal out for her.

"I plan on traveling fast. I want a light load."

He pulled out the gift-wrapped box from his brother and held it up to the light of the window. A ruddy glow seeped into his skin. He muttered a threatening remark in which she caught the name of his brother.

Realization dawned. She, too, turned red.

"Big brother's idea of a joke," he said, seeing her face. He stuffed the box back into the saddlebags. "It's probably a good thing I didn't remember these were available last night. I might have stayed inside and saved myself a hell of a cold bed."

She sprang out of the chair. "Don't count on it."

He stood and draped the bags over his shoulder. "Are you saying you changed your mind? Seems like I remember you were set on having me sleep in the cabin."

It wasn't until he tipped his head up so that she could see his eyes clearly beneath the brim of his hat that she realized he was teasing her. A funny, achy thrill went through her.

"It's every man for himself from here on," she declared.

A grin kicked up the edges of his mouth. "Yeah," he agreed, giving her a once-over that left her feeling scorched.

On that note of wry humor, he went out. She saw him ride off on his pinto, leading the pack horse. The other gelding was cropping grass near the cabin, a hobble on its legs. Kerrigan had left the horse for her, she realized.

When she departed, she'd have to somehow return it to the ranch. She frowned. How the heck was she supposed to do that?

It was a long ride, and she had her car parked at the trailhead in the opposite direction. Going outside, she saw he'd already disappeared from sight.

Several conclusions came to mind. He could be coming back to the cabin. Or perhaps he wanted her to come to the ranch.

She caught a strand of hair and twisted it between her fingers over and over, her thoughts confused. Looking up, she spied the eagles—both of them—riding the early morning thermals on the west side of the gorge.

Something struggled to be born in her heart. It took her a few minutes to realize it was hope. She cautioned herself against it. A sexual attraction did not constitute a commitment between members of the human species.

Chapter Seven

Rachel sat in her blind and watched the male eagle through her binoculars. She'd made three shelters of pine boughs during the past four days, each one close to the three nests she'd discovered about a mile apart along the main branch of Sky Creek, thanks to the use of the horse Kerrigan had left for her. The blinds kept her from being spotted by the eagles and thus disturbing them.

Traveling by horse was usually faster than going by foot, she'd found. She could more easily haul supplies with her and stay overnight if she wanted, rather than going back to the cabin.

The notepad in her lap was filled with observations on the behavior patterns of the female eagle, also on the young male, who seemed determined to stay in the area in spite of the female's less-than-cordial reception each time he approached her.

Rachel's hands tensed on the binoculars. She watched the female eagle dive out of the sky, heading for the male.

Instead of pulling up, the female dropped past him, down into the creek gorge. She landed on a bank of scree. Peering this way and that, she busily looked over the rocks, selected one and lifted off with a mighty flap of her wings.

Rachel caught her bottom lip between her teeth as excitement coursed through her. *The test*. She'd read of this, but had never seen it herself.

The female eagle climbed a thermal and joined in formation with the lazily circling male. She dropped the stone. The male dived after it and caught it in midair. He brought it up and dropped it.

The female ignored the stone. She veered off and landed on a snag directly across the gorge from Rachel's blind. The dead tree, a standing remnant of an old forest fire, was about fifteen feet high and had four stout limbs still sticking out from its gray trunk.

The male landed on another limb. After a few minutes, he flew off, circled, then landed on the female's limb. The female shuffled uneasily. The brash young male gave two comical hops and brushed up against the female.

As soon as he made contact, the female turned on him. She screeched in his face and pecked him on the head. Then she flew off with another warning cry.

The male sat there with his head hunkered down between his wings, looked thoroughly confused and disgruntled.

"Not rocks, dummy, sticks," Rachel advised him. "This is a test. And you're failing miserably."

As if hearing her, the big golden-headed male flew over to the rocky bank and examined the stones as if looking for a clue. He picked up a stone, rose upward and dropped it. After circling once, he drifted off alone, in the opposite direction the female had taken.

He was young and unschooled in the ways of a mating pair, she thought in despair. How many chances would the female give the young male? Three, Rachel decided, then realized that had been the number of times she'd tried to contact Kerrigan. One call and two letters...all unanswered. Because of pride or indifference on his part?

Ducking her head, she climbed out from under the loose network of branches, put her notepad away and started down the rocky ledge. When she reached the creek, something leapt at the perimeter of her vision. She jerked around.

Nothing.

She scanned the area cautiously. Something had moved out there. Just as she started to turn away, she saw it again. This time she smiled. Caught in the branches of an old manzanita bush was a piece of red cloth. She picked her way over a pile of rocks and pulled the bandanna from the branches.

In one corner, printed with a laundry marker, she found the initials *KR*. To distinguish Kerrigan's clothing from Keegan's probably. That would make sense. This must have been the one that had blown out of sight last week when he'd breathed life into her stunned body.

A frisson rushed down her spine. Remembering that incident brought its own excitement. She smoothed the bandanna, then clamped it tightly between shaking hands as longing for that sweet time of wild freedom beat its wings restlessly inside her.

She'd missed him. All those years, she'd missed him.

There, she'd admitted it. She wanted him. Every night she went to sleep thinking of his caresses. Every morning she woke, restless and discontented. He had been her mate....

No. She had to forget that. Humans weren't like eagles.

Tucking the bandanna in her pocket, she returned to the cabin and fixed a lonely supper. Her supplies were getting

low. Soon she'd have to go into town and stock up. She was
also supposed to report in to her forest service contact every
two weeks. That was one of the government rules she had to
live by.

She went outside and watched the twilight after she'd
eaten her meal and cleaned up. Sitting on a stump, she con-
templated the stars coming out one by one, like fireflies in
the sky.

The female eagle was lonely, too. The creature was being
surprisingly patient with the male, who was eager to mate
but didn't yet realize there was more to his duties than that.
Maybe he would make it. Maybe not.

She realized she wanted him to. Very much. *Don't give up,*
she advised, thinking of both of them.

Sighing, she let the darkness still over her. Sticking her
hands in her pockets, she discovered the bandanna in one
and the granola bar Kerrigan had given her in another. She
unwrapped the granola bar and ate it while listening to the
whispering of the wind in the trees. Oh, to be wild and
free. . . .

The brindle cow darted to the right. Kerrigan swore and
took off after it. The cow swerved around a thicket of coy-
ote brush. Kerrigan uncoiled his whip, spurred the cow pony
into a run and caught up with the stubborn beast.

He cracked the whip to the right of her head and suc-
ceeded in turning her around. When she didn't move fast
enough to suit him, he flicked her on the rump. The cow let
out a surprised bellow and ran for the safety of the herd.

Kerrigan wiped the sweat from his brow and grinned in
feral triumph. He coiled the whip and hung it on a saddle
clip.

"You're rough on the stock," Keegan remarked, reining
his horse in. "What's eating you?"

"Nothing."

"Yeah? Well, that *nothing* has you as sore as a bobcat with a thorn in its tail. Chill out or head in," he advised. "The men are tired of walking on eggshells around you."

Kerrigan stuck his bandanna in his pocket. "One thing I've always disliked," he said in a near snarl, "is when you get into your big-brother mode and wax philosophical."

Keegan grinned. "I'm only thinking of your welfare. The men are liable to lynch you if you don't let up."

Kerrigan told him what he could do with his concern.

Ignoring that, Keegan continued on in a serious vein. "It's the woman. You're not over her yet." He frowned into the distance. "Maybe you ought to go see her."

"Stuff it."

"Either get her out of your system," his brother went on, "or find out what's between you."

Kerrigan gave him a threatening look.

"It was pretty obvious you two had the hots for each other last weekend—"

"Back off," Kerrigan warned, in no mood for advice, well intended or otherwise.

Keegan shook his head. "Maybe you ought to take a few days off. Go fishing, go to New York . . . hell, go anywhere so long as you come back in a better frame of mind."

Kerrigan controlled the simmering rage with an effort. His brother was right. He was acting the fool and all because of a woman he couldn't seem to get out of his blood. "Thanks for the helpful suggestions. Maybe I'll take you up on them."

Kerrigan rode off with a visage as grim as a Sierra thunderhead. He glanced back in time to catch his twin shaking his head as if he considered Kerrigan a hopeless case.

After making a remark on his brother's ancestry, which he then realized would also apply to his own, he headed for the ranch house. He was damned tired. And ready for some fun. He'd clean up and head into town.

An hour later he rode into the ranch yard. Wills, the old rodeo clown that he and Keegan had picked up out of the gutter, brought to the ranch and sobered up, met him at the stable door.

"That horse you left with the woman showed up yestiddy," he said, taking the reins of the cow pony when Kerrigan slid off.

Kerrigan glanced toward the house. His heart beat a harsh staccato against his ribs.

"Just the horse," Wills added. "Not the woman."

Fear slammed into him. "She might be hurt—"

"Don't think so. The reins were tied to the horn. Looks like she knows our ways."

Kerrigan remembered how efficient she'd been in the woods. Yeah, she'd known what she was doing. A horse returning to the barn with dragging reins meant the cowboy needed help. Tied reins usually meant the rider had sent the horse back on purpose, no longer needing the animal.

"News said a blizzard was on the way, blowing snow and freezing rain along the coast now. The storm will probably come in by morning. She might not know about that."

Kerrigan shrugged. "She's an adult, a naturalist. She ought to know how to take care of herself in the woods."

"Odd storm. She might not read the signs. Be bad to be caught out in it on foot."

"I'm going to clean up and head into town."

Wills's face puckered up. "Road'll be slick."

Kerrigan gave him a glance over his shoulder. "You're worse than an old woman, Wills. You worry too much."

Wills spat a stream of tobacco juice into the dust. "Somebody has to do it. You boys are wilder than billy goats. You oughta have a woman to look after you."

Kerrigan spun around. "Don't you start, too," he warned, giving the old man a fierce glare that would have made a world-class boxer think twice about saying more.

Undaunted, Wills moved his chaw from one side of his mouth to the other and grinned. "Unnerstand you lost the bet."

"Yeah. I'm heading into town right now to look for a woman who's crazy enough to marry into this outfit," Kerrigan snarled sarcastically. He stomped off to the house.

Damn the lot of them, he swore savagely, yanking off his hat and throwing it toward the rack on the kitchen wall. He'd find a wife in his own good time. He grabbed his shirt, jerked it from his waistband and pulled the snaps open with vicious energy.

Going into his room, he glanced once at the open door of the guest room across from his room. His libido perked up.

"Go back to sleep, stupid," he muttered. "She's not there."

He slammed the door. After getting out of his clothes, he stepped into the shower and turned the water on full blast, then let out a howl as water straight off the Sierra snow-pack hit him like needles of ice.

Town. That's what he needed. It was Saturday. He'd go in, shoot some pool, maybe dance if there was anyone around. Ha! The women in town were either too old, too young, married, or tourists just passing through. But sometimes there was an unattached female in the saloon. Most likely from Pete's, over at the river.

Thinking of anything concerning females reminded him of Rachel. Maybe he should go over... hell, he wasn't her keeper. He wasn't going to ride a horse through a blizzard, if the storm was heading this way, to check on a female who'd let him get beaten within an inch of his life with no warning.

Of course she'd indicated she hadn't known beforehand, but why hadn't she shown up? Answer *that*.

The water warmed, and he scrubbed himself with unnecessary force. That would have been all he needed, he mused. Her there, watching him get the stuffing knocked out of him. Why had he tried to break through three men anyway? Really dumb.

Okay, so he'd had some idea that, if he could see her, she'd tell them she wanted him, that they were going away together, that they were going to be married....

He almost doubled over as pain clawed through him. He would never put himself through that again. He admitted she'd drawn him into her spell while she was there. He wouldn't let it happen again.

Woman-magic. It wasn't to be trusted.

The sound of Rachel's voice came to him. Noble, she'd called him. Well, hell, all nobility had ever gotten the McPherson boys was a reputation as ruffians and several black eyes.

What had brought on this morbid line of thinking? He turned off the shower and stepped out. What he needed was a night out. Yeah, he'd go to town early, pick up some supplies, then stay for some fun. After all, it was Saturday night.

Rachel reached her compact car at two on Saturday afternoon. She slumped in the seat before cranking up the engine.

After riding the gelding within sight of the McPherson ranch yesterday, she'd tied the reins behind the saddle horn and slapped it on the rump. It had headed for the barn and its oats.

Then she'd had to walk back to the cabin, a good five-hour hike. This on top of the three-hour hike to the trail-head today. She was tired.

However, she'd put off heading for town as long as she could. She had to report in and get some supplies.

She pumped the gas pedal a couple of times, then turned the key. The engine growled. She tried again. This time it roared to life. Relieved, she put it in gear, backed from under the tree and headed down the dirt trail at fifteen miles per hour. It would take an hour to get to the paved road, then another to get to town.

Sure enough, it was four when she got in.

The town was busy as usual on a Saturday. She slowed as she passed the logging company to let a truck pull into the traffic. A few men were still at work there, stacking logs in a huge pile. They'd probably be at the saloon later tonight. She'd eat early and leave before things got rowdy.

At the forest service cabin on the south side of the town, she parked and climbed out. Using the key given to her by the local ranger, she went in and checked the place over.

There were two bunk beds against one wall, two chairs plus a wide bench with a pad that served as additional seating for the pine table and could be used as a bed, too. She tossed her duffel bag on one of the chairs.

A tiny kitchen and a bathroom opened off one side. The bath had a shower. Good.

Following instructions, she turned on the hot water heater, then brought in her sleeping bag and spread it on the lower bunk. There. Home, sweet home.

After a hot shower, she felt like a new person. She slipped into clean gray wool slacks and a white turtleneck sweater, then tied a red bandanna around her neck. She lingered for a minute, her hand on the bandanna.

Her thoughts winged back to the bluff where she'd leapt on Kerrigan like some kind of idiot. April third. April Fool's Day would have been more appropriate. Fate had pulled an unkind trick on her, and she'd certainly made a fool out of herself.

That should last for the entire year, she told herself sternly. Don't go looking for trouble. Okay, so it was Saturday night. So what? Not all cowhands and ranchers came to town on Saturday night.

Picking up her duffel, she drove back to the heart of town. Next to the feed store, she located a laundry. She sorted her clothes and stuck them in the washing machines. Once that was taken care of, she went next door to the all-purpose establishment of post office, grocery store and gas station.

Several men lounged around the counter, drinking beer and watching a basketball game on television.

She walked down the narrow aisles. Pushing a shopping cart, she selected beans, cornmeal, powdered milk and dried fruit over the more costly hiker's food. There were plenty of fresh greens to be had in the mountains, so she didn't worry about those. But there was one thing she wanted in the fresh produce department—bananas. She was dying for a banana.

Rounding the corner, she ran into a man hefting a fifty-pound bag of potatoes onto the bottom of his cart.

"Oh, I'm sorry," she exclaimed. "Did I hurt you?"

The man straightened. "No."

She looked into icy blue eyes that seemed to grow colder each second he gazed at her. "Hello, Kerrigan," she said.

He tipped his hat to her.

"Did the horse get to the barn all right?"

'Yeah."

"Good. I wasn't sure what to do with him." She clenched the handle of the cart. "I was afraid to leave him. I didn't know if you'd caught the cougar. You didn't stop by. . ."

She realized she sounded as if she were scolding. He didn't have to report to her on his comings and goings.

"Why didn't you come on down to the ranch?" he asked.

"Well, it was a long hike back. When the ranch came into view, I stopped on the ridge." She looked at him to see if he knew which ridge she spoke of.

He nodded, his face as hard as an oak burl.

"Then I sent him on his way and walked back."

"That was a five-hour walk," he said, his eyes narrowing as if angry with her.

She grinned. "I know."

"Then you had to hike to your car this morning." He looked annoyed about the whole thing.

"Yep," she agreed, forcing a cheerful note.

His gaze skittered down her. "No wonder you don't weigh more than a midget."

"Right," she said, determined not to quarrel with him. "Well, nice seeing you. Thanks for your help last week." She tossed a bunch of bananas into her cart and walked off.

So much for hope reborn. She paid for her groceries and picked up the two bags. A strong hand reached over hers and took one of them. She looked up into stormy eyes.

"Where's your car?" he asked.

"Next door. At the Laundromat."

He carried her groceries for her and stored them in the trunk. She thanked him again. He stalked off to the store. Shrugging, she went in and transferred her clothes to the dryer.

Finished with her chores, Rachel returned to the service cabin and called the ranger station. She reported on her success with the eagle and the arrival of the male. "I'm heading out tomorrow with enough supplies to last the rest of the month.''

''Be careful,'' the ranger advised. ''There's a storm heading this way. It's stalled along the coast right now, but it should move inland in a day or two.''

''Roger that. I'll talk to you in a couple of weeks.'' She hung up and walked around the cabin. The silence nagged at her. Checking her watch, she saw it was nearly six. She'd go eat a hot meal, buy a paperback, then turn in for the night.

She zipped her coat, locked the door and headed down the side of the road. It was no more than a city block to the diner.

When she arrived, she noticed there were several cars out front. The men were in town for Saturday night. She grimaced but continued inside.

Naturally, the first person she saw in the place, seated at a table by himself and looking like a thundercloud, was Kerrigan.

When she hesitated inside the door, he unfolded himself from the chair and stood. With a challenging smile, he shoved the opposite chair out from the table with his boot.

Given such an invitation, how could she refuse? She walked over and sat down. ''Thanks,'' she said. ''I hate to eat alone.'' She gave a pointed glance at his bottle of beer. An empty sat on the table. There was no sign of food.

''Don't scold. Neither you or Wills is my mother.'' He resumed his seat and stared into the distance in silence.

''Who's Wills?''

''The old guy.''

She knew who he meant. There was only one old man on the ranch. The rest were young cowboys.

"He was yelling advice when you and Hank were riding the wild stallion." A flicker of excitement ran through her as she recalled the scene.

"Right. He keeps house for us and generally runs the home area when Keegan and I are out."

"He does a good job. Your house is immaculate."

He made a sound deep in his throat.

"I suppose that's why there are no women on the ranch," she ventured.

"None needed. None wanted." He lifted his bottle in a mock toast before he drank.

Anger warmed her. "You'll need a woman if you ever decide you want children."

He lowered the bottle slowly and set it aside. His eyes bored into hers. "Are you volunteering?"

Heat, like a tiny sun, formed inside her. What would he do if she said yes? She took a breath and said, "No."

Kerrigan felt the tension ease up somewhat. For one gut-clenching moment, he'd thought she was going to say yes. He smiled grimly. Get real, McPherson.

The waitress came over. Rachel ordered the number-three dinner, which was T-bone steak, baked potato and salad. He ordered the same. He realized this was the first time they'd eaten a meal together in public, although in the past there'd been plenty of impromptu picnics in secluded glens.

The tension returned. He heaved a breath in disgust. He couldn't think of her without his libido going haywire.

A couple came in. The man hung up his hat, then helped the woman with her coat. They turned and surveyed the room for an empty table. The woman saw Rachel. A smile broke over her face. She darted across the room.

"Rachel?" she asked, stopping by the table. Her husband stopped beside her. "Rachel Barrett? Is that you?"

"Suzannah!" Rachel exclaimed. She stood and embraced her old friend. She turned to Kerrigan with an anxious glance. He rose to his feet. He knew the amenities.

"Kerrigan McPherson," Suzannah exclaimed, looking from Rachel to Kerrigan. "Do you know my husband, Tom?"

"He's my banker," Kerrigan said in a laconic drawl. The two men shook hands. He wondered if he should invite them to sit with him and Rachel.

It would be embarrassing if they refused. Not that *he* cared, but it might hurt Rachel. The town people had never paid much attention to the McPhersons. The twins had stayed pretty much to themselves, when they weren't working their butts off on the ranch.

Susannah introduced Tom to Rachel. There was an awkward pause after they spoke.

Rachel glanced at Kerrigan. His face was impassive. It was his table . . . well, he'd just have to share it.

"Won't you join us?" she invited. "We'd be glad to have you." She moved over beside Kerrigan and gave him a nudge.

He glanced at her. Then he smiled—it nearly stopped her heart, it was so charming—and asked the couple to please be seated. Rachel could have hugged him.

Tom and Suzannah accepted. "This is our big night out," Suzannah explained. "Mom's baby-sitting."

"How many children do you have?" Rachel asked.

"Two, both girls, thank goodness. If boys are more trouble than girls, I'd go out of my mind." She opened her purse. "I just happen to have pictures," she warned with a laugh.

After the women talked about the children, they all discussed ranching and the economy. Rachel worried about Kerrigan, but she soon found she needn't. He didn't sit there silent as a rock and leave her to carry the conversation like some men did. She was pleased at how pleasant and articulate he was.

Before she realized it, the evening had slipped away. Music started in the next room. A three-piece band set up their instruments, and the dancing began.

"Shall we have drinks in there?" Suzannah asked, her toe already tapping with the rhythm.

"Dancing is her passion," her husband teased.

Rachel glanced at Kerrigan. He met her eyes. An eternity seemed to pass.

"I think I'd better go," she said with a glance through the archway at the dance floor. "I have a long hike tomorrow."

Kerrigan touched her arm. "Come on," he said. "You like to dance. You can sleep late."

Surprised at his perception, she let herself be led to a cocktail table. Kerrigan ordered a margarita for each of them. The other couple ordered the same.

Suzannah and Tom didn't wait for the drinks but went right to the dance floor. They did a Texas two-step in a circle around a gyrating younger couple in the center of the floor.

When the tune changed to a pop-country hit, Kerrigan stood and held out his hand. Rachel went with him to the floor. He dropped her hand and began to move with the beat. She followed his style, which was smooth and rhythmic. He knew the words of the song and sang along with the band.

Beside her, she heard Suzannah's delighted laughter as Tom spun her around and around at the end of the dance. They returned to the table.

"Oh, that makes me feel so wonderful," Suzannah exclaimed. Her blue eyes twinkled at Kerrigan. "I wanted you to ask me out our senior year. I flirted outrageously with you, but you never seemed to notice.''

Rachel gave Kerrigan a questioning glance. That wasn't the way he made it sound the night of his birthday party.

Suzannah spoke to her. "All of us girls had crushes on Kerrigan and his brother, but neither of them ever glanced in our direction. I was totally crushed."

Rachel observed the astonished expression that flickered over Kerrigan's face. He met her eyes briefly. A grin kicked up the corners of his mouth when he spoke to Suzannah.

"Sure wish I'd known that," he drawled. "We figured none of you gals would go with us due to our...uh...rowdy natures, I believe was the way the principal put it."

"Pooh," she said. "That fight at the football game wasn't your fault. Everyone knew Rolly Cawe started it. He and his friends were nothing but trouble and a lot of hot air."

Kerrigan felt his jaw. "Pretty heavy air. Seems I remember he weighed a couple of hundred pounds and packed quite a wallop."

They laughed at his exaggerated grimace.

Suzannah surveyed the room. "I wonder where he and his two pals are? They're usually here as soon as the logging yard closes down." She frowned, then shrugged and turned to her husband. "Come on, honey. I've got to get my fun in while I can."

They went to the dance floor when a slow song started. Kerrigan sat stubbornly silent. Rachel wished he'd show a little more enthusiasm for dancing with her.

The saloon and the diner were full by now. Several other couples joined Tom and Suzannah on the floor.

Most of the people were older couples, she noted. Local ranchers and their wives, Rachel thought. Town merchants. She listened while they greeted one another.

As the hours passed in conversation and dancing—Kerrigan danced only fast numbers and only with her—she observed that she and Kerrigan were included, along with Suzannah and Tom, in the general conversation.

"It's nice to be part of a group like this, isn't it?" she asked Kerrigan when they returned to their table after a rowdy rendition of a popular country hit.

"Yes."

His tone was noncommittal, but she wasn't fooled. He was surprised that people seemed to accept him as one of them. As they should. He'd staked his future on the area just as they had. They had common interests.

Several hours later Suzannah sighed, finished her margarita and stood. "Well, it's Cinderella time. My parents turn into monsters if we're not home by midnight. Rachel, I can't tell you how glad I am that you're in the area. Listen, can you two come to our house for dinner next week?"

Rachel smiled regretfully. "I won't be in town again until the end of the month."

Her friend's disappointed face brightened. "Great. Let's plan a night out then. Meet you here at seven on the last Saturday of the month?" She looked from one to the other.

Rachel glanced at Kerrigan, then away. "I think I can make that. I'll need supplies by then."

A beat of time passed. Rachel felt the blood rush to her face when it became clear Kerrigan wasn't going to accept.

"I have a cougar to track," he finally said. "It'll be a while before I get down this way again."

Tom held out his hand to Kerrigan. "It was good seeing you. Your brother was down at the Medford office the other day. If you want that mortgage, think of us first," he said on a jovial note.

"Tom," Suzannah scolded. "This is our date night. You're not supposed to do business."

His grin was unrepentant as he dropped an arm around his wife's shoulder. "Just a little plug for the bank, darling. The Sky Eagle ranch will be the biggest outfit around if they buy the land next to theirs."

After the other couple left, the pleasant ambience evaporated. Rachel idly stirred her straw through the melting ice in her glass. "I should go, too."

"Why?"

Because you obviously don't want me.

"Because I'm tired. Because I have a long hike tomorrow with several pounds of groceries in my backpack." She shrugged. "Are you really buying more land?"

"We might. The old man on the other side of us had a heart attack. His daughter lives in San Francisco. I doubt if she's interested in ranching. The rancher is ruining the place. It will probably be bankrupt soon."

"How sad," Rachel murmured, "to have a legacy and lose it due to poor management."

"You didn't keep your place," he reminded her.

"But I wanted to."

"Most people have a romantic idea of a rancher's life. They don't know about flies and ticks, being out in the weather no matter if it's hot enough to fry a buzzard's feet on a fence post or cold enough to freeze your buns to the saddle, not to mention winter feed, medicine and vet's bills that eat into your profits."

"You seem to be doing all right. The bank is eager for your business."

"Right. Everyone loves a winner. It's when a man is down that he learns who his friends are."

She gave him a sideways glance and stood. "Remember," she said softly, "I was your friend before you were a rodeo star."

His eyes darkened, and his hand clenched for a second before he released it. "Yeah, I remember," he said.

He pushed his chair back and stretched to his full height. She couldn't stop herself from staring at him. The evening had stirred longings in her that were better left alone. She wanted to be a couple with him, to go home at the end of a pleasant evening and find heaven in his arms.

His hand closed on her arm, and he lowered his head to hers. For one shattering moment she thought he meant to kiss her.

"Don't look at me like that," he said in an angry tone.

"I can't help it."

Kerrigan sighed, defeated. He knew where they were headed and how the night would end. He should have left when he could, when she ran into him at the store.

The band leader announced a final set before their break. It started on a slow number, the theme song from a movie that was so filled with longing, it could make tears come to the eyes just by listening. He saw the shining drops standing on Rachel's lashes.

He locked an arm around her and turned her around. They joined the other couples on the dance floor. For a full ten seconds, he managed to hold her at a distance.

Then, seeing the longing he felt mirrored on her upturned face, he couldn't stand it. He slid his arms around her and pulled her close.

She settled against him, her weight as soft as a sigh.

He ran his hands over her back and felt the malleability of her flesh under his hands. Yet she was strong. It was one of the things that had fascinated him about her—that combination of gentle yielding and strength that she had...that willingness to give herself to his touch, to his bidding, to let him take from her all that he desired.

And in that taking, he'd also wanted to give to her. It had been a two-way surrender.

She made a sound, a murmur against his neck, and he felt his heart swell with a longing so acute that it was unlike anything he'd ever known.

He swallowed painfully. A man would be a fool to let himself be sucked in again. Besides, it was nothing, just the usual man-woman needs, building inside him until he thought he'd kill to have her. Or die from trying.

Right. He'd tried that once, too, and look where it had gotten him—a bruised jaw and a body so sore he'd been unable to ride a horse for a week.

Forget this woman, he advised harshly. But he didn't let her go. He would take this moment. While the music played, she was his.

Too soon it was over.

He knew it was time to take her to her place and to get out of town... before it was too late and he stayed for as long as she would have him. Seven years ago that had been for a month. Four weeks of bliss and then... nothing. How long before she grew tired of him this time?

Chapter Eight

"Well, well," a gravelly voice snarled behind them. "If it isn't one of the McPherson twins, out for a good time on Saturday night. I figured this place would be too small for a big-time rodeo star like you."

Rachel and Kerrigan pivoted together to see a man lounging in the archway between the diner and the saloon. One hand held a beer. The other was propped on the door frame, pulling his shirt tight and exposing a stomach that was already lapping over his belt, although he was no older than Kerrigan. There were two men with him.

"Looks like you figured wrong," Kerrigan said.

The man eyed Rachel. "Who's this? A new girl from Pete's?"

She knew Pete's was a fishing camp on the river where cabins could be rented by the hour. Beside her, she felt the anger in Kerrigan by the way he stiffened. She laid a hand on his arm.

"I'm the new naturalist working with the national forest service," she stated, keeping her tone pleasant but neutral.

"Naturalist, huh? I'll bet you look real nice running around the woods all naturallike." His gaze was an insult.

"Watch what you say, Cawe," Kerrigan warned without raising his voice. "Rachel's a lady."

Rachel looked around. The crowd was watching the scene with a disapproving frown. Was it Kerrigan or the other man they disliked? She noticed there were several single men at the bar now, too. Loggers and cowboys. They'd be game for a fight.

"She couldn't be. She's with you." The man glanced at his two cronies. They laughed on cue.

Kerrigan took Rachel's arm. "Ready to go?"

She nodded, relieved at his good sense.

Cawe and his men blocked the path between the tables. "Running?" he asked with a self-important grin.

"No, but I'm not looking for trouble, either." Kerrigan positioned himself between Rachel and the men. His stance was easy, but alert. "I'd advise you to step aside."

The tension in the room climbed ten notches. Rachel saw some men tense, some grin. They were ready for anything.

She studied Kerrigan's enemy. He was a typical bully, talking tough when he had his foe outnumbered.

The room was quiet as the occupants waited to see the outcome of the confrontation. One of the men at the bar moved down to stand near Kerrigan.

"I'm not worried. You don't have your brother to back you tonight," Cawe scoffed.

"He has me," Rachel said, peering around Kerrigan. The words just popped out. She grinned at Cawe, who looked disconcerted for a second.

He let out a guffaw. "Pretty brave words," he said, "coming from McPherson's wh—"

The insult never got out of the man's mouth. Kerrigan's fist stopped it before the rest of them could move. The bully hit the floor. The other two men lunged at Kerrigan. One of them landed a lucky blow to his nose as Kerrigan shoved them backward.

Just as Rachel decided she'd have to use the self-defense tactics she'd learned years ago, a strange thing happened. There was a shuffling of chairs. Men rose to their feet, leaving their wives and sweethearts at the tables. They moved with a steady purpose. Soon they were lined up behind Kerrigan and Rachel, a solid phalanx of support.

Cawe got to his feet. Kerrigan and his enemy looked equally amazed. Rachel smiled at Cawe. "If you'll excuse us, we'll be going now," she said, striving to keep the triumph out of her face.

Cawe and his two buddies moved out of the way. She shivered at the hatred in the man's eyes as Kerrigan took her hand and led her outside.

He turned to Rachel. "Don't you ever put yourself into my fight again," he thundered.

"I won't," she said. "Unless it's necessary. Here." She handed him a napkin.

Kerrigan wiped the blood from his nose. "I mean it." He looked around. "Where's your car?"

"At the forest service cabin. I walked down."

He muttered some words she didn't catch and started off down the street at a race-walk pace.

"I'm cold," she panted. "Let me zip my jacket."

He released her long enough to open the door of his truck. "Get in," he ordered. "You can zip your coat inside."

She climbed in.

He got in and jammed the key in the ignition. The truck roared to life. He drove the quarter mile to her place in ominous silence.

What next? she wondered as the adrenaline-induced energy faded and fatigue set in.

At the cabin she unlocked the door and turned to him. "Come in. We'll get some ice on your nose."

"To heck with my nose. Get your things. We're heading out to the ranch."

She looked at him in amazement, then shook her head. "I have to go back to the creek. The eagles—"

"I'll take you there tomorrow," he growled, sounding more comical than gruff with the napkin pressed to his nose.

"I'll stay here and drive myself tomorrow," she said calmly, stepping inside and turning the lamp on. "Either come in or leave. That wind's cold."

He came inside and slammed the door. "You can't stay here alone, not with Cawe and his men in town and on the loose."

"I'll lock the door. They wouldn't dare break in."

Kerrigan grabbed her shoulder. "In normal circumstances, no, but you don't know what they'll do after seeing you with me. That makes you fair game. They've been the plague of my life since the moment we moved here."

"Why does he hate you?"

He raised one shoulder and let it drop. "Damned if I know."

She thought about it. "I think it's because he's jealous. After all, you're a lot better looking than he could ever hope to be. Did you hear what Suzannah said? All the girls liked you and your brother. She had nothing but contempt for that bully and his friends."

"I always thought she was a sharp gal," he mocked.

"But something must have put Cawe on your case. What was it? Do you remember the first time he baited you like he did tonight?"

"Our first run-in was the summer my brother and I moved in with our grandfather. Keegan and I won the junior division of a local rodeo. Cawe accused us of cheating and tried to get us disqualified. The judges upheld our win."

"Well, that explains it," she said, satisfied that she'd found the root of Cawe's evil regard.

Kerrigan gave a muffled snort, then grimaced with pain.

"Oh," she exclaimed, remembering his nose. Rushing to the tiny kitchen, she emptied a tray of ice cubes, crushed them in a dish towel with a knife handle and brought them back into the living-sleeping area. "Sit here," she ordered, indicating the bench beside the table.

He obeyed.

She placed the ice pack over his face. With a gentle touch, she smoothed his hair with one hand.

He frowned, took the ice pack from her, pushed her hands away and held it to his nose himself.

"Okay, be stubborn," she said, smiling at him.

She pulled a chair near and watched, unable to keep her eyes off him. Underneath his cynical shell, he was everything a man should be—brave, protective, gentle with her. She wished they could stay like this forever.

The old, useless yearning intruded, and she looked away. If wishes were wings... That month with him had been the most wonderful of her life, a sweet, wild freedom of the soul. She'd never found it again.

Kerrigan wished she'd stop looking at him like he was some kind of hero. He'd only had Cawe to deal with. Pretty easy odds. "You were in a karate stance. Where did you learn it?"

"From my brother. Rafe thought we should be able to defend ourselves in case terrorists tried to kidnap us."

Kerrigan stared at her.

"The life of a diplomat's kids," she said in explanation.

"I never knew it was dangerous," he said with a frown.

"My father had a highly visible post in an unstable area. There were always threats against the family. My brother was protective toward me." She paused, then added, "I didn't know it then, but Rafe found out about us and told the guards not to let you in. He thought he was saving me from a foolish mistake."

"He undoubtedly did," he mumbled around the ice pack.

She ignored his cynical comment. "I thought I could ride off into the sunset with you and be free for once in my life. I didn't mean for you to get hurt. Will you ever forgive me?" she asked.

He felt like a fool, like he should get down on his knees and apologize to her for failing to stick around. Instead he'd crawled back to the ranch with his tail between his legs like a whipped dog. "Yeah," he said. "I forgive you."

She nodded solemnly, then began a search through drawers and cabinets. "The townspeople were on your side. Did you notice?"

"Yeah." He was still astounded.

"They like and respect you."

She made it sound like he'd been at fault all these years, holding them at arm's length. He frowned. Had he? He and his brother had fought taunts constantly in the city where they'd lived with their mother. When they'd been sent to the ranch, they'd run into Cawe and his friends on their first day of school. Kerrigan admitted Cawe's cruelty might have influenced the way they'd reacted to the other residents.

But tonight, Suzannah and Tom had been friendly. Kerrigan had assumed that was because of Rachel. But the men standing up for him . . . And their wives not objecting . . . It boggled the mind.

"You might try being friendlier in the future," Rachel mentioned. Before he could snap at her, she changed the subject. "I only have one sleeping bag." Her voice was muffled by the depths of the closet.

Only the curve of her delectable tush was visible as she went through the contents of the closet floor. He fought a need to get up and go to her, to take her to bed and show her how roomy one sleeping bag could be for two inventive people.

"If you're going to stay, you'll need some cover," she said, backing out and straightening up.

"I have a blanket in the truck. Behind the seat."

She blinked at him in the slow, deliberate way she had. She was clearly not surprised that he would carry a blanket. He felt heat in his ears and knew he was blushing like a kid.

"It's not like you're thinking," he said, feeling defensive.

"How's that?" She closed the closet door.

"That I keep a blanket handy for a quick roll in the hay."

Her gaze flicked to his body, then skittered away.

Hell, yes, he was aroused. *She* did that to him. That's why he'd carefully avoided dancing with her in his arms earlier in the evening. He would never have been able to take it, and he'd be damned if he'd make a complete fool of himself over her in front of half the town.

Of course, he'd done that, too.

"I keep it in case I get stuck out somewhere on the ranch and have to spend the night in the truck," he explained. He sounded guilty as hell, but damned if he knew what for.

"Of course," she said as if she believed him.

A sense of relief ran over him. Not that he had to explain anything to a stubborn female who didn't know to be careful around a bully like Cawe.

She went outside. He kept an eye out for danger while she went to the truck. She returned, closing and locking the door behind her.

"Brr, it's really getting cold. What happened to spring?" she asked. She closed the shutters on the windows.

He watched her spread the blanket over the top bunk, then think better of it. She exchanged the sleeping bag and blanket.

"Change those back," he ordered. "You'll need the warmth."

"I'm going to sleep on top. If you fall off during the night, I don't want you landing on me. The last time that happened, I got the worst of it." She tossed him a grin that had his heart skipping like a stone over a lake.

A groan worked its way from deep inside him. The feel of her mouth under his as he breathed for her returned to haunt him. He closed his eyes and leaned his head against the windowsill. Cold air seeped around the loose-fitting panes, chilling his neck.

Maybe it would chill the rest of him, he thought with grim amusement. Ha, he could be submerged in ice water, and he'd still have this raging hunger for her. It was driving him insane.

"Come to bed," a soft, feminine voice murmured close to him.

He opened his eyes and gazed into her face. She was so familiar—he knew her body as well as he knew his own—yet she was a stranger in many ways...a maddening, impetuous woman who had once seemed to think he was more than he actually was.

For her, he'd wanted to be, he realized. He'd wanted to be a hero in her eyes. But those days were long gone. He was over that illusion. He'd learned, oh, yeah, he'd learned.

"Why did you have to sneak out to meet me?" he asked.

He clamped his teeth together, but it was too late. The words were already out in the open, exposing his vulnerability where she was concerned. He swallowed hard and waited for her answer.

"You were over twenty-one," he went on doggedly, needing to get it out in the open.

"I know," she said. She sat on the bench beside him. "You were the one rebellion in my life. My one wild fling."

"A fling," he repeated. Well, hell, what had he expected?

She touched his hand, her expression incredibly gentle, then withdrew. "Not like that. Not a temporary thing. You were my sweet, wild love. My special secret."

His heart raced painfully. He summoned the cynicism that had sustained him during the weeks after their affair. "Yeah, it was pretty wild."

"I didn't want to share you with anyone. Love can be selfish like that, you know."

Yeah, he knew. He hadn't told his brother about her when they'd discussed the old man's legacy on the phone. He hadn't talked about her until he'd picked Keegan up at the apartment near the hospital where his twin had been taking physical therapy. In light of the bruises, he'd had to render some explanation.

"I could never do anything on impulse—go on a picnic, run out for pizza—nothing like that," she continued in a soft, sad tone. "Every activity had to be planned in advance and approved by the security officer. Going with you was the one impulsive act of my life." She gazed at him without blinking. "The one right act."

It took an effort to keep his defenses in place. "Was it?" he questioned with a sardonic smile. "That wasn't the message I got from your guards that night."

She shook her head and frowned at him. "When you got my letter, you must have realized I didn't know about the beating."

Her letter had been angry. She'd said she'd waited for him for hours. He'd known that was a lie. He'd been there.

"Maybe, but I didn't feel up to taking any more chances at that moment." He'd won his first major rodeo three weeks later, grimly holding on to broncos or bulls—he didn't care what was under him—as if holding on to life, glad for the pain in his body. It drove out the pain in his mind.

"My brother detained me at the house. I did show up, but I was late. Apparently, you'd already left. It wasn't until one of the ranch hands told me about the fight a week later that I realized you'd been there."

He ran a hand through his hair, feeling the fatigue close in. "It doesn't matter," he said. "Listen, let's drop the postmortem and get some sleep. That blizzard is due in sometime soon, and I want to get back to the ranch."

"I have one question—did you get the second letter I wrote?"

"Yeah, I got it."

"Didn't . . . didn't it explain things to you?"

The letter had been in the general delivery packet forwarded by their attorney after settling their grandfather's legacy, such as it was. Seeing her name on the envelope had twisted a hot knife of longing in his gut.

"Either go get her or write her off," his brother had said.

"Hell," he'd said, "a city gal like that wouldn't last a week on the rodeo circuit. Got a match?"

And so he'd burned the letter and never looked back. Except once in a while, at odd moments, like chasing that tawny cougar.

"I didn't read it," he said.

Surprise and something else—anguish?—flashed across her face. "Because you hated me so much by then?"

"I didn't see that there was anything left to say between us. I burned it."

"Burned it," she repeated. "I . . . I see." She took a deep breath. "Well, it doesn't matter now."

Anger saved him from making a fool of himself and begging her forgiveness for some crime he didn't commit. "Look, I thought you'd changed your mind when you didn't show up that night. When I got your call, I thought you'd changed it again. Okay, that's a woman's prerogative, so I'm told, but I wasn't up for any more confrontations just then."

"I understand," she said.

"In your first letter, you were damned mad that I'd stood you up, but I was there on time. You said we needed to talk, but as far as I was concerned, it had all been said. Did you get stuck on the ranch longer than you'd expected and decided you needed some more entertainment?"

"No. I thought we could start over." She gave him a smile that tore his heart to pieces, it was so sad.

He stood and tossed the dish towel of ice on the table. He had to get out. He needed to hit something or—he looked at her, sitting there so silently, almost forlorn—or else he needed to grab her and make love until he could no longer remember that he'd vowed not to make a fool of himself over her again.

"We couldn't then, and we can't now," he stated. "What would be the point? Cheer up. Maybe the female will drive the other eagle off. You'll have done your study and can leave."

She stood and pressed a hand to her head. "I'm going to bed."

He glanced at his watch. After two o'clock. He moved the shutter and looked out the window. The saloon was closed. The street was deserted.

"You'll be safe for the rest of the night. I'll head on back to the ranch."

"Fine."

He turned and looked at her. "Does your head hurt?"

"Some."

He swore under his breath. "Your pills are on the table in my room. I forgot to give them to you."

"I think if I can just get some sleep, I'll be okay." She went to the door, opened it and waited for him to leave.

Frowning, he picked up his hat and coat. Seeing the blanket on the bunk, he grabbed it, too. "Well, good night."

"Good night. Thanks for dinner and everything. And for seeing me safely home."

"It was no trouble." He walked out, feeling that he'd left something unfinished.

After making sure the door was locked behind him, he cranked up the truck and drove off. Outside of town he speeded up, anxious to get back to his own territory, where no women intruded to complicate a man's life.

For years his life had been peaceful . . . after he'd gotten over the weak feeling in the pit of his stomach whenever he'd thought of Rachel. Now everything was in a coil inside him again. Damn her for coming back. And damn Keegan for reminding him of the family he'd thought to have with her.

Chapter Nine

Rachel looked around the cabin. All tidy. She took a bite of banana, slammed the door, then locked it. A minute later she was on the road out of town.

She'd be glad to get back to her solitary pursuits. By herself in the woods, she was more content. Perhaps because she didn't have to deal with people.

The sky was heavily overcast by the time she reached the trailhead. Hmm, the news had predicted possible snow flurries, but there was only a sixty percent chance. She could probably beat it to the cabin. Anyway, a flurry wasn't anything to worry about.

She loaded her backpack with her supplies and put her weatherproof poncho over her jacket. The material was a new fabric put out by Clairmont mills. This storm would give it a test.

Hefting her load on her back, she started off. One thing about walking in the woods—her troubles always seemed to lighten and her thinking, become clearer.

Kerrigan was uppermost in her mind. She thought he'd had a good time with Suzannah and her husband, yet he'd seemed surprised that they'd enjoyed themselves with him. She suspected people like his grandfather and the bully had caused him to close himself off from others.

He and his brother had a lot of pride. By holding themselves aloof, they'd avoided further hurt and possible humiliation. It had been nice for him to hear how attractive he was to someone like Suzannah. Sort of. Okay, so she'd been a little jealous.

It didn't matter. Kerrigan had been hurt too many times in the past to open up his heart again. He would never trust her the way he had that first time. If she'd only told her brother....

It was just that, for once, she'd wanted to follow her heart without having an argument over it.

Three-quarters along the trail, the first snowflakes began to fall, sifting down like giant, loose feathers from the sky.

She sat on a rock and ate the last banana. The snow was getting thicker, falling with soft *plops* on the leaves over her head, making a noise so faint, it was like hearing whispers in the distance, but not being quite sure she actually had.

Pulling her straps tight on the backpack, she carefully pushed herself upright and started out. She wished the trail wasn't all uphill from here.

Twenty minutes later she reached the granite escarpment with its narrow ledge for a trail. Away from the protection of the trees, the wind hit her, and the snow became a blizzard. She staggered and slipped a bit on the rock, then lowered her head and pushed on.

Whiteout, she thought, looking across the valley to the distant mountains, which were lost in a blanket of white. Good thing she had less than a mile to go. She was getting tired.

The trail curved, following the wall of rock along a narrow gorge about twenty feet deep. She labored to draw breath. It was hard work to go against the wind.

As if in answer to her complaint, the wind slackened all of a sudden, and the swirl of snow stopped. She paused with her toes pointed off the ledge and drank in the beauty of the mountains.

The country was rugged with lava debris from a mountain that blew its top millions of years ago and formed Crater Lake. The granite ledge she stood on was formed by the colliding of the North American and Pacific plates. To the southeast was a great flat plateau. A land as varied as the people who inhabited it. And just as tough.

She huffed out a breath, and the air turned milky in front of her mouth. She started upward once more. Just as she did, the wind came shrieking over the crest and hit her full in the chest.

When she tilted sideways, she caught herself and tried to lean to the opposite side. Instinctively, she stepped to the right to balance the precarious pull of the backpack.

Her foot hit the edge of the rock, then slid into air. She lashed out with her arms, but there was nothing to hold on to—no handy manzanita shrub, no cedar or pine bough to grab, nothing but air. Flailing her arms, which must have looked like something in a comedy routine, she went over the side of the gully, landed on her backpack and gently slid to the bottom.

The snow landed on her face like little cold licks.

She pulled herself upright and stared up the embankment. Twenty feet. Almost straight up. Slick with snow. So close and yet so far. . . .

Water rushed along the bottom of the ravine. Good thing she hadn't landed in that, or else she'd have hypothermia to worry about.

She surveyed the gully wall. It was steep, the sides solid rock or loose, dangerous scree that would most likely tumble her back into the gully should she attempt to climb it.

A little chill of worry worked its way along her spine. No, she was all right. Nothing to worry about. She just had to figure out how to climb up a mere twenty feet. Of rock. Slippery, icy cold rock.

The falling snow murmured around her in ominous whispers.

If there had been a tree handy, she could have thrown the rope she used to hoist her pack higher than a bear could reach, over a limb and climbed out. Unfortunately, she could see no such handy tree. She grimaced. Too bad she didn't know how to lasso a boulder. Heck, she'd even lasso a bear if one appeared.

She hunkered down to preserve warmth while she thought.

Wills came into the office with a feather duster in his hand. He swiped along the furniture.

Kerrigan didn't grin at the odd sight as he usually did. Since Keegan and the men hadn't returned to the main house yet, he had started catching up on the ledgers and making up the payroll. Some of the hands would be leaving at the end of the month, moving on north to help with spring roundup and the moving of herds into summer pasture. In the fall they'd head south again.

Sometimes he envied them their carefree life-style. A hard, lonely life-style, he added truthfully. He looked out at the wet blanket of snow covering the quadrangle. It was still falling.

"Bad weather," Wills mumbled around his chaw of tobacco. "Wet snow. It'll melt fast once the sun comes out. Might have some flooding along the gullies and flats."

Kerrigan grunted a reply and went on with the books. He knew what Wills was getting at. He made an error on a check, cursed, voided it, then wrote another. When he entered the wrong amount in the checkbook, he corrected it and threw the pen down.

"That's it," he snarled. "I'm leaving."

"Going over to the line shack?"

"I'm going to track the cougar. This snow will make it easy. The foreman on the next ranch was up near the ridge shooting at something a couple of days ago."

"Check on that little gal," Wills advised, moving his chaw worriedly.

"You're an old hen," Kerrigan muttered. "All right. I'll go by that way."

Dressed in thermal underwear, jeans and a wool shirt with a rainproof poncho over his shearling jacket, he started out an hour later, riding the gelding and leading the pack horse.

"A waste of time," he said to the sky. He didn't know why he'd listened to old Wills. The man was a pain in the kazoo.

Four hours later, he was even more irritated. The line shack was empty. Where the hell was she?

Her camping gear was still there. The backpack was gone, though. She'd surely gotten back from town. So she must be out looking for her eagles. Nah, she knew better. Birds didn't fly when there was zero visibility.

He went outside and stood under the roof overhang and studied the terrain. The snow made little creepy sounds as it fell. He realized there were no tracks in it, not even faint indentations where she'd walked and the snow had filled in later.

Hell, she'd stayed in town. He'd made the trip for nothing.

Rachel's fingers were going numb. She tied the bear rope to her pack, found a fist-size rock, tied the other end to it, then gave the rock a throw upward. It arced over and landed on the trail. Good, now she could pull her backpack up when she got to the top.

Pulling on her emergency gloves, she started searching for finger and toeholds along the cliff face. She longed for the warmth and comfort of the little cabin, which was less than a mile from her. So close and yet so far. . . .

Working sideways toward a slanted crack whose bottom edge stuck out like a pouting lip, she thought if she could reach it, she'd be able to pull herself up and out. She worked carefully, aware of her solitude and the danger. If she fell, there'd be no one to save her this time.

She pressed her lips together, remembering the kiss of life she'd received. *Kerrigan, I need you.* The thought winged through her mind. She shook her head. Wishful thinking.

Hand over hand, step by careful step, she worked her way across the sheer rock wall, finding minuscule creases and cracks to pull herself along. It was slow work.

After what seemed an eternity, she found a place where her foot could support her weight and rested. She felt as if she were the only living being on earth. Being alone in a whiteout did strange things to a person's mind.

Squinting against the snow, she checked to see how far the slanted crack was from her. It didn't look any closer. She sighed and began climbing again. Maybe the cliff was thirty feet. No sweat. It was like climbing a three-story building, that's all.

She reached the edge of the crack. Since it was three inches wide and a foot deep, there was plenty of room for her feet. If she could just get her feet up to it. She felt for hand- and footholds and eased upward. At last she reached a point where she could lift her foot high enough to touch the crack.

On her first attempt, her foot slid off. She stomped the snow out of the tread of her hiking boots and tried again. Made it!

Feeling for new handholds, she pulled herself upward until she could put her weight on her upper foot. She stood and leaned against the rock face, her legs trembling.

After a minute, she began shuffling along. Right foot out, pull the left foot up to it. Find new handholds. Right foot out, pull the left one up to it. Find new holds.

Looking ahead, she saw the crack narrowed to a point about four feet from the trail where she'd slipped. How was she going to get up the last few feet? Could she pull herself over the ledge? She'd worry about that when she got there.

Leaning her head on her arm, she rested, shifting her weight from one foot to the other, preparing mentally for the final phase of the climb. Another twenty or thirty minutes would see her out of this predicament.

The wind moaned down the gorge, tickled her neck and left damp kisses of snow all over her. Shivers raced over her. She realized she was becoming dangerously chilled.

Fear tiptoed around the edges of her mind.

Kerrigan let the horse drink its fill before he headed out on the trail once more. He'd circle around the bluff and check the sandbar at the creek for the big cat's tracks. Maybe he'd get lucky for once and find something.

No such luck.

He grimaced at the snow, which covered the bank of the creek in a pristine sheet. A rabbit had stitched a set of tracks across it. That was all.

Wheeling his mount around, he decided to take the high trail to the line shack. It was too steep at one point for the gelding to negotiate, but there was another trail through the woods, longer but safer, that he could take.

His breath appeared in front of his face each time he exhaled. The day was getting colder, he realized. The snow had been coming down like fat, wet feathers for hours now. Apparently the heart of the storm had arrived.

He kept his mind on his task, searching the ground constantly for cat sign, not letting himself think of last night and the cabin and Rachel.

Rachel.

As soon as the name sprang into his mind, pictures formed like an out-of-control movie—Rachel, looking at him, her smile somehow sad. Rachel, letting him kiss her and touch her, taking him inside her . . . into her warmth . . . loving him . . . letting him love her. . . .

He snapped the shutter closed on those thoughts. He'd never loved her. A fling, she'd said. Yeah, a fling, that's all it was.

Staring at the trail, he concentrated on his task. He had a blasted wildcat of the four-legged variety to find. He jerked back on the reins, stopping the horse, and stared at the snow.

Damnation, a clue and he'd nearly missed it!

He climbed down and knelt to examine the faint track still visible in the falling snow. Not a cat. A person.

Standing, he studied the trail ahead. Rachel, or someone, had come this way after the snow had started. Three or four hours ago, he guessed. The tracks were almost obliterated.

But there'd been no sign of her anywhere near the line shack. A heavy feeling, as if his insides had turned to lead, hit him.

He remounted and rode on, watching for signs on the trail. At the escarpment he pulled up and studied the terrain. The gelding snorted and shook its head, dislodging the clinging snow from its ears and nose.

Kerrigan gazed across the narrow gorge. He could barely see the other side. The mountain peaks in the distance were gone.

Whiteout.

Dangerous stuff, snow. It looked so pretty. It could be so deadly. Enough of those thoughts, he snarled at himself.

Well, no use standing there. He'd have to walk the trail along the ledge. Should he ride through the woods to the other side and leave the gelding there, closer to the cabin?

He gazed up the trail, his eyes on the faint line of prints leading up the escarpment. Was Rachel up there somewhere? Or was he being a fool over her again?

In the silence, he could hear his heart beating, hard but steady. He was probably being stupid, letting Wills's overwrought imagination get to him.

But what if she was in trouble and needed him?

With a curse he hobbled the gelding, removed the rope and the rifle from the saddle and placed a box of shells in his pocket. Grimly he unfastened the pack containing first-aid and emergency supplies from the saddle and clipped it around his hips.

After checking through the saddlebags once more, he started off up the narrow trail. His foot skittered on a slick place as he climbed the granite outcropping. Careful. Slippery snow on cold, smooth rock could be treacherous.

His heart beat faster as he followed the tracks that were rapidly fading to nothing as the snow fell in heavy, sinister silence. Then they disappeared altogether.

Rachel eased her way up the last few feet and stopped. She could go no farther. Her head was still below the ledge where she'd slipped. Blast. She'd thought she would be able to clamber up that last bit, but she couldn't.

"Hello-o-o-o," she yelled as she'd been doing every fifteen minutes. Just in case. The snow seemed to absorb the sound before it had gone more than a few inches. "Hel-lo-o-o."

A hand reached over the bluff and caught her shoulder. "Hi," Kerrigan said.

She gaped at him, totally shocked.

"Nice day for rock climbing, huh?" he said equably. He sounded friendly, but his eyes looked dangerous.

"Kerrigan!"

"I see you remember who I am." He made a slipknot in the end of a rope and dropped it down beside her. "Put this around you," he ordered. "I'll tie the other end to a tree in case you fall."

He disappeared while she slipped the loop over her head and under her arms. He reappeared.

"I'll pull you up," he said. "Don't try to help. Just keep your body straight and still."

"Okay."

When he hooked his hands under her arms at the shoulders, she kept perfectly still. He lifted her up and out of the gorge with one mighty flex of his muscles. It was like riding an elevator. He set her on her feet beside him on the thin lip of the ridge.

She looked up at him, knowing her eyes were shining with love and gratitude, unable to hide her feelings.

"You little fool," he ground out. "You could have gotten yourself killed. Don't you pay any attention to the weather?"

The wind hit her in the back, pushing her into him. She looped her arms around him and closed her eyes.

"Don't," she requested, too near physical and emotional exhaustion to bear a scolding.

He cursed, then his hands clasped her face and turned it up to his. His lips descended, taking hers in a furious kiss.

Rachel recognized the kiss for what it was—a venting of his fear for her safety, a need for reassurance through the sense of touch and an unconscious punishment for putting him through all the other emotions.

On the heels of this realization, the kiss changed. His mouth softened, and she knew the moment he became aware of her on another level. His hands slipped down her arms and settled at her waist. He pulled her against him, bending protectively over her as if he would shield her from all harm.

Oh, love, she thought, and knew how deeply she had missed him.

He eased away from her. "We'd better get off this bluff before we both land in the bottom of the gorge," he advised with grim humor. He untied his rope, recoiled it and hooked it on the side of the emergency kit.

She managed a shaky laugh. "Right." She looked around. "I threw a rock up here somewhere. It was tied to a rope so I could pull my backpack up."

Understanding dawned on his face. He peered over the edge, spotted her pack and visually followed a line from it to the ledge. He walked a few feet past her, found the rope and pulled her pack to the top of the ledge.

"I'll take you to the cabin, then come back for my horse," he decided. "I left him at the bottom of the escarpment."

"The snow is getting deeper," she said, worrying about his being out in it. "I can make it okay from here."

He started to argue, looked at her expression and obviously thought better of it. "We'll compromise. I'll walk you to the fork in the trail. You wait there. I'll come back for the horse, ride him around the back trail and meet you."

She shook her head. "I'll go on. You go back. You can catch up with me."

He frowned darkly at her, but she stood her ground. At last, he said, "All right. I'll carry your backpack. You wait at that boulder with the pine growing out of the middle of it. You hear?"

She agreed to this arrangement. He strapped on her backpack and picked up his rifle. Suddenly he reached out and brushed the snow out of her bangs. The gesture was so tender, it brought the sharp sting of tears to her eyes. He dropped his hand abruptly, turned and walked off down the trail, the wind at his back.

Turning her face to the storm, she continued on her way. As soon as she was off the escarpment and in the trees, the wind could no longer nip her with its aching cold. She walked faster. Soon she reached the boulder with the tree growing through a crack in the middle of it. She settled on her haunches on the leeward side and waited for Kerrigan to catch up.

"Come on, wake up. Rachel, wake up."

She opened her eyes slowly, resenting the intrusion. She was so sleepy. "Leave me alone."

"No way. Get off your tush and stand up."

Rough hands pulled her to her feet. She swayed and would have fallen if he hadn't been holding her. "Tired," she mumbled.

"You're going to walk. Now get moving."

An arm settled around her waist. She had perforce to start walking. She glared up at him. He gazed back at her with his impassive, icy blue eyes.

"You're bossy and mean, Kerrigan," she told him.

"I know. Now walk."

She let out a huff to let him know how angry she was, but she walked. And walked. And walked. The gelding followed placidly behind them.

"A gentleman would let me ride."

"I'm no gentleman."

"You're telling me." She gave him another glare, which didn't faze him. "But," she added truthfully, "you used to be. You were so gentle, Kerrigan. When we made love. So gentle. A gentleman lover." She smiled, liking the sounds of that.

Feeling warm, she tried to take her coat off, but he wouldn't let her. "You have mild hypothermia," he said.

"Oh," she said brightly as if she understood the complications of the illness exactly. "I'm also very tired." She informed him of this fact very solemnly.

"I know."

They continued in silence. The snow licked at them with its icy tongue.

"How much farther is it?" she demanded querulously at one point.

"Less than a quarter mile."

She said a bad word that made him smile. She grinned at him.

They arrived at the line shack after walking just about forever, she thought. Surely they'd taken the long way.

He dropped the reins and ushered her inside. After standing the backpack and rifle in a corner, he quickly built a fire and placed her in front of it on one of the rickety chairs. Then he went out to tend to the horse.

She watched him dreamily through the dirty window. Realizing she could barely see him through the grime, she found the bandanna in her pocket and wiped the glass clean.

There. That was better.

Kerrigan came in and dumped his saddle on the floor. "Did you get the window cleaned to your exacting standards?" he asked.

She didn't care for his tone. "Yes." She pinched her lips together and gave him a haughty stare.

Kerrigan shook his head and fought a maddening need to kiss her prissy lips. She was worn out, suffering from exposure and not quite lucid. None of which she realized. A typical symptom of exhaustion and hypothermia.

He made a bed for her on the straw that still littered the floor, using his two blankets on the bottom and her sleeping bag for the top. He riffled through her pack.

"Where's your long johns?" he asked.

"Umm . . . I have them on."

"Logical. Take off your clothes and get under the covers."

He noticed she was half-asleep again. Resigning himself to the task, he stood and removed her poncho. Then her hat, her gloves, her coat, shirt, shoes and jeans. By the time he was down to the silk long johns, he was in a sweat.

She wore a bra and bikini briefs under the silk, but that didn't stop his imagination from supplying what reality didn't. Although she was slender as a reed—he thought she'd lost weight since the day she'd bushwhacked him from the tree—she still curved in all the right places.

"Okay," he said, hearing the huskiness of desire in his voice. "Get under the covers."

She lay down without giving him an argument and sighed. "I'm so sleepy," she murmured. "Are you coming to bed now?"

A drop of perspiration trickled down his spine. "Not right now. I still have . . . things to do."

She opened her eyes, and it was as if he'd been coated with honey. He could hardly move. "Thanks for your help earlier. I think I would have made it all right, but I was getting tired."

"I know. Go to sleep. I'll fix some supper and wake you when it's ready. Okay?"

"Bossy," she said around a yawn. "But I love you, anyway."

He froze. His heartbeat was suddenly loud in his ears again, like on the walk up the ridge. Had she said that as a joke, or was she hallucinating, thinking they were in another time?

Rising, he went out and checked on the gelding and the pack horse he'd left at the cabin earlier that day. He came back in and quietly prepared supper for them while she slept without moving.

It was completely dark before he had the heart to wake her. She needed calories in her to keep her body temperature up to normal. When he said her name, she immediately roused.

She sat up and stretched. "I feel like a new person. Thanks for letting me sleep."

"Here's your supper."

"Smells good." She ate the reconstituted freeze-dried dinner ravenously, then polished it off with stewed peaches, two granola bars and several cups of sweetened tea.

Kerrigan tried not to notice that the sleeping bag was pooled around her hips and that her long johns fit her like an extra skin. It was impossible. He rose, grabbed a flannel shirt out of her pack and tossed it at her. "Put this on."

Instead of being indignant, she grinned. "Can't take the irresistible allure of my pajamas, huh?" She slipped the shirt on but left it unbuttoned.

With a sigh, she pulled the saddle closer and leaned back on it, one knee drawn up, making a tent of the cover. "Sorry I was such a pain earlier. I knew I was acting stupid, but I couldn't make myself stop. I *am* aware of the dangers of exposure and the symptoms..."

Her voice trailed to a stop. She looked at him as if he had done some wondrous thing.

"You saved my life... again," she said softly.

His throat closed up. He sucked a breath in. "Nah. You'd have made it. There was another wedge of rock off to your left that you could have climbed without trouble."

She didn't contradict him, but her steady gaze said she knew what she knew. He saw her attention wander, moving over his entire body. Feeling hot, he pushed his chair back from the fire a couple of feet. Then he watched her watching him.

It was very erotic to see passion flame in a woman's eyes, he found. It made him burn to see her lips part and her breath come quickly, as if she thought of kisses they might share. It nearly destroyed his vow not to get caught in her woman-magic this time, the way he had before.

He tried to remember the pain of having his illusions beaten out of him. He savagely reminded himself of the weeks and months trying to forget her. All he could think of was how soft she'd be, how smooth her skin would feel under that silk underwear.

When he had himself under enough control that he could look at her again, he saw that she was smiling sleepily at him.

"Lie down," he advised and looked away.

"Make love to me," she said.

He darted a glance at her. There was no smile on her face to indicate she was joking. "You're delirious." He smiled to show he realized they were playing.

"No." She let her eyes roam over him. "I want you."

His body temperature shot right off the scale. If he touched her, she'd sizzle from the heat. "Tomorrow," he said hoarsely. "If you still want me."

"I will."

He rose from the chair. He had to get out and talk some sense into himself before he got sucked in by her. He stayed outside until he was sure she was asleep.

Easing into the cabin, he slipped the bolt into place, then noted the fire had burned down low. Rachel had her coat under her head and the sleeping bag pulled up to her ears. He added a big log to the back of the fireplace and a smaller one in the front. That would keep it going all night.

Being as quiet as he could, he pulled off his boots and shucked down to his thermals. He lifted the cover and slid into the makeshift bed. He'd no sooner sighed in relief than she edged over until her feet and her tush were solidly against him.

Sighing in defeat, he turned and cupped his body to hers. For the first time since she leapt back into his life, he went to sleep almost at once.

Rachel walked quietly around the cabin. The coffee was perked. The bacon was cooked. Eggs were ready to go in the grease. She was hungry, but she wanted to wait for Kerrigan.

He was still asleep. Twelve hours she'd slept. When she woke forty minutes ago, she'd felt sore but rested. She poured a cup of coffee and took it to the window.

"Has the snow stopped?"

She spun around.

Kerrigan rose on one arm. He looked at her warily. Did he think she was a man-eating lioness, on the prowl and ready to devour him?

"Yes. It's still overcast, but the sun is trying to break through. I wonder how the eagles are doing."

She looked out the window, listening to the sounds behind her. She heard him rise and dress, then pull on his boots.

"I'm going out," he said.

"Breakfast is almost ready."

"I'll be back in ten minutes."

She saw him bring the horses out and let them graze in the small open space between the shed and the cabin. Then he headed toward the creek. Judging the time to be about right, she broke eggs into the skillet she'd found in his pack and let them fry in the bacon grease. Holding bread slices on a fork, she toasted them in the fire. The meal was ready when he returned.

He brought the scent of the outdoors in with him—pine and fir balsam, crisp mountain air, the clean odor of soap. She smiled. He'd washed in the freezing creek water. Men were so funny.

"What are your plans for the day?" he asked.

"I'll head up to the cedar bluff to watch the eagles."

"I'm going to track the cougar."

She spooned the eggs onto their plates and laid the toast beside them. "Breakfast," she announced. After they were seated, she asked, "Will you be coming back here tonight?"

He met her candid gaze. "Do you want me to?"

Although his tone was harsh, she wasn't daunted. However, she did pause to think over her answer carefully. Once she'd been impulsive with this man. She had to learn to look before she leapt, as one might say.

He laughed cynically. "Things sure look different in the cold light of day than they do in the hot light of a fire, don't they?"

"I still want you," she said. "I'm just not sure we're not making another mistake. We failed each other once—"

The screech of his chair legs on the wooden floor silenced her as he pushed back from the table. She met his angry glare.

"I was there, right where we were supposed to meet, a full twenty minutes before time, I was so eager for you. You're the one who didn't show up. I still don't know that you did. Or that you didn't tell those men to get rid of me."

"My brother told them to stop you. He didn't tell them to beat you up."

"So you say." He eyed her coldly before pulling closer to the table and finishing the meal.

They were silent for several minutes.

"There has to be trust, Kerrigan," she said softly, feeling the sadness well up in her, "for us to try again."

He washed his plate and utensils, then stored them in his saddlebags. "Who said anything about trying again? A night in the sack doesn't mean a lifetime commitment."

She realized she'd walked right into that one. "I still want it like it used to be—love and passion, all mixed up, inseparable. Giving. Taking. Sharing."

He laughed without humor. "When I was a kid, I used to pretend that my mom and dad were still alive. I'd make believe they were going to come get me and Keegan and take us home so we could all be happy again." He slung his gear over his shoulder, picked up his gun and walked to the door. "It never happened."

The door slammed behind him.

Chapter Ten

Rachel trained her binoculars on the eagles and adjusted the focus. She was farther down the gorge, near the site where she'd pitched her tent earlier that month. Staying in the cabin was much more convenient than tent camping, she had to admit.

Thinking of the cabin directed her thoughts to Kerrigan. Not that he was ever really out of them. It had been a week since she'd seen him, but she knew he was near.

He'd left her a rabbit, cleaned and ready for the pot, one evening. Another time, the pack horse had disappeared and another had been left in its place. She'd seen his footprints at the creek one morning and fresh horse scat, still steaming, and knew she'd missed him by mere minutes.

She'd made a stew from the rabbit with wild herbs and vegetables and left it simmering over the fire. She'd left a note on the table, telling him to help himself. Part of it had been gone when she'd returned from her observations.

The male eagle swooped and landed on the rim of the nest, which was located in the top of a dead tree. He hopped around the edge as if inspecting its design.

"Yeah," she encouraged, "figure out how it's done."

The female took offense. She flew at the young male, causing him to take to his wings. She didn't like intruders in her nests.

Rachel wondered which one the female would choose to be this year's nesting site...assuming she accepted the male as her mate.

The decision had to be made soon. Time was running out on the mating season. The female had avoided the male for several days. However, she hadn't chased him out of the country.

The female lazily drifted down to the ground and selected a stone. She took off again, circled the gorge and dropped the stone, watching it drop to the ground. It landed in the water with a loud *plunk*.

Rachel silently approved when the male scorned the rock. He and the female rode the thermal uprisings for several minutes, each ignoring the other. He maintained a careful distance.

Suddenly the female lofted high into the air, then dived straight at the earth. Rachel's heart plummeted with the daring display of power. At the last minute, the eagle unfurled her wings and, beating the air furiously, arced toward the ground, talons out. She hooked a stick and sailed upward over the lip of the gorge.

At two hundred feet, she leveled off.

The male recovered from his ire at being driven off the nest and circled closer. The female dropped the stick. She dived and caught it. She rose, dropped her toy and dived for it, each time catching it and flying closer to the nest before turning and resuming her play.

The male flew down, landed, and selected a dead twig lodged between two rocks. He pulled and tugged until he worked it free, expending a lot of energy in the task—just like a man, Rachel thought wryly—then he soared upward, leveled off and dropped it.

The female dropped her stick and caught his. She rose high into the air and let the stick go.

Rachel unconsciously clenched her pen. "Please," she prayed.

The male swooped and caught the stick.

"He did it!" Rachel cried aloud. "He did it!"

The male flew upward and joined the female. They rose higher and higher, taking turns catching the stick, playing a game that wasn't a game at all, but a vital test of their future.

Rachel sniffed, then began to write the good news in her report. Later, when the pair tired of the play and flew off to roost, she climbed out from under the loose weaving of tree branches that served as her blind.

Yawning and stretching, she ambled to her knapsack, put her pencil and pad away, then went to a flat rock near the edge of the ravine and watched the changing colors of the rocks as the sun began to set.

"Oh," she murmured, startled.

Kerrigan and the gelding were across the gorge, motionless under the sheltering branches of a fir tree. He was watching her.

She raised the binoculars to her eyes. He dipped his head to her, acknowledging that he knew she was observing him. He didn't smile. Neither did he turn away. He simply looked at her, his expression inscrutable, his eyes filled with . . . longing?

Her heart thumped as furiously as the eagle had beat her wings to slow her plunge to the earth.

What was he thinking? He'd indicated he would come to her, but he hadn't. She wouldn't go to him, not this time.

She'd called. She'd written to him. She'd returned to the scene of their passion. She had told him she wanted him, even that she loved him, although that had been said in a joking manner.

Now he had to come to her.

A test, she explained silently to him, realizing it was true. She, too, had learned a lesson seven years ago. She couldn't trust her instincts as readily as she had then. He, too, had to make a commitment to the future.

She waited all evening, all night. He didn't show up.

Since the eagles seemed most active at dawn and sunset, Rachel took a nap each afternoon before resuming her patrol of the three nesting sites. The next afternoon, she was too restless to sleep.

Going to the natural basin in the boulder by the creek, she stripped to her waist and washed her hair and upper body in the icy stream. Finished, she wrapped her hair and slipped on a knitted cotton shirt, then a flannel shirt.

When she unsnapped her jeans, she paused, feeling a prickle at the back of her neck. She glanced all around. Nothing out of place. A bird called from a tree. A ground squirrel chirred someplace in the woods.

She removed her shoes and the clothing below her waist, washed quickly, then dressed. Then she dunked her clothes and laid them over a bush to dry.

Getting her notepad and pencil, she stuck them in her pocket, looped the binoculars over her neck and headed for the site where she'd last seen the eagles. An hour before sunset, she climbed the steep trail and came out on the lip of the ravine.

Kerrigan was there. A whinny from the woods greeted her as the gelding caught her scent on the breeze.

He sat on the rock she'd used yesterday. She joined him. They each said "hello" like polite strangers seated side by side in a train. Then they watched the play of shadows over the rocky walls of the gorge as the sun sank lower.

The wind murmured sweetly, singing a lover's lullaby. It brought his scent to her—leather, horses, wild sage and soap. His hair, like hers, was damp. He'd recently bathed, too.

A tremor ran over her skin. She wanted to ask him why he had appeared all of a sudden after avoiding a direct meeting all week.

Twin specks appeared in the sky, coming closer. She stared at them intently, afraid to look at him, afraid of what she would see in his eyes . . . afraid of what he would read in hers.

"Will the female accept the male?" he asked. "They've been together for a long time. When is she going to make up her mind?"

"He has a couple more tests to pass. He understands that sticks are good and rocks aren't. She'll show him why."

Kerrigan turned to her. The fiery rays of the setting sun hit his eyes and were trapped there, lighting the coolness of his gaze to shades of rosy warmth. She could feel herself being drawn in. Heat suffused her body, clear down to her fingers and toes.

Nervously she scanned the skyline. "Here they come," she said, excitement clogging her throat, making her breathless. She raised her glasses.

The eagles flew side by side, dipping and gliding on the breeze. The weather had warmed considerably since the blizzard had struck. The two eagles seemed frisky and filled with the spirit of spring.

"Watch," she said when Kerrigan would have spoken. She handed him the binoculars.

The female began the stick routine again. The male joined in at once, catching the hefty twig, rising, then dropping it for her. After one pass in which she caught the stick, she banked suddenly and flew down to the nest.

Rachel sucked in an audible breath.

"What?" Kerrigan asked.

"The female has accepted him," she explained. The effort to speak was almost too much. She ached with needs stirred by his presence and fired by the eagles' instinctive love play.

She felt Kerrigan's eyes on her for a long time. She continued to watch the primitive pair.

The male studied the situation while the female worked her branch into the nest. He suddenly dived, picked up a sturdy twig and landed at the nest. He tried to ram the stick into the network of limbs. The female shooed him away and put it into place.

Tears rushed into Rachel's eyes. "He did it," she whispered in a choked voice. She turned to Kerrigan. *"He did it!"*

She looked into his eyes and couldn't look away. The sunset was reflected in those light blue depths. All that she'd ever dreamed of seemed to shine in his eyes.

He reached out and touched her cheek. His fingers caressed her face, her mouth. Passion welled upward, pushing a muted sound from her throat.

"You didn't come back. Tomorrow, you said. But you left and didn't come back," she accused, yearning to caress him as he did her, but afraid. So afraid.

"I had to think."

She waited, but he didn't add to the statement. Closing her eyes, she rubbed her cheek against his hand when he touched her face again. "You decided to come to me?"

"No." He laughed, a bitter sound of defeat. "I decided, if I knew what was good for me, I'd head for the high country until you were gone for good."

"Did I hurt you that much? I'm sorry," she murmured. She turned her head and kissed his palm, then lingered and ran her tongue over the smooth center. He had calluses at the base of each finger. A working man's hands. Strong. Reliable. Gentle.

He said something—she didn't catch the word—but she understood the desperation, the need, the pain, in his tone. She felt all that, too. There was more.

Between them there existed a drive that forced them together whether they willed it or not. She'd known, the first time their eyes had met. She'd felt it. And she'd known.

"Need you," she said, a catch in her voice. *Like the need for air, for food, for shelter. Primal. Essential.*

"Like the flowers need the rain," he said, shaking his head at the inevitability of it. He gathered her close. "The words of every love song ever written. I need you."

He touched her forehead with his lips.

"I need you."

He kissed the tip of her nose.

"I need you."

He kissed her trembling mouth.

"I need you," he whispered against her lips.

She clung to him, nearly weeping.

He turned her, and they walked down the trail. In the woods the gelding and the pack horse waited. Kerrigan placed her on his horse and climbed up behind her.

She leaned into him with a shaky sigh. The muscles of his arms contracted on each side of her. She felt his breath, then his lips, on her hair. Then he clicked and the horse started for the cabin.

They were riding west. Into the sunset.

But this wasn't the end of the movie. There'd be no fade-out, then a list of credits. It would be just them, alone, the way it used to be, all those years ago when they'd fallen in love.

At the cabin he dismounted and lifted her down. Without looking at him, she went inside. She checked the pot of beans, barely simmering over the fire, and the potatoes wrapped in foil and leaves and covered with hot ashes.

She made biscuits and set them to baking in a skillet. Tremors ran over her every so often, like tiny earthquakes denoting the flaming passions underneath the calm surface.

Kerrigan came in from tending the stock.

"Smells good," he commented, bolting the door. "It's getting cold out there."

"I have plenty of firewood. I chopped some this morning."

"I heard you."

She glanced up, then down at the pot of wild greens she'd cooked earlier. "Were you . . . did you . . . were you in the woods when I was down at the creek?"

"You mean when you were bathing?" He grinned slightly. "I was going to stop in, but I saw you were busy. So I rode on."

She laughed, a throaty sound. "Thank you. I wouldn't like being . . . looked at. Not like that."

He placed the saddle on the floor, tossed his hat on a nail and slung the saddlebags into the far corner. With casual efficiency, he made up their bed as before.

"I think supper is ready."

They filled their plates with the simple fare. He ate the way hardworking men did, silently, hungrily; then he complimented her on the meal. He made her sit still while he cleaned the dishes.

"There's stewed fruit and cookies for dessert," she told him.

"Later," he said, settling in front of the hearth with his coffee cup held between his hands, resting on his flat-as-a-table stomach. He watched the dying flames licking over the logs.

Rachel covertly watched him. The sky darkened to night, and the stars came out. The tiny cabin seemed a warm, safe haven from the outside world. If they could only stay there forever.

When he saw that she was finished with her coffee, he drank the rest of his. Then he stood and set his cup on the table.

He set hers on the table, too.

The tremors started again. Deep inside her. When he started on the buttons of her shirt, she stood utterly still. He undressed her down to her rib-knit shirt.

"Let's get the rest," he suggested. He caught the bottom edge and lifted it over her head. When he dropped the shirt on the chair, her bikini briefs were tossed aside, too. "Now, under the cover," he ordered as chills ran over her.

She slid under the down-filled sleeping bag onto the soft wool of the blanket. Each heartbeat seemed to shake her whole body.

Kerrigan watched her as he undressed. Again he found it erotic to know she was intent on his every move, her brown eyes with their golden streaks luminous in the firelight. By the time he stepped out of the last piece of clothing, the hunger was a red haze of need, blinding him to everything but her.

He took his place beside her, not touching, but close enough to feel each other's heat. He reached out, then stopped.

"I'm shaking," he told her, holding his hand so she could see. "I'm not sure how good a lover I'll be. I'm too... hungry. Hell, *famished* is the word."

"I know." Rachel pressed her hand flat against his, palm to palm, and reveled in the contact.

Suddenly he moved, so fast she could hardly comprehend the action. His hard body pressed her down on the blanket. One thigh slipped between hers. And he was kissing her, holding her, moving his hands over her, all over her, as if he couldn't get enough of touching her, in every way he knew how.

Kerrigan felt her response when he ran his hands over her breasts, drawing them into hard points that thrust against his palms when he cupped them. She was as lithe as a willow wand, this woman, and she wove her magic spell around him with her hands, her mouth and her sweetly curving body.

When she opened her mouth and took his tongue inside, he groaned with the needs that pressed against his control until he ached. He broke the mouth-to-mouth contact.

Resting his head beside hers on the saddle, he fought for breath and for command over his impatient body.

"You don't have to be so gentle," she murmured, her lips running over his chest, her tongue sneaking little licks against his skin.

"Don't I?" he questioned. "You're burning me alive. If I don't hold myself back, it'll go too fast. I want the magic to last. All night."

He kissed her face, learning its tastes and textures, checking the present against the past and finding that they merged. The feeling was the same, exactly the same.

With a burst of insight, he realized the danger. He was letting himself get sucked in again, letting himself think he had to have this one woman to complete his world. He knew better.

All the lessons from his past warred with his need of her. She was just a woman. This was only passion. He could handle it. This time he wouldn't let himself be fooled into thinking desire was more than a physical thing.

Rachel forced her eyes to open—her lashes were so heavy—when Kerrigan pulled back and stared down into her face.

"Don't go," she whispered, afraid he was going to leave.

He laughed briefly, almost bitterly. "I couldn't if my life depended on it."

She experienced the hurt along with the passion. Once, they'd made love so naturally, and neither had looked back or counted the cost.... For a moment, she remembered how high the price had been—a month of bliss followed by seven years of loneliness.

Kerrigan saw anguish in her eyes. "What is it?"

"Sometimes fate demands a ransom for loving that's too high to pay," she said. "Do you want to stop?"

He shook his head, knowing it was hopeless. He was already caught. Running a hand into her hair, he bent to her. "Kiss me again like you just did. As if it meant the world."

She tried to answer, but he silenced her with his mouth. He wanted only her passion, he reminded himself savagely. He didn't need anything else.

Rachel held him close. She ran her hands along his spine, feeling the splendid hardness of his muscles under the satin texture of his skin. The kiss deepened, absorbing them both in the tactile world of touch and taste. She moaned and cried out when he kissed her breasts.

"Yes," he encouraged. "Tell me how much you want me."

"I want you so much, I ache," she said. She writhed against him, feeling his arousal against her thigh.

"Here?" He sucked at one taut nipple. "Here?" He took the other into his mouth. "Here?" He slid low on her body and lowered his head.

She clutched the blanket in wanton desperation as he pressed his face against her and gave her the most intimate of kisses she'd ever known.

Kerrigan tasted her again and again, her hot pleasure driving him higher and higher, his senses filled with her—her flavor, texture, scent, the heated glow of her body, the demanding little cries that urged him to give her completion.

He drank in the womanly essence of her, utterly free to do with this woman what he'd done with no other. With her, he could experience every ounce of passion's intrigue. He felt it drawing him in, changing him, making something in him soften while his body ached with a hardness that demanded appeasement.

She moved her legs restlessly, inviting him inside.

"Not yet," he said in a barely audible voice. "We have the whole night. I intend to take it...minute by slow minute."

Rachel held back her whimper of need and let his words murmur over her like the flow of water over smooth stones. She was like sand, and he was the river. He soaked into her, filling every pore with the wonderful elixir of his desire, making her want him with a passion so intense, she ached for release.

He paved a trail of kisses up the middle of her body until he reached her lips again. She learned the taste of her passion from his mouth.

With the gentlest of caresses, he explored her intimately with his lean fingers, slipping into the hot center of her, making her tremble with suppressed needs. His tongue thrust into her mouth at the same moment. He moved his chest so that he stroked her nipples into hard peaks, a sensual abrasion that made her writhe helplessly against him.

"Come to me," she pleaded against his lips. "I want you."

"In a minute," he promised. "I want to give you more than this, much more."

He refused to give in to her urgent demands and impatient pleas. Instead he held himself in check while he caressed the swollen nub of desire he'd summoned from her body. With his thumb, he spread a blanket of liquid fire over the sensitive point.

Tension grew in her. She stopped breathing. The world contracted to the place where he touched her, then it exploded, wiping out all her senses in one burst of pure pleasure.

Kerrigan nearly came apart himself when she gave a throaty little scream and sank her teeth into his shoulder. She held on to him, her body rigid and utterly still; then she tightened her arms around him. He felt her go limp.

He watched her as she let her head fall back on the saddle, her eyes closed, the dark lashes like little fans on her flushed cheeks.

Woman-magic. She had it in spades. He was as caught in it as the first time he'd kissed her, even without entering her and getting his own pleasure yet.

"Wildcat," he said.

Rachel heard the rough tenderness in his voice. It brought tears to her eyes. She looked at him, but was unable to read more than passion in the depths of his.

Reaching up, she brushed the hair off his forehead, then let her hand slide around his head until she could bring his mouth to hers. As their mouths joined, she felt him smile.

Still kissing him, she rolled over him and pushed him down. She kicked the cover off and lay down on him, marveling that he could take her weight with no discomfort at all. She tasted the salty flavor of sweat on his neck and licked it off, slowly working her way down to his chest and beyond.

When she would have taken him into her mouth, wanting to give him the same wild pleasure he'd given her, he stopped her with a hand in her hair.

"I've been dreaming of this for days. Let's not rush it," he said in a warm, lazy voice that didn't match the blaze in his eyes at all.

"For someone so...hungry, you seem determined to take an awful long time at it."

"You were always impatient," he teased, wrapping his hand around her hair and bringing her back to lie on him.

"You were, too," she retorted, feeling a blush rise from her breasts to her face.

He traced the rush of heat up her throat to her cheeks and raised his eyebrows in question.

The blush increased. "It's been a long time since I...since, that is...well, love play and all," she finished incoherently.

She pressed her face to his chest and groaned, knowing she sounded ridiculous. After all, it was only passion they shared.

When he laughed, she could hear it in his chest, a plangent sound like the chant of ancient runes in a chapel.

"You weren't shy the first time we made love," he reminded her. His hands began moving on her again.

Her pulse, which had steadied, upped its rate as he slid a hand along her back and over the curve of her hips. He moved her slightly and found the treasure he sought.

But she wasn't without defenses. She opened her legs and trapped him in the embrace of her thighs. Sliding against him brought them both a surge of pleasure so strong, they gasped.

He caught her hips between his hands and held her still. "Let me up. Just for a second," he said at the surprised disappointment on her face.

With ease, he flipped them over, then rose. Going to the saddlebags, he removed the box of condoms with its gaudy birthday paper. He tore the paper off, throwing it in the fire. He opened the box and removed a packet.

She watched him without blushing. This, too, had been a regular part of their lovemaking.

When Kerrigan came to her again, he positioned himself between her thighs. "The total kiss this time," he said, straining to keep from sliding inside and going for instant gratification.

"The meeting of the body and soul," she whispered, gazing up at him. Her eyes glowed like warm honey. He saw things he didn't want to see.

"A meeting of the body," he corrected, refusing to let it be more. Then he plunged straight into the hot, melting core of her. He groaned, fighting a battle with his senses over control.

Not yet. Not yet.

When he opened his eyes, she was still watching him. Her lips parted as she breathed in quick little breaths. Seeing how much she was affected increased his pleasure. He fought another battle.

"Don't move," he said.

"I won't," she promised. "Unless you touch me," she added truthfully.

She was beguiling in her passion. He'd seen her out of control with the pleasure he gave her. He'd seen her teasing and playful. He'd seen her serious and intent. She was playful now.

With her fingertips, she circled his nipples until they stood out in his chest hair. "You're giving me warts," he said, letting himself enter into her erotic play.

"Cute warts." She dipped her head and kissed each one.

Bolts of electricity shot through him. When she lifted her mouth to his, he took it roughly. He couldn't play at love-making this time. The need was too great, too driving.

When she raised one leg and caressed along his thigh, he couldn't stop the leap of passion that ran through him. He moved involuntarily against her. That was his undoing.

"Rachel," he warned, on the brink of losing control.

He pulled back, almost all the way out, until the contact was a mere whisper between them; then he sank back into her, into the hot, slick depths, the dew of her passion surrounding him.

It was all there for him, just as it had been the first time with her and all the times since. The sweet woman-magic, taking him in... making him... whole.

It's just passion.

He hoped that wasn't a lie. He knew he was becoming lost in her. He fought the need, the awful need that he hated. It was a weakness to want someone this much. He had learned long ago not to depend on women. They took your love and abandoned you....

But now, caught in her spell, he was sinking deeper... helpless...the way he'd been when the guards had held him, hit him and laughed at his dreams of him and her and a lifetime together....

She moved under him, and he could feel the internal ripples that went through her, pushing him closer to the edge. He withdrew slowly, paused, then thrust...*slowly, slowly*...into the welcoming passage. Through the roar of blood in his ears, he heard her say his name, a low moan of need as her hunger returned.

He moved his hand between them and stroked the incredibly smooth surfaces. She caressed him wildly, every place she could reach, stroking her hands all over him.

Woman-magic.

When she cried out, his control slipped. Everything evaporated in the flame of his desire for her.

The past—which he should remember, *tried* to remember—no longer seemed important. He forgot the betrayals, the small, numerous humiliations, the fact that no one had seemed to care very much about the McPherson boys after their father died.

Except for Rachel. She had said she cared. She'd looked at him one time and seen his soul. She'd taken him into her and given him peace and bliss. And left him to the mercy of three bodyguards who wouldn't let him go to her.

He tried to remember that final betrayal, but it faded into nothing. There was just her, beneath him, letting him in....

Woman-magic. He tried to hold back, to keep that one bit of himself, his soul, whatever, private, but it was no use. With Rachel, nothing worked but letting go.

He groaned as the mind-shattering release swept through him. Past, present, future merged into one, into this moment, this magic, this woman.

Rachel met each of his thrusts with an equal and opposite force, wanting to give him as much pleasure as he'd given her. Little pleasurable aftershocks darted through her at the point of his gliding contact, and she enjoyed those, too.

She felt his body go rigid against her. He pushed deep and stayed there while a tremor coursed through him. His climax gave her another jolt of pleasure as he pulsed within her.

At this moment he belonged to her again. She felt a deep peace steal over her. It was only a meeting of the bodies, she reminded herself. He hadn't given his heart. She knew that, had sensed, even in the throes of her passion, that he held part of himself back.

Rogues didn't give their trust easily a second time. He'd been hurt and wounded because of her. It would take a while before they could become friends as well as lovers. But for now, she'd take this.

She rocked against him, wanting to stay like this forever, knowing that all good things must come to an end. She saw it in his eyes just before he eased them to their sides and let his breath catch up with his body's needs.

Chapter Eleven

Rachel stirred when Kerrigan quietly eased from their bed and tended the fire. She hoped he would come back. He did.

With a sigh, he cupped his body to hers and ran his hand over her side before sliding it up to her breast.

"Is it morning?" she asked, snuggling against him.

"No. Go back to sleep."

"If I do, are you going to sneak off without saying goodbye?" She rolled against him and peered over her shoulder. She caught the quick flash of his smile.

"No. I'll probably want you again. In about two minutes."

The hardening of his body against her buttocks told her it would be much less than that.

She turned to face him. "I want you, too." She held her breath as other words rose to her throat. Pressing her face to his chest, she moved her lips against him. "I love you."

Did he understand? He gave no sign.

She moved over him and made love to him. They slept again. He turned to her once more as dawn pinked the sky.

Later, she laughed huskily and asked, "Isn't it your turn to cook breakfast? I don't think I can move."

He smiled at her; then he touched her lips with the tips of his fingers. Next he touched her breasts, just the tips, which were a little sore from their lovemaking; then he touched the dark gold curls.

Rachel swallowed hard against the sudden urge to cry. He looked as if he were memorizing her body...so he could recall it when they had long parted.

"Don't," she pleaded.

"What?" He glanced at her. A look of surprise crossed his face. He sipped the tears that caught on her lashes.

"You looked as if you were saying goodbye."

"Every moment we live is a moment closer to dying," he said.

She was reminded of the shortness of time. "We could have a child," she said impulsively, realizing how very much she wanted it. "Our gift to the future."

He pushed himself up and away from her. The cold rushed in along her side where he'd lain.

"Don't even think it."

"Why?" Her voice trembled ever so slightly.

"Because any child of mine will be legitimate. It will also be raised at the ranch. With me." He pulled on his clothes, his motions angry. "You're just feeling soft due to sex. It'll do that to you. You have to watch that you don't take it for more."

With that advice, he walked out.

She watched him go to the lean-to and lead the pack horse out on a hobble to graze the sparse meadow grasses. He brought the gelding out and dropped the reins, leaving the animal ground hitched until he was ready to leave.

Despair engulfed her. This time there'd be no wild ride to ease the pain. She rose and prepared their breakfast.

When he came in for the saddle, he glanced at the food. "I'm not hungry."

"It's almost ready," she informed him in a level tone. "You may as well eat."

He reluctantly took his place across from her. When she sat down, she looked at him, finding his gaze on her in a disquieting study. She picked up her fork. They ate in silence.

Rachel stood on the bluff alone. Her binoculars hung around her neck like a millstone, but they weren't as heavy as her heart. Kerrigan had ridden out three days ago, and he hadn't come back.

That should teach her a lesson about her irresistible allure. She'd thought, once they'd made love, he would be unable to stay away. She turned from the bluff and headed for the cabin.

The eagles were busy with their nest. She had watched them mate that morning, the young male brash and eager, bringing a smile to her face. He and the female would meet here each spring and share the duties of raising their young.

Until death do them part, she paraphrased to herself.

Restless, she hung the binoculars on a nail at the cabin and packed her knapsack with a light meal. She would take a long walk and work some of the kinks out. She'd been sitting in the blind too long and too much of late.

She chose to hike along the ridge trail, going past the point where she'd leaped upon Kerrigan from the tree. She ate her lonely supper there. Munching on some trail mix for dessert, she ambled on, coming out at the trail where she'd fallen during the whiteout, and Kerrigan had helped her up the last few feet.

Stepping close to the edge, she peered at the rocky bluff. Yes, there was another ledge to her left. She could have climbed out on it with no trouble. Just as she started to walk on, she spied a movement down in the gully. She leaned over the edge for a closer look.

A cow was trapped between two boulders. No, not trapped. But it couldn't get up. She surveyed the opposite bank and saw where the ledge had given way beneath the cow's weight. The creature had slithered to the bottom in an avalanche of rocks. Rachel thought its leg was broken.

Her first thought was to go to it. She immediately thought better of it.

Another movement caught her eye. Rachel exclaimed softly, sympathetically. The cow had a calf. As she watched, the calf struggled to its feet. It was obviously very weak as it tried to find its mother's milk, but there was no way it could reach the teats with the cow lying between the boulders.

Pivoting, she rushed back along the trail, heading for the cabin. When she arrived, breathless and flushed thirty minutes later, she glanced around for Kerrigan. No sign of him.

Inside, she left a note on the table, telling him where she was and the problem. She hurriedly packed her knapsack with food and first-aid supplies, then tied her bear rope to the straps.

Heading out the door, she caught the pack horse and put the pack saddle in place. She climbed on, using a stump in the clearing and rode off down the trail.

At the bluff, she hobbled the horse and left him to graze where he would. Taking her pack, she went to the edge of the ravine and checked on the animals. Still there. She placed the pack on a rock, then tied the rope securely to a tree.

After tying several knots in the rope to give her hand- and footholds, she threw it over the side. Strapping her knapsack on, she wriggled off the bluff to stand on a narrow ledge. She began her descent, rappelling down the rocky cliff face using the rope.

As soon as she reached bottom, she picked her way across the rushing water by stepping from boulder to boulder. Soon she stood by the injured cow. It bellowed weakly at her.

A quick examination proved her earlier diagnosis was correct. The animal had broken a leg during the fall. It might have other injuries Rachel couldn't detect.

She got a pan out of her pack and filled it with water. While the cow was drinking, she went to check on the calf. It could hardly lift its head when she knelt beside the tiny creature. Its cry of welcome broke her heart.

Going behind the cow, she decided she could reach the udder, but she'd have to prop the cow's leg out of the way. She retrieved her pan, glad to see the cow had drank all the water, and returned to her task.

As soon as she touched the cow's leg, it started kicking, not with a great deal of strength but enough to be dangerous near her head. Rachel glared at the cow in disgust.

"I need milk for your baby," she said in what she hoped were soothing tones. She tried sneaking up on it. That didn't work.

She tried rubbing calf slobber on her hand, letting the cow sniff it, then going right to the teats. That worked for thirty seconds. When she tried propping the cow's leg over her shoulder to hold it out of the way, the cow displayed a burst of energy and kicked like mad.

"You sure you got the right end?" a voice called to her.

She looked up, shielded her eyes from the sun with one hand and glared at Kerrigan, standing on the bluff.

"If you know so much, you come do it," she challenged.

With a lazy grin, he accepted.

After checking her rope against his weight, he drew the coils of his own rope up his arm so that it rested on his shoulder. Then he came down the bluff the same way she had.

She couldn't keep from watching. And yearning.

He was lean and wiry. His strength was evident in every move. It was almost like watching a choreographed ballet as he skimmed lightly down the cliff.

At the bottom, he strode across the boulder field without a misstep and came to a halt beside her without getting a drop of water on his boots. He ignored the pan she held out. Instead he stepped back to study the situation.

"The cow has a broken leg," he said after a minute. He checked the animal carefully. "And some broken ribs, probably internal damage. She's not going to make it."

"I know." Rachel drew a breath and faced the decree head on. "Do you have your gun?"

"Yeah."

"Could we feed the calf and get it back on its feet first?"

He turned his wintry gaze on her. "What for?"

A jolt of surprise swept through her. "Why, so we can haul it out of here."

"And then?"

She frowned at him. "Then we take it back to the ranch. You said the pack horse wouldn't mind carrying the cat. It surely won't be bothered by a calf."

Kerrigan had begun shaking his head before she finished.

"Why not?" she demanded, feeling belligerent because he could so easily walk away from her and stay away for days, then return as if nothing wonderful had happened between them.

"This situation is made to order," he informed her coolly. "I tracked the cougar back this way. She's bound to discover the cow and calf. When she does, I'll have her."

Rachel stared at him in shock. "You'd use them as bait? When they're hurt and helpless?"

He hooked his thumbs in his belt. "You want I should get them well and then use them?"

"No!" Rage blew through Rachel like a sudden spring squall blowing in off the ocean and hammering the mountains.

Kerrigan took two steps and leaned down to her. "I suppose you're one of those bleeding-heart conservationists who thinks meat comes prepackaged on the hoof, that you just pluck a steak off the cow with no more to-do than picking an apple—"

She threw down the pan. "No, I don't. I've already admitted the cow can't be helped. But does that mean we have to let the calf be sacrificed, too?"

They glared at each other, angry and stubborn. At last he heaved a sigh, picked up the pan and bent to the cow. When the animal tried to kick him, he slipped a loop over her leg and tied it out of the way. Then he squirted the pan full of milk and handed it to Rachel.

"Thank you," she said stiffly.

He didn't say anything. She went to the calf and tried to get it to lap up the milk. It was too weak to catch on. She rubbed its head while it bawled pitifully.

"Can't you do something?" she asked, giving Kerrigan an anxious appeal from eyes filled with tears.

"Why do women always expect men to fix things?" he snarled. "Try dipping your fingers in the milk and letting him suck it off."

She did, but it was slow work. "If I had some rubber gloves, I could stick a hole in one finger. That would work."

"Do you carry them in your pack?" Kerrigan asked.

"No."

"Me, neither." He checked the cow again and shook his head at her questioning glance. The animal was getting weaker.

Watching him, she thought of how capable he was. She realized she had expected him to fix the problem and make everything all right. He was a rancher, not a miracle worker.

An idea came to her.

"Kerrigan, do you have any work gloves with you—those unlined leather ones used to work on barbed wire fences?"

He looked blank for about two seconds, then understanding dawned. "In my saddlebags."

"Would you let me try one on the calf?" she asked sweetly.

"The calf won't like the texture," he warned.

"But we won't know until we try, will we?"

Muttering imprecations about women in general and one dark-eyed blonde in particular, he pulled himself up the rope and got one glove. After skimming down the rope again, he picked his way across the boulder field and dropped it into her lap.

"There's already a hole in the middle finger," he told her, not bothering to hide his skepticism.

He watched her check the glove and find the split in the seam. She opened it a little wider with one finger. "That should do the trick," she decided.

Scooting closer to the calf, she laid its head in her lap. Then she dipped the glove in the pan, filling the fingers with milk. Holding the seam closed, she stuck the middle finger of the glove in the calf's mouth.

A pulse beat out of control deep inside him. Seeing Rachel with the helpless animal, seeing her concern and her efforts to help, did things to him. He wanted to hold her and comfort her.

He hardened his heart against her allure. It was probably all an act, anyway. Women could be tender one minute and hard as nails the next. He knew from experience.

"That's about one slurp," he advised.

"Well, what's your suggestion, Mr. Know-It-All-Rancher?"

He ambled over and squatted beside them. Picking up the pan, he held it in position. "You feed. I'll pour."

The calf, after some hesitation, sucked down the milk greedily after that, seeming to gain strength with each swallow. She fed him until all the milk was gone.

When the task was completed, she twisted her head around to beam at Kerrigan. "It worked," she said triumphantly.

A muscle clenched in his jaw for a second; then he muttered, "Yeah," rose and walked off.

While he examined the cow's leg more closely, she petted the calf. The deep, abiding melancholy that had lived in her since their parting long ago swept over her.

She felt a bond with the cow and calf, with the eagles and all of nature. From deep inside came the knowledge that it was time to start her family. She wanted a child . . . with this man.

"What is it?" Kerrigan asked, dropping down to a rock beside her after a minute of restless pacing.

"Nothing," she said. "Why?"

"You looked sad there for a minute, then happy."

She was surprised at his perception. Managing a smile, she asked philosophically, "Don't we all, at one time or another?"

He frowned, obviously dissatisfied with her quip. Nodding toward the calf, he told her his plans. "We'll haul the calf up and take it to the cabin. The cow won't last through the night. I'll give the cat until tomorrow to come around. If she doesn't, you can take the calf to the ranch and let Wills tend him. I'll stay here and trap the cat."

"Okay."

With the help of the pinto gelding, they hauled the calf out of the ravine. With Kerrigan's help, she managed to feed the calf several times during the day. As evening approached, Kerrigan made one last effort to milk the cow. There was very little in the pan this time.

"Here, take the calf to the cabin," he advised after Rachel finished feeding the creature which had now adopted her for its mother. He made a halter out of rope and tied it on. After a few minutes of shaking its head, the calf accepted it.

"Will you be coming in?" she asked.

"Maybe. It's according to what happens this evening."

All the way down the trail, she worried about him and the big cat. What if it attacked him instead of the cow? It could easily climb a tree and leap out on him the way she had.

A gunshot echoed faintly off the hills around her. She realized Kerrigan had put the cow out of its misery. The calf bawled as if it understood, and she patted it sympathetically.

At the line shack, she tied the calf to a post in the flimsy corral and went in to see about supper. The beans were done. After collecting fresh salad greens, she built up the fire, made cornbread, put on a pot of coffee and waited. Twilight came.

When another shot rang out, every nerve in her body leapt with fright. Still she waited.

It was almost dark before she heard the pinto clomp across a rocky place near the shed. She sprang from the chair, grabbed her coat and rushed outside.

"Stay back," Kerrigan ordered in a subdued tone.

She watched him slide out of the saddle and go to his pack horse. Tied across it was the cougar.

In the fading light, the creature was beautiful, tawny and lithe, harmless looking in her drug-induced sleep, especially since she was wearing a muzzle. However, nothing was foolproof.

"I'll keep her in the shed tonight and take her to the ranch at first light."

"And then what?"

"The park service will bring in a chopper to take her high into the back country."

"Good. What about the calf?"

He gave her one of those looks that men bestow when they indulge a woman who's being difficult. "I'll send one of the hands back for the calf tomorrow."

She gave him a look of surprise.

"With the cat out of the way, I'll have no reason to come up here again," he told her with a hard glance. "I have a ranch to run. Now go back inside in case of trouble."

"Give me the gun." At his wary expression, she added, "If the cat gets loose and attacks you, I'll shoot it."

Kerrigan looked heavenward for a second before loading the gun with another tranquilizer and handing it to her. She stayed on guard under the porch overhang while he manhandled the big cat off the patient pack horse and into the shed.

There he checked the ropes that held her huge paws immobile, made sure the muzzle was secure, then gave her a shot to keep her asleep or drowsy until morning. For another moment he lingered, letting his fingers brush over the tawny fur...so soft and warm, reminding him of another female's softness and warmth.

He paused before facing the woman who waited for him at the door of the shack. A man could do worse than a woman like her. A funny feeling ran over him as he recalled her standing by him against Cawe and his cronies. She was a hard worker. Smart, too. Compassionate. She'd be a good mother....

Bloody hell, what was he thinking! A little sex and *he* was going soft in the head. He got up and walked across the clearing.

The warmth of the fire greeted him, and the mingled aroma of food and hot coffee. For a second a fantasy came to him—he and Rachel as pioneers, alone on their land, in a cabin they'd built with their own two hands, eating food they'd harvested...the two of them, building a new life, raising a family.

He swore savagely to himself and forced the images aside.

"I'm starved. I waited for you before eating. Are you hungry?" she asked, her tone innocent.

Innocent, ha! About as innocent as that cat out there, who'd tear him apart given half a chance. It was in the nature of cats and females to render a man senseless.

He grabbed the bucket and went down to the creek for water. He washed in the icy stream, hoping that would dislodge any notions he had about them when he returned.

But when he walked in and saw her setting out the meal for them, the fantasy stormed back, stronger and more beguiling. Her beauty grabbed him by the throat and wouldn't let go. He breathed deeply and forced his trumpeting libido to quieten.

Hell, she wanted him. Why should he deny them the pleasure? He was being a fool. Why not take the moment?

And when she left, he would be prepared for it. He wouldn't think he was going to die just because he couldn't have her. That was a boy's fantasy. He was a man now, and he saw things from a man's point of view.

Boldly, he walked up behind her and put his arms around her. She stiffened, then relaxed and leaned into him. Sliding his hands up her slender torso, he found her breasts and covered them with his palms. She didn't tell him no.

His need to bury himself in her overcame any other thoughts. She was ready, willing and able. And he sure as heck was.

With a groan, he bent to her neck, pulled her hair aside and alternately kissed and bit at the succulent flesh there.

"Dinner's ready," she murmured, her breath catching on a tiny gasp when he gently squeezed her breasts and caused them to form hard little peaks under her sweatshirt.

"I've a hunger that won't wait," he told her, his voice thick with desire.

He slipped his hands under her shirt, needing the feel of her bare skin. He caressed her breasts until he had to turn her and push the shirt up and taste the sweet, yielding flesh.

She sighed and moaned and whispered his name, her hands busy in his hair as he knelt in front of her. Closing his arms around her, he swung around and laid her lightly on the bed. Before lying down, he knelt there on his knees and gazed into her shining eyes.

"This is just for tonight. It doesn't mean anything," he told her fiercely. "This is sex, a meeting of the body and nothing else, you got that?"

The glow left her. Guilt at his brutal denial of emotional involvement attacked him. Hell, women always expected soft words, but he wasn't going to lie. She'd have to accept that.

"What if it becomes more?" she asked, startling him.

He scowled at her. "It won't. I'll make sure of that." He studied her for a long moment, puzzled by her mood. A flash of emotion passed through her eyes, that odd sadness he'd seen in her several times now. He hesitated, then lay beside her.

Putting her arms around his neck, she whispered, "Kiss me, Kerrigan. Make me forget everything but this moment."

Still he paused. He wanted her, yet there was something about her that bothered him...as if she held back some part of her from him. Ah, hell, what did it matter?

He reached for her mouth. At the first touch, he forgot everything but the wonder of making love...*with her*, some part of him echoed.

Only with her.

He blocked the words out, deepening the kiss until his mind reeled with the power of his lust for her. "Lust," he mumbled, pushing his hands under her shirt and finding the warmth there. "That's all it is."

She drew back, a stricken look on her face. "No."

"Yes," he snarled at her. He had to think that or go crazy from the fantasy that refused to stay buried in his mind.

"You're wrong—"

He kissed her with a fiery hunger, feeding her needs until her desire matched his. With trembling intensity, he helped her undress. She did the same for him. He forced himself to remember his vow and retrieved the gift package of condoms from the saddlebags. Then he glided into her and felt life flowing into him like a river, from her to him, from him to her...a river flowing with life...with all the promises of tomorrow in the wet, silky depths of the current....

"I meant to go into town and have dinner with Suzannah and Tom yesterday," Rachel said drowsily. They were still in bed, watching the first light of dawn. "I forgot about it when I found the cow and her calf."

Kerrigan made a noncommittal sound in his throat.

"Thank you for helping me with the calf," she said, kissing him on the shoulder and snuggling closer while the fire warmed the cabin. He'd been up and out earlier, checking on the animals and had returned to bed only moments ago. "Did the cougar run very far after you hit her with the dart?"

"No," he said. "I got in a good shot. She dropped almost at once."

"I hate to see her removed from the area," Rachel murmured with a trace of regret. "But that's the way of things. I couldn't see any signs that the cat has had babies, could you?"

"No. She hasn't found a mate. I don't think there are any others in this area. There will be up in the forest."

"Good."

He turned toward her, resting his leg over her thighs. She felt the stirring of his body at their intimate contact. She traced whorls over his chest with one finger, knowing the desire was building in her, too.

With a gentle motion, he stroked her body, from her breasts to her thighs. He let his caress end at the mound of tawny curls at the apex. He covered her with his palm and rested his fingers on the vulnerable softness between her legs.

"Morning dew," he murmured huskily, bringing his fingers to his mouth and tasting her flavor.

A blush crept up her cheeks at her obvious readiness.

"You're more easily embarrassed now than you were seven years ago," he observed. "Why is that?"

She shrugged, then kissed his chest, tasting him with loving forays of her tongue.

His voice had deepened when next he spoke. "You were a virgin, yet you let me do anything I wanted. I remember your shock the first time I kissed you . . . here." He pressed his hand against her. "But you accepted my touch. You trusted me completely."

At the note of anguished wonder, she raised her head and met his eyes in a candid perusal. "It seemed right and natural. We were both so innocent, Kerrigan."

She closed her eyes tightly and fought the rage of emotion that threatened to overcome her. He didn't want tears or any kind of emotion, only passion.

"So innocent," she repeated. "How did we lose it all?"

"I don't want to talk about it." He leaned over and kissed her, stopping the useless probe into the past.

She gave herself to the kiss, feeling the perfect rhythm of their hearts beating together. The pleasure mounted as the twin caresses of his mouth and hands continued.

He moved away just enough to reach the gift box on the floor beside her head. She wished . . . No, don't think about it.

Looking into his eyes, she realized she wasn't part of his future, not even briefly.

"You don't plan to come back, do you?" she asked, already knowing it was true.

His smile was mocking. "I wasn't able to stay away this time. What makes either of us think I will the next time I think of you?" He paused at her smile. "Does it please you to have that much power over me?"

She laid a hand on his cheek. "You have the same power over me," she told him honestly.

The cynical smile faded. "That's the only thing that saves my ego," he said with equal candor.

He moved over her and the twin caresses became three as he established a new rhythm, his mouth wild on hers while his hands and body created waves of hot, bursting pleasure in her sensitive, love-starved flesh.

But before the sun rose above the far mountain, he was gone.

Rachel muttered a distinct curse when the calf jerked the glove out of her grasp and powdered-milk solution spilled over her clean pants. She jumped back, but the damage was done. The calf bawled and sucked at her shirt.

"There's nothing here for you," she scolded. "I'll have to make up another batch."

In the cabin she removed her soaked shoes and socks, deciding to go barefoot until the feeding was done. She stirred the lumpy powder until it was dissolved in the creek water. With much coaxing, she got the calf to drink the strange milk concoction.

"You have to keep your strength up," she explained. "It'll be hours before anyone can get here for you."

She returned to the cabin and put on dry pants. After rinsing her clothing out and laying the items on bushes to dry, she tried reading a book she'd brought with her. It was no use. She was too restless to concentrate on the words.

Grabbing her binoculars, she started out to observe the eagles, but paused as the calf bawled from the corral. "You can't go," she called to it. "Someone will come for you later."

Would Kerrigan return? He'd said he wouldn't.

Sighing, she went about her work. It was terribly important to her that the eagles succeed with their family. She realized she had transferred all her hopes and dreams to them.

Foolish. Nature could be as cruel as humans.

Chapter Twelve

Rachel stared moodily at the nest across the gorge. The male had brought food to the female, who was busily devouring it while he went off hunting again. For the next thirty-five to forty days, they'd be busy incubating their eggs. The pair seemed to have settled into domestic bliss. Rachel was glad...and yet...

Well, really, it was ridiculous to be envious of a couple of birds. But she was. She climbed out from her blind and stretched, her body weary from a long day of waiting. She hiked to the cabin.

The calf bawled happily upon seeing her. She unfastened the rope from the post and let it loose. It followed her while she bathed in the granite basin and then did her evening chores.

"He probably forgot all about us as soon as he left," she told the creature. "Out of sight, out of mind. I suppose I'll have to walk you over to the ranch before I can leave."

The trip would normally take four or five hours on a horse. On foot, with the young calf in tow, she'd be lucky to make it in six. Then she'd have to spend the night and hike back.

The prospect of begging the McPherson brothers for hospitality for a night didn't please her.

She checked her meal, frowning as she thought of how tired she was of beans and stewed fruit and wild greens. It would be good to be back in civilization again. For once, she thought she'd had enough of the wilderness.

The calf bawled outside the open door where she'd tied it to keep it from coming in the cabin. "Just a minute," she said.

She stirred powdered milk into water. Sitting in the doorway, she tried to teach the calf to lap the milk. It bawled hungrily and sucked at her fingers. Giving up, she retrieved the glove. The animal guzzled all the milk.

"There. Even powdered milk is better than nothing, huh?"

She scratched the calf on its horn buds and rubbed its ears. Suddenly it jerked its head around and watched the woods. In a minute, she heard the sound of horseshoes on the granite.

Kerrigan rode into the clearing a few seconds later.

Rachel stood, the glove limp and forgotten in her hand. Her heart beat heavily, almost shaking her in its rapacious excitement as she watched him dismount.

She suddenly realized why none of the cosmopolitan men she'd met through her family's diplomatic connections had appealed to her. Kerrigan was the man of her heart, the other half of her soul. She'd known it the moment they'd met. He still was.

Although he denied them a future, she knew she was as bonded to him as the eagles were bonded to each other.

For life.

"Hi," she said. "I was just going to eat. Join me?"

"I was hoping you'd ask." He swung down from the horse. There was no pack horse with him this time.

While he took care of his mount, she busied herself with supper. When he brought the saddle inside, she retrieved his cup, fork and plate and put them on the table with hers.

"Did you get the cat moved without any trouble?" she asked when they were seated.

She thought he looked tired. Also incredibly handsome. The force of his masculine appeal swept over her. Just as it had the first time she saw him. Her instincts had been correct—they belonged together.

"I wouldn't exactly say it was without trouble," Kerrigan drawled, his passionate, sensual mouth drawing into a grin. "The cat apparently woke up but was playing possum. When one of the rangers started to lift her into the chopper, she took a swipe at him. Scared three years off his life."

They laughed together.

Kerrigan told her the rest of the tale while they ate. He described staying with the wildlife expert until the big cat had recovered completely from the drug, then springing the cage open so she could escape. He *didn't* tell her of his mixed feelings watching the cougar run for high ground, the sun striking the tawny coat, turning it golden, nor that the sight would forever remind him of Rachel.

While they cleaned their dishes and put them away, she told him about the eagles, that they had two eggs and were taking good care of them.

Over coffee he told her the happenings on the ranch.

Silence fell between them as twilight deepened into night.

Rachel looked at the steam coming off her coffee after he poured them each a fresh cup. "I didn't expect you."

His snort of laughter was self-mocking. "I told you I couldn't stay away."

"Did you mean to?"

"Yes."

The stark admission hit her like a sword, thrust into the heart. She'd asked. He'd answered.

He stood suddenly and paced the tiny cabin. "I didn't mean to get mixed up with you again, to get ensnared in the woman-magic you weave around me—"

"The what?" she broke in, her head jerking up.

He scowled at her. "The spell you women cast over men. You get us all tied up inside until we don't know whether we're coming or going, until we'd rather die than miss a smile from you."

"Is that the way you feel now?" she asked, her breath sticking in her throat.

"I want you," he told her, his anger evident as he admitted it. "I thought if I had you once more, I'd be satisfied. I could ride off and be done with it." He slammed his cup on the table. "Instead, I nearly lamed my horse getting back here." He paced some more, then stopped in front of her.

She looked up at him.

He made a growling sound in his throat. "Why are you crying? You should be laughing. It's funny, isn't it?"

"No." Rachel put her hands over her face. "I can't bear it that you were hurt. You came for me, honest and trusting in your love and I failed you."

"So you didn't mean to meet me that night," he said.

"Yes, I did!" she cried. She bit her lip, knowing she had to be totally honest. "But I was nervous about the elopement. I'd never done anything like that before. It was exciting but frightening, too, going off into the unknown with a man I wasn't quite sure of."

"You didn't trust me?" he questioned incredulously. "We were going to be married. I'd never mentioned that to a woman before."

"My brother warned me that you needed money—"

Kerrigan muttered a savage curse. He turned from her and hit the door with his fist. The cabin reverberated with the sound, as if a shudder went through it. It didn't satisfy the rage in his blood. "So you were slumming, and I...I was out to get a fortune through marriage. Is that the way of it?"

He heard movement behind him, then felt her light touch on his arm. "Kerrigan, we were both wrong. Don't you see? We let others influence what we thought about each other. We failed the test."

"What test?"

"We didn't believe what we instinctively knew the moment we met. We didn't trust our love. Because of my uncertainty, I let my brother detain me. Because you thought I'd betrayed your love, you wouldn't answer my call or my letters."

Pain twisted his insides until he burned with the need to hold her, to pour out the misery he'd felt when he'd realized she wasn't coming to him. The feel of fists pounding into his flesh hadn't hurt nearly as bad as the knowledge that she hadn't wanted him the way he'd wanted her, that she'd abandoned him....

He reached for the door, knowing he had to get away before the need for her overcame wisdom and he fell at her feet, begging her to stay with him.

"It wasn't love," he said. He walked outside into the night.

Damn women for always making something simple into something complicated. He'd come up here for sex.

She'd offered it every time she'd looked at his mouth yesterday, every time she'd touched him while they worked together. She'd made it plain she wanted him. Hell, he was just responding to the invitation. That was all.

And spent almost ten hours in the saddle since morning in order to get back to her.

He was too tired for frolics, anyway. He would bed down under the stars. The night was clear, the weather warm for the end of April. The temperature was at least ten degrees above freezing.

Realizing he'd have to go inside to retrieve his saddle and bedroll, he glared at the cabin.

The soft spill of firelight from the window stopped his rapid stride forward. He saw Rachel's slender form outlined against the flames. While he watched, she removed her clothing and pulled on the silk underwear she slept in. In spite of his fatigue, his body went into high gear, swelling against his jeans and inciting a riot of pleasure and pain in him.

Grimly he turned away, waited a few minutes until he was sure she was tucked up in her sleeping bag, then went to the door. He paused, then knocked self-consciously. When he didn't get an answer, he opened the door and went in.

The scene hit him like a kick in the stomach.

Rachel was sitting in front of the fire, huddled in a small, delicate ball of misery, her arms around her drawn-up knees, her head bent forward in dejection.

She didn't hear him but sat lost in her thoughts.

Kerrigan swallowed hard as emotion choked him. He tried to remember that he wasn't dumb enough to get trapped by a woman's wiles again. But she looked so...hurt. And he'd never meant to hurt her. It was just that he couldn't afford to get caught up in wanting her too much again.

"Rachel," he said, so hoarse he could hardly speak.

Her head jerked up. Then he saw her eyes.

He dropped to his knees beside her and clenched his fists against his thighs, every muscle in his body tight and aching.

"It's no damned good. It's just no good," he muttered, his eyes closed against the sight of her.

He heard her voice say his name, so softly he might have imagined it. Then she touched him, her fingers landing lightly on his arm, then darting off like a startled butterfly, only to land on his shoulder, then in his hair.

"What is it?" she asked, concerned.

"You," he replied, looking at her. "Me. This." He gestured between them.

"I know." The sadness returned to her eyes.

Rachel stroked through his thick, dark hair where the coolness of the night lingered in the strands. He sat there for a second more, then his arms reached out and closed around her.

"Need you," she heard him whisper against her breasts. "I need you." He pushed her down on the pallet. "I need you."

Then his mouth touched hers, and she knew the magic he'd spoken of. Woman-magic. Man-magic. Whatever. It was there, drawing them together, wrapping them in splendor in a night she hoped would have no end.

She turned her lips from his. She had to tell him how she felt. "Kerrigan..."

"Don't talk," he said. He kissed her cheek, her temple. "Words don't mean a thing. There's only this." He crushed her to him and made love to her.

It was beautiful; it tore her heart to shreds.

* * *

With the morning came regrets. As usual. He was determined not to be trapped by love's magic again. The barriers were all up and in place.

"I never meant to do that," he said, anger with himself at what he perceived as a weakness obvious in his expression.

The long night of wild lovemaking had left them both tired and sated, yet she knew it hadn't been enough for either of them. "I know."

She met his cold, unreadable glance, her composure shaky but intact. Last night, after their first tempestuous rush to completion, she'd cried in his arms, her tears falling on his bare chest. He'd simply held her, not asking why she wept.

But she knew.

She'd cried for all the things they'd lost and all those they would never have. It was hard to give up a dream, to accept only the sweet, wild passion and forget the rest.

"We both received pleasure so... no harm done." If her heart was broken, she had no one to blame but herself. She'd known she might not reach his heart. He'd barricaded it well.

"Did you receive pleasure?" he asked, almost harshly.

She nodded, not sure she could speak.

His voice dropped to an intimate level. "Your cries woke the calf. He bawled his head off after you went to sleep."

"Poor baby," she murmured. "I didn't hear him. I was too exhausted by then."

"Yes." He continued to study her for another minute.

She moved uneasily about the cabin, loading her backpack for the long hike out. A frown creased between his eyes.

"What are you doing?" he asked.

"Packing. I'm leaving today."

Ten seconds ticked off. "What about the eagles?"

"They'll be on the nest for a month. If no one disturbs them, they'll be fine. The male is feeding the female. He relieves her while she takes a break." Rachel managed a smile. "Then the female has to wait until he's hungry before he'll give up the eggs. The instinct to brood is very strong, even in the male...." Her voice wobbled and trailed off.

She didn't look at Kerrigan. Instead, she busied herself with the coffeepot, setting it off the coals to cool, so she could wash and pack it.

"So last night was goodbye." The cynical edge was back in his voice. "Where are you going this time?" he asked after a minute. "Do you have other eagles to study?"

"No. My brother is throwing a birthday party for me next weekend at the resort."

"Your birthday isn't until a week from Tuesday."

So he remembered the exact day. "Yes, well, he's having it on Saturday so people will have time to arrive. Some will have to fly in."

"Sounds like a real event."

"Will you come?" she asked.

He laughed. "The wild goose among the swans? No, thanks." He went out with the bucket.

When he returned, she was all packed. He drowned the fire and stirred the hot coals, cooling them with the rest of the water.

She followed him outside. "I'm not finished up here. Is it okay to use the cabin when I come back at the end of the month?"

"Sure." He saddled the horse he'd ridden over, a large mare with a red glow to her brown coat. "Hold the mare's head while I heave our young friend up."

Rachel held the reins while Kerrigan placed the calf across the saddle and loosely tied its legs so it couldn't kick free. He paused before climbing on.

"I doubt if I'll see you again," he said. "I've been asked to judge a couple of rodeos and will be gone most of the summer."

She wondered when he'd decided to do that. She opened her mouth and breathed slowly, striving for a calm that was eluding her. Her life seemed dismal and so lonely she couldn't bear it.

Of all the eagles in all the national parks in the United States, why did you have to choose that *one to study?* he'd asked.

She'd had to come back. She'd had to see if there was a chance for them. Now she knew. He'd loved her once, but he wouldn't let himself trust her again.

It came to her that everyone he'd ever depended on or trusted had forsaken his love—his father through death, his mother through grief, his grandfather by whatever had made him a hard, bitter man, and she by not being there when he'd needed her. By letting herself doubt for even a minute, she'd cost them a lifetime.

She swallowed hard, acknowledging that while she still wanted him for her mate, he no longer trusted her enough to take a chance on her love again. Who could blame him? Not her, not anymore.

A touch on her chin brought her face up to his. His eyes were dark and fathoms deep. He gazed into her eyes for a long time, his thoughts unreadable.

Then he bent and kissed her—softly, tenderly, surprising her and melting her heart with love—then climbed into the saddle.

She stood there, unable to move as tremors passed through her like a harsh wind through the mountain willows. Helplessly she petted the calf, who was nuzzling her shirt, getting it wet where he sucked on the material.

"Goodbye, little one," she said. She looked up at Kerrigan. "You will take care of him, won't you?"

"Yeah," he said gruffly. "Just what every rancher needs—a pet calf following him around." He smiled, a tight, hard smile, but she thought she saw understanding in it.

Aching inside, she put her head against the calf's neck. The calf licked her shirt. Raising her head, she rubbed its horn buds and gazed into its large, soulful eyes.

"Well, if I'm going to hike out today, I'd better get going," she said. She forced a smile. "Goodbye and thanks for all your help."

The muscles in his forearm contracted as he tightened his hold on the calf. The animal bawled and nuzzled Rachel. She absently patted it on the head, then let it suck her fingers.

The wind murmured along the creek and ruffled her hair as she and Kerrigan remained motionless.

"Right," he finally said. "I'll have the men at the ranch check on the eagles when they're up this way repairing fences."

"That would be nice."

"I'll make sure the line shack is available for you . . . in about a month, did you say?"

"Yes. I have to give a paper on raptors at a conference in San Diego. Then I'm supposed to report to division headquarters to help write up an environmental study I took part in before I come back for the great event."

"Great event?"

"The hatching." She paused. She wanted to tell him how very much she regretted it that they hadn't eloped almost eight years ago. Last night, after they'd made love, she'd cried for the family they would never have. Unlike the eagles, she and Kerrigan weren't going to make a life together. She had to accept that.

She stepped back and let him go.

Chapter Thirteen

Kerrigan took a deep breath of cold air when he entered the hotel lobby. God, he was tired. He wasn't sure what city he was in, but it was hotter than hell. He gave a silent snort of laughter. Hell was the right place. He felt like the very devil.

He was traveling the rodeo circuit again, hired on by a national television network as the sports commentator, the person who was supposed to supply the insider information on rodeoing.

Yeah, he could tell 'em a few things. Like how it felt to live in the back of a pickup truck for five years so you could save every penny you were lucky enough or stubborn enough to win. Like how it felt to come home to a lonely hotel room at the end of a grueling day and find... emptiness.

Home? What a laugh. After a couple of weeks, all rooms, all hotels, all cities, started to look the same. Dreary.

Sounds like a bad case of self-sorry-itis, he told himself with a halfhearted attempt at humor. It didn't work.

Striding across the lobby, he detoured into the bar and, sitting at a tiny cocktail table, ordered a beer and watched the recap of the rodeo on the news. A woman came over and paused by his table. He glanced at her, then away, offering no welcome.

She was persistent. "This chair taken?" she asked in a sultry, friendly tone.

He could invite her to join him, he thought. He could ask her to have dinner with him. She'd be someone to talk to....

Except she wasn't the right one.

He stood and gave her a sardonic smile. "No. In fact, the whole table is free." He went to his room, showered and flopped on the bed with the TV remote control in his hand. Flipping through the channels, he came across a nature show on hawks.

A pain settled in his chest. The big birds, the hilly country in Texas where the show was filmed, all reminded him of the ranch. Hell, it reminded him of Rachel and her eagles.

A weak feeling washed over him. Just thinking of her coiled his insides into a tight knot.

He shifted restlessly on the king-size bed. Finally getting up, he stood at the window and watched the ceaseless moving of traffic on the street below.

Today was Tuesday. Rachel's birthday. She was twenty-nine. Eight years ago he'd met her, a woman who'd turned his heart around the first time their eyes had met. He hadn't gotten headed straight since. He didn't know which direction to go.

He sighed, unable to turn the memories off. If he and Rachel had married all those years ago, they'd have most likely been divorced by now. It was just as well their involvement had ended when it did.

Except he kept having visions of how it could have been. If she'd loved him. They'd have had kids by now. That thought wrung a new twist of pain from him.

That damn bet with his brother. Every time he'd seen Rachel after that, he'd thought of making a baby with her. He'd *wanted* to. In a flash of insight, he knew, with absolute certainty, he'd never take another woman in her place.

He swallowed hard against the bleak reality of the future. A need to go to her rose in him, choking and bitter.

No, dammit, he'd never do that again!

A picture of a boy—seven, eight, nine years old—clinging to his mother, begging her not to go out, not to leave them that evening . . . but she always did. And one night she hadn't come back.

The old scars went deep, he acknowledged. He and his brother had learned not to trust anyone but themselves. Together they'd taken on the world and they'd won. Life had been fine until each of them had let a woman into his life; then it'd been hell all over again. A man who didn't learn from his past mistakes was a fool.

The shrill ringing of the telephone had him spinning around, his heart kicking into a staccato beat. He answered on the second ring. It was his brother.

"How's it going?" Keegan asked.

"Fine." Kerrigan ignored the sense of disappointment. As if he expected anyone else to call, he mocked himself. "How're things out there?"

"That's what I'm calling about. In case it was on the national news. We've had a couple of fires."

"Close to the home place?"

"No, so far they've been over around the eastern boundary where you caught the cougar."

"Touched off by lightning or arson?"

"Lightning. It's been bad. The thunderheads come over, but we don't get a drop of rain from them," his brother explained. "They just bombard us with bolts of fire. The weather forecast is more of the same."

"Doesn't sound good."

"You know that country better than anyone else. We could use your expertise in case we get a really bad blaze. When are you coming home?"

Kerrigan's thoughts flew to Rachel and the line shack, the eagles and their nest in the old tree. He wondered if she was back yet, observing the mated pair. A worried frown puckered his forehead. Was she in any danger?

"Have you checked out the line shack? Rachel was due back the end of the month. She could get trapped on that ridge between the gullies..." He thought of her alone, terrified, walls of fire rushing toward her, closing her in....

"I sent Hank over. There were no signs of anyone at the cabin that he could see."

Relief and disappointment hit him at the same time.

"Well?" Keegan demanded.

"I don't know," Kerrigan said. "I've been offered a three-year contract as a sports commentator to cover the rodeo circuit. I'm thinking of taking it."

His twin swore mightily and long.

"You know the land as well as I do," Kerrigan added in his own defense. He was tired of traveling, but he didn't want to return.

"You're needed here," Keegan stated in a hard tone.

"Right, the cows probably miss me like hell."

"You're heartsick again," his brother concluded.

"Yeah," Kerrigan agreed, surprising both of them. "Want to hear the kicker? Same woman."

There was a tense silence on the line. Keegan spoke first, and this time his voice was softer. "Are you going to let her run you off your own land?" he challenged.

"Well, I'll have to leave next year, anyway," Kerrigan said.

There was a brief pause, then, "Forget the bet. It was a damned stupid thing, anyway."

It was as close as his twin would get to an apology, Kerrigan realized. "I'll think about it," he hedged, not sure what he was going to do. They talked briefly about business, then hung up.

Kerrigan flipped through the TV stations again. He stopped at the nature show and watched as the young hawk flapped his wings and rose over the nest. Suddenly he gathered his courage and took the plunge over the side. He flapped desperately, then caught an updraft. With a graceful glide, he rose, banked and managed to land in a tree. He was fledged.

The announcer explained that the parents would return next year to the same area and raise a new family.

Kerrigan glanced around the dark, empty room. He knew he couldn't take it anymore. He'd had enough of this life.

Tomorrow he'd tell the TV producer he didn't want the job. He'd finish out the month, then he would take off. He wouldn't let a woman, studying some dumb birds, keep him away from his home.

"That dress is lovely," Mrs. Barrett said, complimenting her daughter when they found themselves alone for a minute.

Rachel looked down at the gold silk evening dress that cupped her breasts, then fell in a long, slender line to her feet. "It was a gift from Rafe."

She glanced across the room at her brother, very handsome in a dark formal suit. He had given the party in her honor, but she detected her parents' diplomatic hand in the invitations. The governor of the state was present. So were several officials on the federal level—a judge, a cabinet member, a financial adviser to the president.

Plus several handsome, eligible bachelors, any one of whom would be acceptable to her parents as a son-in-law. Her mother had said as much at dinner that night.

"I'm too busy to think of marriage," she'd said with a laugh.

"You're twenty-nine," her mother had said, a brisk reminder of the biological clock, Rachel had thought.

"If a man wants to interest Rachel," Rafe had teased, "he'll have to find a pair of eagles or some such and camp out in the woods with her."

Rachel wondered if her parents knew her heart was already lost. *To a rancher whose heart had become as stony as the hills around his ranch.*

"The jewelry goes well with the dress," her mother decided, looking at the intricately carved gold-and-brown tigereye set that had been a birthday gift from her and Rachel's father.

"Yes. Thank you for getting them for me."

"I found a charming diamond pendant in a star-burst design, but of course you never cared for diamonds."

Not from my parents. "I'm not much for jewelry," Rachel said apologetically. She'd be glad when the party was over. The social chatter, the glitter of jewels and scent of expensive perfume made her feel stifled. She longed for the outdoors and the solitude of the eagles and the woods.

They observed the crowd milling around the elegant room. Her mother nodded toward a tall, good-looking man across the room. "Kirby is making quite a name for himself in Washington. He's looking for a wife now that he's established in the law firm.''

''Oh, Mother,'' Rachel said softly, regretfully.

''You could do worse,'' her mother said firmly, determined to speak her piece. ''He's interested in you.''

''But I'm not interested in him.'' Rachel turned to her mother. ''I know you pressured Rafe into having this party for me, to bring me to my senses by making me see what I'm missing. I know you and father are worried about my future.'' She swallowed the tears that formed. ''I appreciate your concern but . . .''

''But you prefer trees and rocks and birds to people,'' her mother finished with an exasperated sigh. To Rachel's surprise she smiled and added, ''I suppose you're old enough to know what you want. I won't force you to endure this again.'' With a sweep of her hand, she indicated the party and the men she'd selected as possible husbands for her daughter.

''Thank you.'' Rachel suddenly wished she could tell her mother about Kerrigan, about how he made her feel—so wild and free. He'd never demanded anything of her that she didn't want to give.

That was one reason she'd been attracted to him, she realized. He'd wanted her love, nothing more. He hadn't asked her for anything else.

''I think I'll be leaving in the morning,'' she said. ''Father will be conferring with the presidential aides, and you'll have to entertain their wives. Rafe will be busy with the resort.''

''Don't you ever get tired of communing with nature?'' her mother asked with wry humor in the question.

''Don't you ever get tired of political intrigue?'' Rachel countered. She met her mother's hazel eyes, so like her own.

"Touché," Mrs. Barrett conceded after the first shock of the question passed. "Have a good trip. Be careful."

Rachel gave her mother a kiss on the cheek. "I will." She went to her room after saying good-night to her father and brother and telling them of her plans.

The next day, when she climbed into her car and drove off, she felt as if she were let out of a cage. A gilded cage, but a cage nevertheless. She knew she'd never willingly return to it no matter what her future held.

His twin met him at the Medford airport. "You home to stay?" Keegan asked, casting a wry glance over Kerrigan's city clothes, then looking at his own dusty jeans, shirt and boots.

"Yeah." Kerrigan tossed his luggage in the back of the pickup and climbed in the front. They took off up the highway on the long drive home. "Everything looks good," he remarked when they were out of town. He inhaled deeply, taking the scent of the woods deep into his body.

Home, he thought, and felt the tightening in him. He let the breath out in a sigh.

"Are you okay?" Keegan asked.

"Yes." The tightening clamped down and became pain. "How's everything at the ranch?"

"Pretty good. Still dry, but the grass is holding out." He paused. "The naturalist was here for a week, waiting for the eggs to hatch. I went over and checked on her. I told her it might be better if she didn't stay in the cabin—"

Kerrigan whipped around, fury in his eyes. "Did you order her off the place?"

"No. I think that's your department," Keegan said. "My only concern was her safety since she was on our land. I told her to keep an eye out for forest fires and to get out if any started in that section. That's all. I figured if you wanted her gone for good, you'd handle it.''

Kerrigan ignored the barb. He managed to get air past the knot in his throat. ''How is she?''

''She *was* fine. I don't know how she is now. She left.''

A hollowness settled in Kerrigan's stomach. She'd come and gone without waiting to see him. Well, hell, what had he expected? That she'd be hanging around like a rodeo groupie? Women found it easy to leave a man. He knew that.

But his reasoning didn t fill the bottomless pit inside him. He swore savagely.

She probably didn't want to see him again, not after he'd made it clear he wasn't coming back when he rode off with that damned calf. That was for the best.

He closed his eyes, too tangled up inside and too tired to figure it out. He didn't speak on the rest of the trip to the ranch. When they arrived, the first thing he saw was the calf, running at old Wills's heels like a puppy.

A picture formed in his mind. Rachel petting the calf, a towheaded youngster at her side, laughing with her over the antics of the playful critter.

The pit widened and deepened. A kid. Rachel and his child. If he'd read her second letter, the one that had explained everything and said she wanted to try again, if he'd swallowed his pride and gone to her, they might have had a kid by now. Maybe twins. If he went to her, if he asked, maybe she'd stay. . . .

He cursed the imagination that produced pictures of them being happy together . . . loving . . . laughing . . . Hell, hadn't he learned anything about life? You bet he had.

As soon as the truck stopped, he leapt out, went to his room, changed to ranch clothes and headed out on the pinto gelding. Four hours later, he pulled up at the bluff. Across the ravine, one of the eagles was busy tearing up the day's catch for two young eaglets, who were screeching in their high, raucous voices.

Rachel wasn't in the blind. Neither was she at the cabin. He looked around. He saw few signs of her presence there.

The straw was gone, and the floor was neatly swept. A broom was propped in the corner. He could see her hiking in with it, intent on cleaning the place. The windows were clean, too, inside and out.

He dropped into a chair and covered his eyes with his hands, but that didn't stop the images from coming. Rachel, in her silk underwear, smiling up at him from their pallet. Rachel, letting him undress her, letting him touch her, make love to her.

Rachel, happy in his love, big with his child.

He rushed from the cabin, riding hard for the ranch, but he couldn't outrun the images in his mind.

A man has his pride, he argued against the gut instinct that urged him to find her. He'd had the hell beaten out of him for daring to dream of a life with her.

If they'd married, she'd probably have left, anyway. Better that it had ended before he'd gotten used to having her around all the time. Yeah, better, so why did he feel so miserable?

At the ranch, after rubbing the gelding down, he left the stable and stood by the corral fence, remembering how Rachel had watched him ride the stallion without saying a word, although there had been worry etched in the lines between her eyes. He'd been showing off for her, like a kid in front of a girl he was sweet on.

The loneliness of the years without her bit into his soul. Knowing her again, having made love to her, stirred up all the pain and loss of that other time. He rested his head on his crossed arms and stared at the ground. Coming home to the ranch wasn't soothing his soul the way it used to.

Hearing steps near him, he looked up.

His twin came over and stopped by the fence. "You're grieving again," he said. "Like you did before."

"It'll pass." He watched the twilight deepen on the hills. "It did the other time."

"Maybe."

"It will." He headed for the house. "I'm going to shower. Tomorrow I'll head out and ride the fences."

"Will that stop you from thinking about her?"

Kerrigan didn't answer. He packed up and spent the next seven days in the saddle, ranging the hills, driving strays to the lower pastures and mending fences. By working until he was dead tired, he slept without dreaming. But there was no place he could go that didn't remind him of her.

When he ran out of food and fences, he went in and worked the home pastures. His inclination to see other people lessened with each day, he found. He wanted solitude.

"Me and the boys are heading for town," Keegan told him when the weekend rolled around. "Why don't you join us?"

"I'll pass."

He took care of his horse, stored his tack and headed for the house. The rowdy calls of the men getting ready for Saturday night in town grated on him. He stomped across the porch.

After a long, hot shower, he went into the kitchen. Two filled plates were on the table. His brother poured two glasses of ice tea. "Thanks," he muttered, sitting down and picking up a fork. He ate in silence.

Keegan finished and pushed back from the table. "There's a new band playing at the saloon."

"I'm not interested."

Keegan gave him a narrow-eyed once-over. "We could stop by Pete's later."

"I said I'm not interested," Kerrigan snarled. Hell, couldn't a man find any peace in his own home!

"Maybe it's just one woman you need."

"Think again," Kerrigan advised.

His twin shrugged, not at all intimidated by the icy glare he received. He finished his meal, put the dishes away and stood. "Well, I'm off." He headed for the door, then paused. "She said she'd be back tomorrow to observe the fledglings until they left the nest." He walked out.

Rachel paused by a boulder. She swung her pack off and propped it against a pine tree. Sitting on the boulder, she wiped her face, then unscrewed her canteen and took several swallows.

It was hot for mid-June. Humid, too. She looked at the clouds forming along the peaks. They were flat and charcoal gray on the bottom, rising in great billowy heaps that could extend forty-thousand feet or more into the air.

Boomers, she thought. Big thunderheads that could strike without warning, throwing violent shafts of lightning to the earth below. Without rain to cool things off and wet the dry grass, the lightning could start forest fires.

Although there were local showers, the area got about two inches of rain during the summer, she recalled. With a grimace, she stood, loaded up and started out again. She wanted to reach the cabin before noon, then check on the eagles.

Walking along the trail, she breathed in deeply the resin-scented air. She was glad to be back. She mentally paused and considered that statement.

An understanding had been established with her mother. Their hugs had been affectionate and a little sad when she'd left yesterday morning. Her mom was finally willing to let her go her own way.

She was worried, though, about her brother. She wished he could find someone special.

The way she had?

She sighed and trudged along the steep path. No use thinking along those lines. If Kerrigan couldn't get over his distrust of people, she couldn't help him.

He should be home now, according to his brother, who had ridden over to check on her at the line shack. Keegan had said his twin had decided not to take the sports announcer job. He'd be back at the ranch at the end of May.

A tremor cascaded over her. Today was Saturday, the sixteenth of June. She was twenty-nine, but she still felt as if she were twenty-one—full of yearning for something that was never to be hers. Why did she have to be so picky in her choice of mates?

Why do birds fly? she mocked her foolish heart.

At the cabin she looked around. No signs of anyone having been there. The broom kept a lonely vigil in the corner where she'd put it. After unpacking, bringing in a bucket of water and eating lunch, she took her binoculars and headed for the ridge.

The baby eagles had had lunch and were napping, their heads hunkered down in the fluff that passed for feathers. They were utterly ridiculous with their scrawny necks rising from bodies that looked huge because of the downy feathers.

Faces that only a parent could love, she acknowledged with an affectionate smile. A pang hit her heart. She ignored it.

For the next two hours, she took notes, absorbed in her work. A loud crack behind her brought her back to the real world. She climbed out of the blind and looked around.

The clouds had continued to gather while she was occupied. They covered the sky with an ominous coating of black. While she watched, lightning sizzled from cloud to cloud. She counted the seconds the sound took to reach her. Eight. Divide that by four. Two. The *hot* clouds were roughly two miles from her... and closing in fast.

She turned her face into the wind, which was picking up. It came from the northwest. The boomers were north of her, stretching from west to east across the horizon. Lower clouds scudded over her head, moving rapidly like restless ghosts.

Turning back, she noticed both adult eagles were on the nest. The fledglings were awake and squawking for food. The male busily answered their demands. The wind ruffled his neck feathers into a collar around his head.

The female sat on the rim of the nest, her wings tucked tight against her body. She seemed to be watching the clouds, her head cocked to one side.

Rachel put her glasses in their case and slipped the strap around her neck. She headed off along the ridge overlooking the gorge, wanting to get to the cabin. Her shirt wouldn't be warm enough if the temperature dropped rapidly and the clouds dumped hail as they often did in a summer storm.

The air felt heavy. Lightning flickered all around her as the clouds rolled across the sky until no blue showed. The thunder cracked like whiplashes in her ears. She picked up the pace, blinking when the wind blew dust into her eyes.

She was anxious to get over this section of the trail. Where the gorge curved to the north, the path turned west, dropping down and into the woods. She'd be safer from the elements there.

Suddenly, she felt a prickling sensation all over her scalp and arms. Lifting a hand, she realized the hair was standing in a halo around her head. She threw herself down on the ground and rolled into a shallow depression between two boulders.

Lightning struck a lone tree directly across the gorge. Its accompanying clap of thunder deafened her. As if in slow motion, she saw the tree split along one side. Half of it fell to the ground, teetered, then disappeared over the edge of the gorge.

The prickling sensation lessened. Rachel jumped to her feet and ran. She wanted to be off the ridge before the next strike.

She didn't make it.

When her hair rose on end, she threw herself down as flat as she could and clung to the earth for dear life. She inanely recalled that scientists figured lightning strikes occurred at a rate of one hundred times per second over the entire planet. That was six thousand times per minute.

Here, they were happening about every thirty seconds. As soon as the thunder cracked, she was up and running. The trail veered off into the woods only a hundred yards in front of her.

The length of a football field. She could make it.

The next strike was directly in front of her. She saw the lightning hit, form a glowing ball around a sharp boulder, then disappear. She paused, stunned, then started running again.

When she felt the next tingle run over her skin, she dropped down. She wondered if the eagles were safe as she hugged the ground. Their nest in the tree snag was below the rim of the eastern side of the gorge, giving it fairly good protection from wind. She thought the somewhat sheltered location would help in a thunderstorm, too.

Just as she started to rise, she heard another rumble. Her heart beat wildly for a second; then she realized it was the sound of pounding hooves. Standing, she saw a horse and rider come out of the woods below the ridge. Kerrigan!

"Come on," he shouted.

She ran. When she reached him, he grabbed her pack and swung her up behind him on the saddle. She clung to his lean waist as he turned the big pinto horse. They were almost to the woods when the next bolt hit behind them. A tree exploded into shredded wood.

The gorge reverberated with the crash of thunder. Rachel pressed her face against Kerrigan's back as the trees whipped past them. He slowed the horse as the trail narrowed and dropped down off the rocky ridge. A few drops of rain fell on them before they reached the cabin.

"Get inside," he told her. He took the gelding to the shed and put him up before running across the tiny clearing and leaping through the door she held open.

Lightning momentarily blinded her as she slammed the door. The thunder boomed furiously. The storm gods were angry that she'd escaped.

She leaned against the door and stared at her rescuer. He took his hat off and wiped his face on his sleeve. She saw him draw a deep breath before he faced her.

"That was close," he said.

"Yes."

"I figured you'd be watching your eagles instead of the sky. The ridge is a dangerous place during a lightning storm."

She laughed, giddy with relief. "Tell me about it."

He didn't answer. Instead he continued to look at her, his expression closed and unreadable. She wrapped her arms across her chest as a shiver attacked her.

With a low curse, he went to the fireplace. He quickly laid a fire and got it going.

"I'll make some coffee," she volunteered. She busied herself with the task and tried to put her thoughts in order. "What are you doing here?" she asked while waiting for the coffee to perk.

He pulled the two chairs close to the fire and sat in one. She took the other.

"Old Wills was worried about you," he said. "The lightning has set several fires up on the national forest land. Unless this storm dumps enough rain to put them out, they're going to be hard to control."

"Are the smoke jumpers coming in?"

"Yes."

"I'd better report in. I'm trained—"

"The forest service is using the ranch as a staging ground. I talked to your supervisor before I left. He said for you to head back there in the morning. I'll take you on the gelding."

So they'd both be spending the night in the cabin. A tremor ran over her. She was nervous with him, she realized.

She removed the coffeepot from the fire while he retrieved his cup from his saddlebags. She poured the coffee. They resumed their seats, drinking in silence and watching the flames.

The sky darkened behind the clouds as evening came. They fixed a quick supper and ate. The light faded to inky black that was illuminated by hot flashes of lightning.

A strange kind of peace came to her. If the cabin was hit, what would it matter... as long as they were together?

"Damn," Kerrigan said.

She looked up when he leapt from his chair and went to the window. Then she saw the flickering light.

Chapter Fourteen

*F*ire. Rachel went to the window and peered around Kerrigan. He moved and let her stand in front of him. Together they watched the flickering tongues of fire dance over the earth. A sudden flare of light glowed brightly as a pine tree burst into flame, its dry needles burning furiously. For a minute its limbs were visible, like a dark skeleton in the center of the flames; then the glow faded as the needles were consumed. The blaze continued its destruction along the base and lower limbs before finally climbing to the topmost branches.

"The wind is dying down," Kerrigan observed. "Maybe we won't get a crown fire."

Crown fire...a terror that raced along the tops of the trees like sheet lightning with a sound like a hundred locomotives thundering through the forest, its speed terrifying. Nothing could outrun it.

"We should be safe," she said. "The wind has been out of the northwest all afternoon."

"Yes, that'll keep the fire on the other side of the gorge. Provided it doesn't turn on us."

A forest fire could generate its own wind, which could easily soar to gale force as the fire sucked in fresh air. Like a huge, sentient beast, she thought, knowing it had to have oxygen to keep itself going.

They continued to stand at the window. Rachel was aware of him at her back, looking over her head at the danger. She wanted to lean into him and tried to think of all the reasons she shouldn't. None seemed important.

His body tensed as she let herself settle against his chest. He didn't move for a second; then he raised his arms and laid them on the window sill, enclosing her, making her feel safe.

They stayed that way for a long time. Finally the wind died completely. The fire flickered and became an ember glow creeping through the night.

"You'd better get some sleep," he suggested. He moved back and dropped his arms.

"What about you?"

"I'm going to watch a bit longer."

She started to protest, then realized it would do no good. "Call me in a couple of hours and I'll spell you." She spread her pad and sleeping bag, then laid his blanket over them. After removing her shoes and bathing her face with a damp bandanna, she crawled under the cover and went to sleep.

"Rachel."

She woke immediately to the sound of her name. "What is it? Is the fire worse?"

"The wind is picking up, straight out of the north. The fire is moving south on the other side of the gorge. It's near dawn. When it's light enough, we'll get out of here."

"Okay."

He had coffee ready. They ate trail mix and dried fruit. After filling two canteens, they headed out. The clouds that had caused all the trouble had moved on, dropping no rain. Smoke filled the air with a yellowish overcast.

Kerrigan dampened a bandanna and tied it like a loose feed bag over the gelding's nose. "Give me yours," he advised. He wet their bandannas from his canteen, and they tied them around their faces like bank robbers of the Old West.

Riding at a fast, steady walk, they hit the trail and started toward the ranch. They came out of the woods onto the ridge.

"Wait," Rachel said, grabbing his arm. She stared across the gorge at the flames almost directly across from them. "The eagles."

Kerrigan studied the fire, crackling no more than five hundred feet from them but across the deep gully with its trickle of water. "They should be all right."

"The wind is blowing due south. There're trees close to the ledge above the nest. The fire will get those."

She leaned her head against his shoulder to look up at him. He looked at her lips, no more than two inches from his. He'd carefully stayed out of her bed last night, but his control wasn't ironclad. Looking into her brown eyes with their golden streaks, he knew he couldn't refuse.

"Just a quick peek," he murmured.

She settled her body against his as he turned the big pinto and headed along the ridge. He traveled as fast as he dared, but he noticed the fire kept pace with them.

The wind was stronger, swirling the smoke in great roiling billows around their heads. His eyes stung and watered. He urged the surefooted gelding faster. They could see the nest now, sticking out from the ledge a bit below the rim.

"The pine tree," she gasped.

He saw what she did. An old pine tree, probably full of pine borers, was covered with dead needles. They'd burn like tinder. Sparks driven by the wind were hitting it, flaring, then dying out. It was only a matter of time...seconds...before it caught.

The adult eagles had left the nest. He could hear their cries as they circled above the smoke. In the nest the eaglets squawked in hoarse terror.

"We've got to save them," Rachel said.

When he stopped on the ridge opposite them, she slid to the ground before he did. He tied the gelding to the side of the trail and went to stand beside her.

"Get your rope," she ordered. "I'll rappel down—"

"Then what?" he demanded. "Climb halfway up the cliff to the tree, climb it and carry two frightened birds down with you."

"Yes." She gave him a defiant glance, then turned back. "Oh, no," she cried.

The pine tree burst into flames. Part of it split off and hit the ground. Burning branches broke and scattered. One of them fell over the ledge. It lodged in the side of the nest.

"Get the rope," Rachel shouted above the sounds of the fire. She struggled against his hold as she tried to get to the rope tied on his saddle.

"You can't save them," he told her savagely.

She stared at him with something like hatred in her eyes, then with a sob she turned to watch the destruction she couldn't stop.

The eaglets moved instinctively away from the flames that licked around the rim of the nest. Kerrigan knew the fire would encircle the birds in a matter of minutes. One eaglet, then the other, hopped to the rim of the nest next to the gorge.

"Jump," he ordered. "Jump." It was their only chance.

The two birds flapped and screeched helplessly. Rachel wiped helplessly at the tears that streaked down her face. Behind her, she was aware that Kerrigan had moved away from her. In a second, he was back.

He looped his rope and circled it over his head. With a mighty toss, he flung the rope toward the nest. Missed. He reeled it in and tried again.

This time, the lariat fell in a circle over the babies. He pulled it toward him slowly, then gave a sudden yank. The rope leapt up, hit the eaglets and pushed them over the edge.

Flapping their stubby wings, they plummeted into the ravine and landed in a shallow pool of water. They picked their way to a dead branch and climbed up on it, their cries momentarily stilled as they shook themselves and looked around as if stunned.

Rachel cheered. "We've got to get them out," she said, her delight gone when burning branches began falling from the nest. "The snag might catch on fire and fall on them."

Kerrigan started to say something, then changed his mind. "I'll let you down on the rope," he told her.

He put the loop over her shoulders and tightened it under her arms. After tying one end to the saddle horn, he braced himself for her to go over the side.

"Give me your bandanna," she requested. When he did, she tucked it in a pocket and started down the ledge. At the bottom, she approached the young birds carefully, tossed the bandannas over them and tied each of them into a rather odd bundle. Then she opened her shirt, tucked a bird in each

ide, and hoped she could make it to the top while they were
till quiet and confused.

She had only to keep her feet against the cliff and one
and on the rope, she found. Kerrigan and his horse knew
heir business. They pulled her up effortlessly.

"What now?" he asked when she gently laid the birds on
he ground and stood beside him. He smiled at her.

She glanced at him. Their eyes met. For a moment she
ouldn't move. Although they didn't touch, it was almost as
f they shared a kiss . . . the sweetest she'd ever known.

A cloud of smoke rolled over the canyon, obscuring the
ircling adult eagles. Rachel drew back, confused.

"What do we do with the birds?" he asked.

She stared at the bundled bandannas. "There's another
est about a half mile up the gorge, on a ledge. We can put
hem there and see if the parents will come to them."

"Let's go," he said.

She saw his gaze go down the gorge; then he quickly un-
ied the gelding and boosted Rachel into the saddle with her
undles tucked into her shirt again. While he swung up be-
ind her, she saw what had caused the flicker of worry to
rease his face.

"The fire has leapt the gorge," she said.

"Yeah, we need to hit the trail." He was calm, almost
natter-of-fact.

"You should have left," she said.

He gave her a terse smile as he prodded the gelding into a
ast walk along the cliff trail. "Would you have gone?"

There was no need to answer. She wouldn't willingly have
eft before attempting to rescue the soft bundles snuggled
gainst her, but that didn't relieve her guilt at putting him
nto danger.

Where the path widened, he urged the gelding into a can-
er. Rachel watched the tops of the trees to their left. The

wind was behind them, from the southwest, blowing the fire
up the ridge. She wondered how fast it was coming.

Risking a glance over Kerrigan's shoulder, she sucked in
a sharp breath of dismay. "Crown fire," she said.

He cursed briefly and put his heels into their mount. She
leaned forward and held on to the saddle horn, one arm
protectively holding the eaglets. The fire demon was at their
backs, slowly gaining as the wind became stronger and the
fire fed itself.

When the gelding tired, Kerrigan let it drop to a trot. He
looked back. The crown fire was spreading rapidly toward
the west, more slowly to the north. Right now the sound was
like that of a distant train rumbling along loose tracks. As
it came closer, it would increase until it was a locomotive on
their tails.

He tightened his grip on the woman who rode with him,
their bodies moving as one with the horse. Watching the
spread of the fire, he realized it was going to cut them off.
They wouldn't make it to the ranch.

"We'll have to go down into the gorge," he told her.

She nodded.

He realized she'd figured out their predicament, too. Her
courage touched something deep and hurting in him. He
didn't have time to think about it now, but later... if they
survived...

"Get us to the eagle's nest," she said. "Do you know
where it is?"

"No."

She told him. He kicked the tired gelding into a run. A
half mile up, the ridge opened to a wide rocky outcropping.
He was off almost before the horse stopped. He set Rachel
on her feet, jerked off the saddle and slapped the big pinto
on the rump.

"Git outta here," he shouted. He threw a couple of rocks at it. The gelding gave a snort at the blows and took off for the barn and the bucket of oats that awaited him there.

Rachel had the rope off the saddle and was tying it around a big fir tree.

"Let's use a rock," he suggested with a grin. He looked back to see where the fire was. Coming faster now. "Quick."

He tied the rope to a rock, then wedged that rock into a crack in a huge boulder. He packed dirt into the crack, wet it, then added rocks over that, hoping the fire wouldn't get to the rope.

"Ready?" he asked.

She nodded.

"Leave the eagles. I'll hand them down to you."

She removed the bundles and headed over the side.

The other nest had been used the year before, he thought, glancing at it from the rim of the gorge as she started her descent. It was about ten feet down the side of the ravine, positioned on a triangular outcropping of rock jutting out from a shallow cave.

"I need some pine resin," she announced. "To help disguise my scent," she explained at his questioning glance.

He looked around, spotted a likely pine and went to it. In a minute he returned with a hunk of partially hardened pine sap. He tossed it to her, then carefully lowered each eaglet.

After checking the fire's progress once more, he lowered the saddle as far as he could and let it drop into her waiting arms.

"Hurry," she called to him.

"Coming." He grabbed the rope and went down. "Empty the canteens on the birds and the nest and give them to me."

She followed instructions without question. He let himself down into the bottom of the ravine. He refilled the canteens and pulled himself back up the rope. They wet down the nest and the birds, then themselves. He filled the canteens once more.

With the birds between them, they squeezed under the overhang of rock. He pulled his saddle under with them. There was nothing to do but wait out the fire storm.

Already smoke was roiling over the ravine in thick billows. An updraft kept it above their heads. Kerrigan relaxed. They would be safe enough in their aerie. He looked at Rachel. She met his eyes with a steady gaze. Courage, she had it in spades.

Rachel felt her heart contract with love for Kerrigan. *For this man, no other.* Her first impression of him all those years ago had been right. He was wonderful, simply wonderful. She looked at him with shining eyes.

"We did it," she whispered.

His eyes, cool, wintry eyes, skimmed over her. They were no longer cold and unreadable. Passion flamed in them. He reached out and touched her face...gently, so gently. Tears, not caused by smoke this time, filled her eyes.

"You did it," he said in a strained voice.

She tried to study his expression, to determine what was wrong, but there was no time. His lips settled on hers, soft at first, then harder, seeking a response. She opened her lips and gave him everything he wanted.

It was a time out of time, and she knew it wasn't real. It was danger that drove the passion, not love. But she would take the moment. And later, when she was alone again, she'd remember how wonderful it had been to be in his arms.

Just as his hand slipped behind her head to deepen the kiss even more, a shout had them both jumping in startled surprise.

"Fan out. We'll hold it here," someone said.

"The fire fighters," Kerrigan exclaimed with a grin. He ducked from under the overhang and climbed the rope. "Yo," he called.

Rachel followed him more slowly. She realized she hadn't wanted the intimacy of the shared danger to end just yet. She stepped onto the ledge. Men and equipment were everywhere. They were already hard at work containing the fire. It was almost anticlimactic after the mad race to the bluff.

Kerrigan's brother walked over to them. "Thought maybe you two were roasted meat by now," he said.

Then, to Rachel's utter shock, he threw his arms around both of them and hugged them until she thought her neck would crack.

When he finally let them go, he muttered, "It was a hell of a long night. When the pinto came galloping in, I was afraid—" He stopped and struggled with emotions too raw to suppress.

Kerrigan laid a hand on his shoulder. "We had to rescue the eagles. Rachel wouldn't leave without them. There's a nest just over the ledge."

"Oh, the babies," Rachel exclaimed. She headed for the edge. Letting herself down, she placed the eaglets in the middle of the nest and removed the protective bandannas after rubbing her hands with pine resin to cover her human scent. They blinked comically and looked all around. Then they turned to her and screeched.

"I'm not your momma," she said with a laugh. "Let's see if your folks will claim you ugly ducklings." She hung the canteens over her shoulder, then spotted the saddle. "Hey," she yelled.

Kerrigan appeared above her with another rope. "This what you need?" he asked. He smiled at her. It caused chills to rush over her—such a serious smile with meanings she couldn't begin to guess flickering through it.

"Yeah." She tied the rope onto the saddle, and Kerrigan pulled it to the top. She climbed back up. Strong hands were there to help her. "Thanks," she said.

They looked at each other a minute; then the business of beating out the fire took their attention.

"The cabin is gone," Kerrigan said.

She peered through the smoke. With the trees bare of needles, she could see through the woods to the clearing. The cabin was a smoldering ruin, one side caved in, the other ready to go. An ache lodged in her heart. The place where their passion had bloomed so wildly was gone. End of an era, she thought.

"Rachel," a man called out, coming toward them with a relieved smile on his face. "I'm sure glad to see you're all right."

She turned to her supervisor. "Anything I can do?"

"Sure is. How about manning the radio unit?"

For the rest of the morning, they were busy. By noon, the fire was out. It was time to pack up and head out. A crew would remain to keep an eye out for any flare-ups, but everyone else could leave.

"My car," Rachel remembered. "It was at the trailhead near Sky Creek."

"Safe," someone answered. "The wind turned before the fire got that far."

"Your camping gear is gone," Kerrigan reminded her coming up to them. "It was in the cabin."

She couldn't look at him. Staring out at the blackened land from their vantage point, she said, "Well, that can be replaced easily enough. I was worried about my car, though I'm not sure I'm covered for forest fires."

"Who is?" the fire fighter nearest her quipped, drawing weary laughs from his fellow workers.

When everyone was ready to go, she hung back.

"There's a truck at the bottom of the ridge," Keegan told them. "You can ride back to the ranch."

"I'm going to stay awhile. I want to see if the eagles will find the nest here." She saw the two brothers exchange glances after she made this pronouncement.

Kerrigan's mouth curved into a wry smile. "Me, too. I have a vested interest in those birds."

"Right," his brother agreed sardonically. "I'll have one of the ranch hands leave your truck at the end of the logging road."

After the crew left, except for a dozen men who roamed the perimeter of the hill keeping watch, Rachel broke off several branches from a fir tree and made a blind between two boulders on the ridge. Kerrigan did the same.

She could hear the two eaglets squawking indignantly from the gorge. Keeping her eyes on the horizon, she tried not to think of the man who waited with her. It seemed forever, but was actually less than an hour, before she saw one of the eagles coming toward them, gliding easily on a thermal rising from the ravine. She held her breath. Yes, it was the female.

The male came into view. Rachel exhaled in relief. They were looking for their family. When they reached the ledge, the two eagles circled warily; then the female landed on the rim of the nest while the male kept a sharp eye out for enemies.

Rachel leaned forward. She could see part of the nest from her cover. Now was the crucial moment. The female cocked her head from side to side. She stretched forward. The young eagles pushed nearer to her, wanting food. The female let them touch her beak, then she gave them food.

Tears ran down Rachel's face. When the female lifted off the nest to go hunting, Rachel backed out of her blind and headed for the trail. Kerrigan joined her.

"Looks like the female accepted them," he said.

"Yes, they'll be fine now."

"A family."

She glanced at him, trying to read his expression. "Yes, that's right, a family."

They drank from their canteens and hiked down the ridge to the logging road. Kerrigan's pickup truck was waiting. Three hours later, they arrived at the ranch.

Wills greeted them with a big smile. "Well, you're back," he said, seeming to find great satisfaction in this fact.

"She needs a shower and then some rest," Kerrigan broke in. "We don't have time for your jawing."

Wills grinned and headed for the stable.

Kerrigan directed Rachel to the guest room she'd used before. Grateful, she undressed and went into the shower. With the warm water pelting over her, she realized just how tired she was. For no good reason, she felt teary-eyed and sad.

No, there was a reason. She knew that after the eaglets were fledged, she'd leave and she wouldn't return. There were other studies that needed doing. The world was full of natural wonders.

Finished, she dried off, wrapped the towel around her and went into the bedroom. The blue-plaid shirt lay on the bed. Her sooty clothing was gone, and the bed was turned back. She put the shirt on, hung up the towel, then sat in the chair and looked out at the hills. From here, she couldn't see any burned areas. Except for the smoky haze, the fire might never have happened.

A knock on the door had her turning in that direction. "Come in," she tried to say. She had to clear her throat and try again.

Kerrigan brought in a tray with two bowls on it. "Lunch."

He set it on the piecrust table and took the other chair. He handed her a napkin. She put it in her lap. It suddenly seemed much too confining to be eating with him in a bedroom. Her breath came unevenly. The sooner they finished, the sooner she could get dressed and leave. She didn't want to sleep there.

She managed to eat the soup and bread sticks. He handed her a glass of tea, tart with lemon. She took a drink.

"If you could spare someone, I'd like to get my car this afternoon. I'd feel better having it in town and out of the woods." She smiled lightly.

Again she couldn't look at him. The tears were too close. But she was aware of the mingled scent of his after-shave, shampoo and soap—that clean, masculine fragrance that was his alone. He'd dressed in clean jeans and a shirt after his shower.

"Oh," she said. "I need my clothes."

"They're in the dryer."

"Well, when they're ready, I'll leave," she said brightly.

He took the glass out of her hands and set it on the tray. "What about your study?" he said, his voice hoarse and strained.

Her gaze was drawn to him against her will. He was watching her, his face set in harsh lines. He looked so formidable, a fortress she couldn't breach. "Well, I . . . I'll finish it. Right now I need to go to town," she managed to say past the tears that clogged her throat.

"Why?"

Because I can't stand being near you, yet locked outside your heart. "I need to get a new pack and . . . and things."

"Will you come back to watch the eagles?"

She nodded. "Until they're fledged." She gazed at the far peak. "When the eagles leave, I'll be going, too."

"And you won't be coming back."

"No," she agreed. "I won't be coming back."

Chapter Fifteen

Rachel paused and drew a deep breath. The air was cool and crisp, feeling more like spring than summer. She adjusted her new backpack and began her journey again. She'd been gone almost all of June, writing up the notes on her study thus far and turning them over to the experts who would write the final report for the foundation. Now she would watch the final sequence as the young birds joined their parents in the sky.

Moving on, she reached the ridge trail at midmorning. She hiked along it, memories flooding her mind. Fireweed, one of the first plants to come back after a fire, was up, some of it already in bloom. If not for the blackened ground, one would never suspect danger could lurk in the peaceful scene.

She reached the ledge where the eagles nested. She stopped but a minute, not wanting to worry the parents over an intruder. The male was busy with the young ones, feeding them. Their plumage was changing, and they were growing real feathers. She quickly went on before she was noticed.

Pausing at the high point, she viewed the land. Her mouth dropped open in surprise.

The cabin, last seen burnt and lopsided, was standing in its little clearing, new and shining and neat. The trees along the creek had black trunks, but they hadn't burned, nor had the manzanita shrubs rising behind the cabin. It looked pristine, utterly charming and very inviting.

Rachel walked down the trail off the ledge, her heart thumping. When she reached the clearing, she heard the babbling of the creek and the trill of birdsong. Peaceful.

Yet her heart raced.

A porch had been built all across the front of the cabin. The two chairs that used to be inside were on it. They'd been sanded and varnished, she thought. She opened the door and went in.

Loosening her pack, she swung it off her shoulders and stood it in a corner. The fireplace stones had been cleaned. A mantel of varnished wood was mounted over it. Pewter plates and cups lined the mantel. A clock perched in the middle of it.

A new table was placed to one side. It had drawers in it. She opened one. Paring knife, cooking spoons, can opener and flatware. She closed the drawer. A bench had been built against the wall. It had a brightly colored pad on it. She raised the lid on the bench.

Firewood filled one half. A divider kept the wood from rolling on the pillows, sleeping bags and blankets on the other end. She looked around the room, feeling rather dazed. Rather than the original two, windows were now in every wall, giving views in all four directions.

"Oh," she said, distressed.

She could see Kerrigan coming out of the unburned woods on the other side of the creek. He walked across the meadow. In a few seconds he would be at the front door, which she'd left open. She tried to compose herself, but her heart wouldn't cooperate. It beat so wildly she had to press a hand against her chest.

He stepped onto the porch. Then he was inside. He stayed just inside the door.

She glanced around. There was a door in the back wall. She could escape through it. . . . Really, don't be ridiculous.

"I'm glad to see you returned," he said, "else all this would have been in vain." He gestured to the cabin.

"I'm impressed," she managed to say. She pressed harder. Her heart was going to leap right out of her chest.

"It's for you." He watched her without smiling.

She didn't know what to say.

"All the men at the ranch pitched in, even after working a full day. They came up on their own time. Keegan, too." Still he didn't smile or move forward. "You can use it to watch the eagles for as long as you want."

"Please thank them . . . that's very kind . . . they really shouldn't have . . . I mean, I won't be back . . . after this season."

"The study will be finished?"

"Well, no. We're going to try and keep track of the pair and their offspring for several years."

"Then you'll need the cabin."

She drew a shaky breath. Her control was slipping. She didn't want to make a fool of herself in front of him. "Someone else will use it—"

"No," he said sharply. "My brother and I will only give permission for you to stay here."

She stared at him.

He stepped forward one step, paused, then another. "Rachel's aerie," he said softly. "Ours...if you'll let me stay."

"I don't understand," she whispered past the painful constriction in her chest.

Suddenly he was very close. His hands clenched and unclenched at his sides. The air grew thick. She couldn't breathe.

"Rachel," he murmured, a desperate expression crossing his face. "Have I failed you beyond forgiving?"

"What are you talking about?"

"You failed me once, or so I thought," he explained. "But I failed you many times by not taking your call or answering your letters, by not coming to you when I knew we belonged together. I thought I was a fool for falling under your spell, but I was a bigger fool for wasting eight years."

She pressed her fingers to her temples, not sure she was hearing right, and closed her eyes as tears rose precariously near the surface. A hand lifted her chin. Her eyes were blotted with the gentlest of touches.

"I was afraid to trust you," he said. "But as soon as I saw you, I was caught in your magic again."

Her eyes flew open. His were no longer cold and unreadable. She saw anguish in them. And tenderness. And...love.

"Is it too late?" he asked, a worried hesitation in the question. "I rebuilt the cabin for us. When we were here before, I used to think of us as pioneers, building a new life in a new land together. I want that."

He brushed the hair back from her temples with a hand that trembled. An answering tremor went through her.

"Don't make me live without you," he whispered hoarsely. "The future is nothing without you."

She lifted a hand and touched his lips with shaking fingers. "Forever?" she asked.

"God, *yes*." He swept her against him, holding her. "Love," he said. "My love."

There were words to be spoken, but not now. Love wouldn't wait. They had to be together. The bench was quickly changed into a lover's nest with sleeping bags and pillows to cushion the hard pine planks. Clothing fluttered to the floor.

And then they were together, with nothing between. He paused before entering into the final ecstasy with her. "Do you have any objection to starting a family right away?"

She shook her head.

With all the gentleness she'd learned to expect from him, he lowered his strong, powerful body to hers. They moved together and became one. "Woman-magic," he said, smiling down at her.

Her heart beat wildly, happily. She was home.

* * * * *

Silhouette SPECIAL EDITION

MORGAN'S MERCENARIES

by
Lindsay McKenna

Morgan Trayhern has returned and he's set up a company full of best pals in adventure. Three men who've been to hell and back are about to fight the toughest battle of all . . . love!

You loved Wolf Harding in HEART OF THE WOLF (SE #818), so be sure to catch the other two stories in this exciting trilogy. Sean Killian a.k.a. THE ROGUE (SE #824) is coming your way in July. And in August it's COMMANDO (SE #830) with hero Jake Randolph.

These are men you'll love and stories you'll treasure . . . only from Silhouette Special Edition!

WILD RIVER TRILOGY

by Laurie Paige

Come meet the wild McPherson men and see how these three
sexy bachelors are tamed!

HOME FOR A WILD HEART, July 1993—
Kerrigan McPherson learns a lesson he'll never forget.

A PLACE FOR EAGLES, September 1993—
Keegan McPherson gets the surprise of his life.

THE WAY OF A MAN, November 1993—
Paul McPherson finally meets his match.

Don't miss any of these exciting titles—only for our readers and
only from Silhouette Special Edition!

MEN MADE IN AMERICA

Fifty red-blooded, white-hot, true-blue hunks from every
State in the Union!

Beginning in May, look for MEN MADE IN AMERICA!
Written by some of our most popular authors, these
stories feature fifty of the strongest, sexiest men, each
from a different state in the union!

Two titles available every other month at your favorite
retail outlet.

In July, look for:

CALL IT DESTINY by Jayne Ann Krentz (Arizona)
ANOTHER KIND OF LOVE by Mary Lynn Baxter
(Arkansas)

In September, look for:

DECEPTIONS by Annette Broadrick (California)
STORMWALKER by Dallas Schulze (Colorado)

You won't be able to resist MEN MADE IN AMERICA!